Here Lies Buried

CATHY ANN ROGERS

This is a work of fiction. Names, characters, businesses, places, events and incidents are either the products of the author's imagination or used in a fictitious manner. Any resemblance to actual persons, living or dead, or actual events is purely coincidental.

Deborah J Ledford, Editor
Cover design by JD Smith Designs

ISBN-13: 978-0-9914843-0-0
ISBN 10: 0991484304

www.aquitaineltd.com

DEDICATION

To my parents who told me I could do anything if I applied myself.

PROLOGUE

Rogers Lake, Arizona
Winter 1881

J osefina Paralelos sat high in her saddle as she and her five
companions rode on horseback toward a solitary cabin at
Rogers Lake, Arizona. She listened to the horse's hooves
pounding into the frozen earth, rhythmic deadened thuds,
repetitive and hypnotic. She glanced over at the San Francisco
Peaks and marveled at the eerie beauty of the snow-covered
mountains. The innocence of nature calmed her. A landscape
untainted by human indulgences or immoralities. Pristine and
pure, unlike she and the company surrounding her.

She rested back on her saddle as they stopped short of the
cabin. The stiff material of her husband's pants rubbed the
sensitive skin of her inner thighs. Magda, Natalia and she had
cut their hair short, wore loose-fitting jackets and long pants to
disguise their gender. Josefina smiled. The deception had
worked so far in the stagecoach and train robberies. The sheriffs

and their posses looking for a gang of six male outlaws instead of three upstanding married couples.

Amused with her own thoughts, worry crept back in when Josefina looked at her husband, Ricardo. Something had changed in him. She knew Nicholai Rodchenko and Borja De Velasquez sensed a strain by the absence of the easy camaraderie that had once existed among them. They moved in unison in silence to the front of the crude cabin.

The six slid off their saddles, leading their horses by their reins up to the post in front. She heard shuffling sounds inside, and then saw faces covertly peering out through stained curtains. She heard them racking their shotguns, poised to fire. She did not flinch at the sounds. They rarely took exception at caution. When the men inside recognized them, they opened the door and stepped out onto the porch.

"Wasn't sure who you were at first. You sounded like an army," Henry said, inviting them through the door.

Josefina welcomed the heat radiating from the potbelly stove. The cold had seeped into her bones during the ten-mile ride from Flagstaff. She looked around the room with its spare furnishings, two cots and a table with two chairs, and wished she were back in Mexico.

"We need to be back in Flagstaff by morning so we best be getting to it," Ricardo said.

Henry pulled out eight large gold bars stolen from the Tip Top Mine in Gillette four days before. "Here ya go."

"What about your take from the stagecoach robbery in Flagstaff yesterday?" Ricardo's accusatory tone had the intended effect on Henry and his companion, Ralph.

"About that. We was going to tell you," Ralph said. "Just that we thought that'd be a bonus, you know. We was here already just waiting anyway."

"When you go don't follow the plan, things can go wrong. People can be caught. Sometimes people *die* from making mistakes," Ricardo said. "Get the coins and the gold bars and load them up in those wooden kegs over in the corner."

"We don't get to keep none of it?" Ralph said. "We did that

on our own." He turned to Henry for support, but Henry would not meet his eyes.

"No. That's the price of disobedience," Ricardo leaned forward to meet Ralph's stare. "You have a problem with that?"

"No," Henry said, "We don't."

Josefina saw the fear in both men's eyes. Ricardo had that effect on almost everyone, except for her. She had known more frightening men than her husband and killed a few, as Ricardo well knew. She had learned how not to be afraid, even when she had been sure she was about to die. She observed that fear either breaks you or makes you stronger than your opponent. She could slit a man's throat as easily as shoot him square across his forehead if it meant living another day.

Borja, Nicholai and their wives stood to the side, not speaking. Josefina knew there was nothing else to say. Ralph and Henry pulled a job that was sure to bring the sheriff and his posse here by noon tomorrow, thereby forcing them to change their plans. They had planned to pick up the gold from this stash house after the first posse moved away from this area. With a fresh second posse looking for Henry and Ralph, they had to come tonight to pick up the gold, or lose it.

Now, she and the others studied the pair. She was positive they would talk. They were weak. Just like right now, cowering before authority to save themselves. Successfully concealing their identities after all the robberies, Josefina did not see a situation where they could trust these two to keep the secret.

Once Ralph and Henry placed the gold bars and the coins into six kegs, arranging one on each horse, Josefina motioned to the other women to join her outside. They were on their horses when they heard the gunshots. The three men came out of the cabin, mounted their horses and they started back toward the road to Flagstaff.

"This is the first time we've had to kill one of our own. I don't like it," Nicholai said.

"We don't let the ones who commit the robberies ever see us. That was foolish, Ricardo," Borja said.

"I took care of the problem," Ricardo said. "All we have to

do is to keep low for a while before doing another job. No one will connect us with either of these robberies, so stop bellyaching about it."

"Ricardo," Borja said. "Don't forget that we are equal partners in whatever we do. You do not take it on yourself to make arrangements without us again."

Josefina cringed. She knew her Ricardo. He would never forget that admonishment, even though he had it coming.

CHAPTER 1

September 15, 2006
Cincinnati, Ohio

Pilar Sagasta tapped the touchpad on her Apple PowerBook and closed the window on the scanned documents she had been reading the last three hours. Full of dangerous encounters with defending armies, political unrest brought about by the struggle for human rights, espionage, intrigue, and betrayals by the government and by their own families, the ancestry she had compiled read like a sweeping saga of heroic deeds. The idea that she could have learned so much more about her great great-grandparents if her *abuelo* had been less guarded when he spoke of his Mexican roots and their immigration to the United States.

"Mexico is our past. The United States is our future. Dwelling in the past keeps you from moving forward," he would say when she would ask about his parents. Bitterness toward Mexico stayed buried beneath his skin, exposed when someone picked at the scab encrusted over the wound that never healed.

"One thing I will tell you, *mija*, is that Josefina Paralelos was the gentlest and the bravest woman. Tender to her family. Ruthless to her enemies. No, I take that back, your *bisabeula* was the bravest person I have ever known. If you want to look up something from our past, look up the *Soldaderas*. When my father and uncle fought in the Revolution, she was there with the other wives and single women doing what they could to help. She rode a horse on an astride saddle, concocted homemade medicines for the soldiers' injuries, cooked over an open fire, as well as being a quick draw with the two ivory-handled *pistolas* she carried in two bandolier holsters. She did all of this in the middle of battle."

Pilar winced, her memories bringing him alive in her mind. She grinned as she replayed the story he had told often, her fingers moving along the silver frame holding his photograph.

Then she believed he was in the room with her. His weathered faced, creased from a lifetime of smiles, would softened at his own memories. "I remember her bandolier and how I counted the bullet loops on the front, and the shotgun loops on the back while she worked in the kitchen. As a boy, I thought it was normal for mothers to wear their pistols while cooking breakfast. I was so proud of her grace and strength. The saddest day in my life was the day I knew I'd never see her again," he had said, ignoring the instinct to conceal his emotions.

Remembering the few stories he had told her about their crossing from Mexico to Eagle Pass, Texas, she held the leather notebook that safeguarded those few family stories close to her. She imagined their escape with Obregón's soldiers close on their heels, hunting them down like criminals. Preserving her grandfather's stories and adding to them as she learned more, kept him close, at least in spirit.

Loss swept over her as she thought about the gentle, wise man that had raised her after her parents died. She knew the sadness did not come from the absence of lost family members, but from the loss of her guardian angel, her spiritual guide, and her best friend, a void she feared no one would fill again.

Now, mental images played in her mind from those documents. Like the reels from a 1920's silent film, she saw dashing young men, brave and fearless, fighting for justice and a better life alongside the likes of Pancho Villa and Emiliano

Zapata. They risked their lives in the face of death warrants issued by corrupt government officials, coupled with hostility from family and friends afraid of the retribution. Known as the *Villistas* and *Zapatistas,* her ancestors struggled for equality that had eluded them for decades. Yet, many like her *abuelo* and his family fled across the border into the United States for safety, often never returning to the country they had fought to change.

Optimistic, Pilar blinked back tears as she moved to the kitchen. She opened the window over the sink and looked out onto the lush backyards of the homes in her neighborhood. Inhaling the fragrance of freshly mowed lawns lingering in Cincinnati's moist late summer air, the breeze rushed over her like the embrace of a long lost friend. Energized by her resolve, she refilled her coffee mug, treated herself to a handful of chocolate wafer cookies, and started back to her computer.

The ringing telephone caught her off guard, giving her an adrenalin jolt. "Hello," she said reaching out for the cordless to stop its insistent ringing.

"Glad I caught you. What are you up to?"

"Hi, Tammy." She smiled hearing the voice of her closest friend since grade school.

"I've been going over the research I dug up on Pete's side of the family. I found two phone numbers of ones still living in Arizona. Pete's sister Virginia is still alive. At least she has an active number"

"I'm not sure about this. It's creepy to invite strangers into your life. All you can be sure of is you share the same blood."

"Is that so," Pilar said with an edge of challenge hanging on the words.

"They could be any kind of degenerate or murderer, and there you go, walking right into the lion's den never to be heard from again."

"I don't know how you can say things like that. You don't know anything about them."

"That's the point. Neither do you," Tammy said. "Alright then, who are these wonderful people you found that's never shown any interest in you your whole life."

Pilar reached for her family book to pull out a handwritten list. "As I said, there's Virginia Rodchenko, Pete's sister. She lives in Flagstaff where she and Pete grew up. The other names are Rod and Sylvie Folsom. I found a second number for Virginia in Phoenix with the Folsom name listed as others in the household. That must mean relatives.

"Or caretakers of the asylum."

"Good grief, Tammy. You're too cynical for your age."

"Someone has to point out the obvious. Since I've known you longer than anyone outside your family, that's my job."

"I know what I'm doing. Don't worry. I'm not as gullible as you think."

"Right."

◆　◆　◆

Tammy had exhausted her. Now, she needed more coffee to regain her focus before she spoke to the new relatives. She glanced at the clock and figured she should be good with the two-hour time difference between Arizona and Ohio this time of year. She took a bigger sip of the freshened coffee and settled back into her comfortable chair in front of the computer.

She took a deep breath, and placed a hand over her churning stomach. She had lost some of the earlier confidence. *Damn that Tammy.* It was now or never, she thought, taking the receiver and punching in the first phone number.

"Hello."

"My name is Pilar Sagasta. I'm the great granddaughter of Peter Paralelos. Am I speaking to Virginia, his sister?"

Without hesitation, the woman said, "Well, well, now. As I live and breathe, I never thought I'd hear from the likes of you people again. What do you *want*?"

You people?

"Uh," Pilar said, unsure how to answer that question. "Well, I guess I want to meet you. Pete died not too long ago and I thought it would be a good way to …." Her voice trailed off when she realized her reasoning was no more than an abstract feeling for family connection.

"You thought you'd feel he was still around by being around me. Not unreasonable. Don't know if it will work, but come if you want," Virginia said, her raspy voice as rough as the welcome she extended.

"Well, I'm driving out. I expect to get there by Saturday."

"I hope you get what you expect. Come by when you get to town. Call first," Virginia slammed down the receiver in Pilar's ear without another word.

Left with her mouth open, Pilar lost the chance to give the speech she had rehearsed about looking forward to meeting her, and developing a personal dialogue to learn more about their mutual histories. She had not expected this stinging dismissal.

God, if Tammy turns out to be right, she will never let me forget it.

She called the number for the Folsom's. More reserved for this call, unsure of the reception she would get.

"Hello," a soft voice said in such contrast to Virginia's that it startled her.

"Hi. You don't know me but my grandfather was Peter Paralelos, Virginia's brother. I'm coming to Arizona and wondered if I could meet you." Pilar braced for more rejection.

"We'd love to meet you. My husband, Rod, is the relative. I'm Sylvie, the insignificant outcast daughter-in-law."

Pilar let out a hasty laugh, "It's nice to talk with you. I'm looking forward to seeing everyone. In fact, I spoke with Virginia a little while ago. She invited me to visit her too."

"Listen. Why don't you meet her while I'm there? It might be easier. I won't burst your bubble, but let's just say her attitude is an acquired taste."

Pilar let out a nervous giggle in spite of her manners.

"Come to Phoenix and stay with us. We have plenty of room."

Meeting them together could be the best if the situation went south, Pilar thought. If the reunion went well, she had the opportunity to get to know them better staying with them.

"You sound like the family navigator."

"Something like that," Sylvie said through a forced laugh.

"Thanks for your hospitality. I'll call you with my itinerary."

"That sounds fine," Sylvie said. "And don't worry."

As she disconnected the call, Pilar set aside her uneasiness, but then wondered about Sylvie's parting words. *Don't worry about what?* She carried her coffee with her to her front parlor, started a fire to take off the damp edge of the season, and grabbed up the latest Sue Grafton book. As she read, her mind trailed off to both conversations. Nothing for her to worry about as Sylvie indicated, but she knew from the past that an alternate plan B was a good idea. From her travel guide, she made a list of the places she could visit in Arizona if the family turned out to be a bust. It *will* be an adventure and I *will* have fun, she told herself, in spite of the uneasy prickling in her stomach.

CHAPTER 2

February 2, 1918
Flagstaff, Arizona

Josefina Paralelos hesitated midway down the stairs that lead to the basement dining room. "*Dios mío!*" she whispered. A premonition of tragedy and ruin seized her, forcing her to pause to catch her breath. Her husband and their closest friends sat around the kitchen table without speaking, their sober faces staring back at one another. The rattling water bucket hanging outside the cellar door interrupted her thoughts and brought her into the moment. She eased down the final steps, careful not to let her trembling hands spill the bowls of soup she carried on a large serving tray.

A sudden gust of wind slammed metal tools against the wood rack where they hung outside and she shuddered. When she took the last step down onto the tiled floor, she heard the gentle snorts of the horses stabled in the structure across the yard. Their reassuring sounds calmed her nerves, but she could not shake off the sense of impending death.

She walked to the buffet behind her seat at the table, set down the tray next to a silver coffee pot, and turned to look at them. The flickering light from the kerosene lamps cast shadows across their faces like dancing demons. She resisted the prickly feeling in her mid-section that had also proved a forecast of looming bad times.

The insistent banging of the metal bucket echoed inside her. This night, the cold, the mood in the room, put her body into the fearfulness she had not experienced since Mexico before a battle. As the bucket outside would never keep its original condition after repeated pounding, a relentless wind of change in the world's political climate ensured they would not see a return to the old ways. That finality she had accepted, but she would not accept Ricardo's proposal to disband their group, and suffer another emotional blow. Maybe anticipating that loss caused her to fear something bad was coming. *"Another whimsy,"* as Ricardo often said.

She filled their coffee cups, laid out biscuits, and placed the bean soup in front of them before sitting in her chair opposite Ricardo. Lowering her small frame onto the chair, she took in the aromas of the meal and found a temporary peacefulness. This ritualistic signaling to the start of the meeting had become a subconscious act no one had initiated or noticed but had agreed to in passive acceptance long ago.

"Ah," Ricardo began. "The time has come. The six of us might have started out as outlaws, but we ended up as compatriots fighting rebels in our homelands. My brother arrived yesterday to tell us that Pancho Villa's *banditos* raided our home and Carranza's land reform methods have left us nothing. By now, they have converted our land into *ejidos* for the *Mestizos*. This is our tragedy. I once prayed to return, but I fear we can never go back. General Diaz believes we can fight for the others not yet touched by this plundering, but I do not agree. We must move forward. The world changes and we must learn to move with the times."

Nikolai Rodchenko, a Russian man, nodded in agreement. His wife, Natasha, seated next to him, watched him glance over at her before he spoke, "Word has come to us since our last meeting. Lenin has claimed victory and removed the royal family from the palace. Lenin and his Bolshevik *Cheka* execute anyone who challenges them. Most of my family escaped, except for one brother who has chosen to stay. Our many friends who have not been lucky will never see the light of freedom again or they look forward to a death warrant. How can a few expatriates like us make a difference now that "Iron Felix" Dzerzhinksy and his *Cheka* security police have achieved such strength?"

Borja de Velasquez, a Spaniard from the Basque area, sat next to Ricardo. Borja contrasted against the light olive skin of his wife, Magda, sitting next to him. Josefina saw how the passion between them ignited when she touched him, like now. Magda rested her hand on his shoulder, and Josefina saw the subtle shiver that caused him to hesitate before he spoke.

"From the outside we see the reality, but inside the vision is narrow. Public spirit overtakes their conscience. Still, I am hopeful. Anarchy has not yet prevailed in Spain. But I, too, question if what we do matters." Borja turned his intense dark eyes to Ricardo.

"In American money, our individual shares have an estimated value of sixty thousand dollars. That does not include what we have used over the years for living expenses, or what we have held to liquidate later," Ricardo said, "We have the gold from the stagecoach robberies, but that's identifiable. We need to melt it down."

The other two men moved with imperceptible nods while their wives eyed their husbands in anticipation.

Nikolai continued to nod his head, keeping his eyes fixed

with appreciation on the miniature boxes resting on the center of the table. "We're taking our shares now? Going our separate ways?"

Ricardo looked at Josefina and for a few seconds did not speak. "If our time working together has ended, we should take our shares now. We have been safe here, but if anything were to happen to my wife and me, you might lose everything. These three small tins hold the keys to this basement and to the storage places that we built. As long as we are the only ones who know, I will continue to use the same hiding place down here and keep our key in the bank's safe deposit box."

Magda looked at the group, her eyes full of tears, and spoke as if the words burst from her, "Our three families have become one in these unsettled times. For me, I have known no other sisters as well as Natasha and Josefina. We met as strangers so long ago, grew to be friends and since then have lived through dangers we cannot speak of outside our own company. We can never return to the past and the United States is now our home. I would be heartsick to lose this family we've become after all that I have already lost." Magda lowered her moist eyes to watch her husband lovingly envelop her delicate hands.

"This is not the end of our friendship, Magda," Josefina said, smiling. The moisture in her eyes created a translucent light to their darkness making them appear like shiny black marbles.

"Of course not," Natasha said, as an involuntary rush of tears poured from her eyes and down the sides of her nose. The watery character of her light blue eyes against the ashen tones of her thick hair gave her an eerie quality that amplified her distress.

"What else could this mean but that we are saying good-bye?" Magda said.

Josefina wanted to rush to hold Magda, the soul of their

group, the one who reminded them of their humanity despite the circumstances. Magda had voiced her feelings, reminding them that no one wanted this to end. This unity was more about family than about the money.

Ricardo appeared irritated and uncomfortable. "There is no hurry to this. I can see our emotions are running high. Let us consider for a moment that we stay in Flagstaff. We had not considered that option before, but we can live here as well as anywhere else, can we not?" Ricardo paused. When no one spoke, he continued. "These people believe we are wealthy immigrants. We would not want them to grow suspicious of our absences, especially if anyone were to put thought to the dates of our trips out of town with the robberies."

"We have become attached to this part of the country," Nikolai said, looking at Natasha. "We want to stay, but you are right that we do not need trouble from the authorities. Like your children, my son and daughter need stability and safety. I believe we have enough to provide comfortable lives for our families with what we have. Instead of taking our shares and leaving as we planned, let us wait. We are safe, respectable here in Flagstaff. We should consider allowing ourselves to settle into our new lives, and see what happens. I have no problem keeping our share with you."

"Agreed," Ricardo and Borja said in unison, while the women exchanged nervous smiles.

CHAPTER 3

September 24, 2006
Flagstaff, Arizona

Driving into Flagstaff for the first time, Pilar saw the town as a winter wonderland. The tall Ponderosa Pines dusted with powdery snow and the gray snowcapped verges outlining Interstate-40 like road markers to a destination, its tranquility acted as a sedative for a wired traveler. Cold as the air had to be outside the coziness of her vehicle, she surprised herself by pulling over and stepping onto the cold damp ground. Blinking, the air puzzled her, cold yet not cold. The winter air she knew was wet and biting, one that penetrated protective clothing to sink through to the skin and flesh, down to the very bone. Here, the chill stopped at her car coat and black riding boots. Inhaling the thin air and watching her breath blow out as steam, she stood still to take in the wooded area to remember later.

Once she found Virginia's house and pulled up to the curb, she started to lose her nerve. As irrational as she considered this to be, she wanted to give into the urge to flee, to drive off never to return, but commonsense held her foot on the brake. She considered the house, a cross between Queen Anne and Prairie centered on an acre parcel, the three-story home and its dormer windows had an imposing presence against the surrounding tall pines. Peering out beyond the slight upgrade to the porch, she caught sight of a *porte-cochère* on the home's south side. The French name translated to carriage porch, as her mother had explained when describing the side porch of her own childhood home in Ohio. Memories clouded her vision recalling where she pretended to be a princess and her brothers transported her on a makeshift carriage made of thick wooden slats. She saw an old-fashioned station wagon there and pictured horses drawn to the covered entrance for passage of the women from the carriage into the house to keep their clothes shielded from the dirt and mud before pavement.

A tapping on her passenger side window gave her heart a leap and she was back in the present. Looking over, she saw an auburn haired woman looking every bit like Wilke Collins' "*The Woman in White*," appearing out of nowhere with eyes that were pleading and warning at the same time. Maybe she had set the tone by her daydreaming about the past, but for a minute, Pilar's heart pounded with terror. She hoped the woman had not seen her reacting in a childish manner, and pressed the button to lower the window.

"Pilar? I'm Sylvie. I hope I didn't scare you. I wanted to meet you out here to prepare you."

"Oh, thank goodness. I mean, thanks for meeting me out here. Is anything wrong?"

"No, but these people have a way of, well, not being nice. There's no other way to describe it. You'll see. Don't take what they say or do personally."

Pilar's anxiety returned, enough for her to hesitate before closing the windows and shutting off the car. Sylvie met her as she stood up and gave her a hug. "Welcome." Pilar paused to assess Sylvie. Her hair gently clung to her neck, stopping at diminutive shoulders. Everything about her was ghostly, her frailty, her pale complexion, even her stylish clothes in pastel winter hues.

As they walked up the steps to the front porch, Sylvie's small talk had an unnatural quality that confused Pilar.

"How was the drive across country?" Sylvie asked, giving Pilar's arm a squeeze. "I've never done anything so brave in my life."

"No incidents. I had a good time seeing the country as I drove."

"Every Sunday, we have to drag our butts up from Phoenix to visit Virginia. She insists on it. Everyone jumps because of her money. Don't let on to Rod that I said anything. He hates gossip, even when it's true. Family pride and all that crap."

"I see. So Rod's here?"

"Actually, he's not. He and the kids are sick so I'm the emissary. Virginia and Madera don't like me, so that makes it amusing. You'll see. Remember what I said," Sylvie said as she turned the doorknob to lead Pilar inside to the living room.

That fear came back as Pilar looked around the living room at the angry eyes staring at her. Something about their expressions told her they resented her, but she brushed that aside.

"Everyone," Sylvie said. "This is Pilar Sagasta. She's come all the way from Ohio to meet you."

"Who is this again?" Virginia's demanding acidic tone did not match her elderly appearance.

"Pilar Sagasta," Pilar said. "Peter Paralelos was my grandfather, Virginia's brother. I'm thrilled to meet all of you."

When no one spoke, Sylvie took over, and said, "This is Virginia, and her daughter, Madera. Madera's husband, Bert Folsom, and their daughter Lenore Santos."

Standing before them, Pilar reached out to shake hands but Virginia did not accept her offer. Madera, a woman who looked in her fifties or sixties based on her sagging eye bags and droopy jawline, stayed sitting, giving Pilar a suspicious glare. No one else uttered a word. Pilar gave them a wide smile. *What's with these people?*

Virginia leaned forward, and said, "I'm sorry to hear Peter's dead. I hadn't spoken with him since our mother died. I was arranging to visit him sometime. I don't know why, though, since he never made the least attempt to visit me or have anything to do with my family. It's odd that you show up here wanting to be family out of nowhere. What on earth do you want from us?"

The atmosphere of the house was smothering in mood and temperature. Dry heat blasted down on her from the wall registers, the stifling air making her lightheaded. She blamed it on the hostile mood in the room more than the temperature.

Sylvie directed her to sit in a nearby side chair. Pilar sat, wondering how to break the mood. "I guess you wouldn't know, but my parents and two brothers were killed in a car accident when I was nine. It seems my aunts and uncles all died from various illnesses or accidents. The only one left was Pete and his late wife's sister, Marian. Pete took me in, but he wasn't good at the little girl stuff so Aunt Marian came around a lot," Pilar said, using the pause to swallow to keep her emotions in check. "He died last autumn of pneumonia."

Madera stared on, waiting for her to continue, showing no sign of sadness or regret about the loss of her uncle. Bert displayed his disinterest by turning on the television and leaning away from the group. Virginia made indistinguishable remarks under her breath. Lenore sat silent, her dark eyes darting back and forth, while Sylvie still stood at the entrance looking amused.

"Are you a lesbian?" Madera said.

"No," Pilar said, caught off guard by the crude question.

"I was just wondering since you look like you're into sports. Not really a feminine thing to do, competing with men. And you don't seem to be too concerned with your appearance."

"Excuse me?" In a flash, she was back in grade school tormented by the bully that terrorized her for three years. Pilar decided she was too old for this. She knew that the more you engaged with an abusive personality, the more power you lost. "I'm sorry but I think it's time for me to leave."

"Suit yourself. You're the one who invited yourself here," Madera said.

Sylvie moved over to place a comforting hand on Pilar's

shoulder and said, "Enough is enough. How can you treat your own flesh and blood like this? I don't understand you people,"

"She's probably only here because she wants something. Well, the bank is closed, sweetie. No handouts here," Virginia said, her bulbous eyes protruding and bloodshot.

"Here we go," Sylvie said. "Everything's about money. Did you ever think that some people are looking for a family connection?"

"Listen to you talk," Virginia said, aiming her arthritic forefinger in Sylvie's direction. "Here we are, supposed to be celebrating *my* birthday and Rod and my grandchildren are nowhere to be seen. Some family connection you are. Sure, he's sick. Sick having to work himself to death to support you. You never should have had three children for my son to provide for while you sit on your lazy ass. And now you've got him paying for that tramp of a mother of yours."

Sylvie lunged forward, aiming her right forefinger at Virginia. "For your information, you old bat, Rod is the one who wanted three children and for me to stay at home to take care of them. As for my mother, she's a hell of a sight better than your sniveling daughter who only kisses your ass expecting a reward once you're dead. If you didn't have an inheritance to dangle in front of everyone, no one would get within a mile of you, you sorry ass excuse for a human being."

"Get out! Get out of my house right now before I call the cops," Virginia screamed, waving her fist in Sylvie's direction. "And take that other freeloading bitch with you. If Peter wanted us to be family, he should have made an effort when he was alive."

"Come on, Pilar. Let's get out of this madhouse," Sylvie said, helping a stunned Pilar to her feet. Around them, the room had grown silent. Bert had even muted the television. Virginia and Madera glared while the others pretended to be invisible, eyes lowered and lips pressed together so hard, they looked glued down.

"It will be a cold day in Hell when any of you get to see my children again. Suck on that for a while," Sylvie said as she and

Pilar crossed the threshold to the outside.

Pilar thought her shaking knees would topple her down the steps. She accepted Sylvie's hand for balance while she pressed her other hand on her stomach to keep from throwing up.

"I'm so sorry you had to go through all that. I didn't think they would be that cruel. They're vicious as a rule, but that went beyond anything I've ever seen. I can't wait for that old woman to drop dead and make my life easier."

"You're not the only one," Pilar said. "I've never been talked to like that in my entire life. What horrible people."

"I hope this hasn't changed your mind about visiting us. Please come to our house for a couple of days. Rod is not like them, I swear. He wants to know you and all about Peter. Please. Let us make this up to you."

"If you don't mind, I need to be on my own and pull myself together. I read about a hotel, Little America. I thought I'd try to get a reservation for one night."

"I love that place. That'll do you good. Get some great food, relax by the big fireplace, and take a long bath. You'll feel better tomorrow. You have my address. Just come down in the morning or when you feel like it."

"Okay. I need a good workout before I do anything. Sweat out the poison. "

After hugging, Pilar took a last look up at the house before getting into her car. Shaking, disillusioned and disappointed, she could not hold in her emotions any longer. Pulling away from the curb, tears obscuring her vision, she drove a block down the street and around the corner to park and gave in to unrestrained crying before driving on.

Still stinging from the emotional beating, Pilar stopped at the front desk of the Little America and asked for a room for one night. After getting past the business of check-in, she followed the porter as he led her past the Gift Shop to the last available King room with a view. Action is what she needed to distance herself from nasty situations.

After a hard workout and a shower, she sat on the edge of the bed staring at her pile of research. She shook her head. Not even Sylvie's welcoming invitation was enough to encourage her to stay in Arizona now. What would be the point in trying to get to know these people? Maybe Pete had been right when he said to look at what is in front of you and not behind you. Maybe there was not always a treasure to reveal when trying to uncover a buried past.

CHAPTER 4

September 24, 2006
Flagstaff, Arizona

Lenore lifted her eyes when her grandmother began to speak after the Sylvie and Pilar passed through the front door. She had never understood Virginia and Madera's capacity for cruelty toward strangers. But she compounded their crime by remaining silent. That shamed her, but she knew she did not have the fortitude to speak out against them.

"I could strangle that bitch with my bare hands," Virginia said, loud enough for her words to reach Sylvie before she was out of earshot. After they heard the door slam shut, Virginia added, "Well, I never liked her. Rod should never have married her. She's not good enough and never could be. She came from nothing. That social climber waltzing around us with her uppity manners and modern ideas. I can't imagine where she gets such airs. She might be a white, Anglo-Saxon Protestant, but she's white trash more than a WASP. When Rod hears how she talked to us with that trench mouth of hers, she'll get the boot. Mark my words."

Lenore watched Virginia eye Madera through squinted eye, while Madera shook her head and rocked back and forth.

Madera Folsom looked worried as she studied the print on the rug beneath her feet. Twisting hands pulled at themselves as her feet twitched and toes wriggled inside her black nursing shoes. She heard Virginia clicking her tongue, and said, "Maybe we shouldn't have said all those things."

"What's the matter, Madera?" Virginia said. "Having another nervous breakdown? Stop your whining and grow up. If you were any kind of mother, your children wouldn't have turned out the way they did. It's your fault Rod married her in the first place. He couldn't wait to get away from you and your blubbery weakness. Oh, I warned you. You can't say I didn't. "Then she turned to Bert and said, "Turn off that god dammed television. Electricity ain't free. You think I'm made of money?"

Bert pressed the power button on the remote, tapped his index finger on the loveseat arm, took deep breaths, and closed his eyes.

Madera started to cry, speaking in gulping sobs. "Shut up! Shut up!" her voice rising to a shrill. "I can't bear to lose another child. Tasha hasn't come around me for years and Rod's all I have left. Oh, my son! My son! Oh, I don't want to miss seeing his children grow up and—"

With a sharp intake of breath, she stopped speaking, the color in her face and neck rose with the heat of embarrassment and panic. She turned to her left at Lenore, silent with her downward stare and crossed arms.

"Oh, Lenore, I didn't mean it like that. Of course, Rod isn't *all* I have left. I meant, well, that he's my only *son*, and without him, well, you know what I mean. A son is a rock. A son is a ... is a ... well, you know what I mean." Madera reached over to rest her hand on Lenore's shoulder.

Lenore Santos looked from her mother to her grandmother with the tortured expression of one who wished for once that someone cared about her feelings.

"All you ever do is to praise the mighty Rod for all his accomplishments. His disciplined children. His beautiful home. How great he is with money. There isn't anything Rod can do wrong. I don't blame him; I blame you for being an insensitive bitch who does not consider my feelings." She did not care if God struck her down for saying it, but she had said it. No, wait a minute. She had not said anything, she realized. It was that same speech she had rehearsed so many times that it *felt* real.

"Yeah, it's okay Mom. I knew what you meant. Listen, I've got go. Allegra should be home soon and I'd like to be there when she gets home. It's a two hour drive back to Phoenix, you know." Lenore raised her sinewy form from the chair.

"Ah, honey," Virginia said, her voice this time soft and syrupy. "Don't go. We haven't had dessert yet. I made your favorites, pecan pie and carrot cake with cream cheese icing."

"No, really. I have to go. See you next Sunday, I guess?"

Grinning, Virginia said, "Sure honey. Next Sunday, as usual. Now, don't you worry about anything your mother says. She doesn't think before she speaks and half the time says things she doesn't mean. You know out of all the grand kids, you're my favorite, don't you? And don't we all know that what's important is what I think anyway," she said, winking.

"Sure, Gran," Lenore said, leaning over the frail woman and kissing her paper-thin rouged cheeks. Yuck, she thought. The things I do for that inheritance money, she reflected as she raised her head and smiled. She nodded to her parents as she grabbed her coat and scarf on the way out. As the cold, bitter air hit her face, she wished she had Sylvie's nerve. Looking back toward the house before pulling away, Lenore thought again, how difficult it was waiting for someone to die.

Grateful for the darkening landscape, Lenore stared ahead to the road delivering her back to Phoenix. Living in Arizona all of her life, the partially lit section of Interstate-17 did not intimidate her. Her familiarity with the winding roads with plunging depths beyond the guardrails on one side and towering mountain slopes on the other, gave her that comforting confidence she experienced nowhere else.

Keeping a lookout for oncoming vehicles to switch off their bright headlights, Lenore had flashes of blindness during the seconds of the change, but her sense of place kept her from veering off too much in one direction or going straight on a curve. To her relief, as a respite from that alertness, she found herself alone on the road for the stretch through the Camp Verde exits. Settling back to enjoy the peace she found within the inky darkness, she frowned when she noticed a dark SUV approaching from behind at a dangerous speed.

She pulled to the side to allow the SUV to pass, but instead of passing her, the driver rammed into the back of her car. The impact gave her a bobble head action that snapped her head forward then back with a disorienting force. Her awareness disengaged for several seconds. Adrenalin surged through her body warning her to keep alert. Looking up in time to see the guardrail three hundred feet in front of her, she grabbed the wheel, turned it into the curve, and slammed her foot on the brakes. She came up just short of ramming the side of the mountain head-on. She swore under her breath watching the offending vehicle disappear into the darkness. Her sweaty hands turned the steering wheel toward the direction for Phoenix and she eased into the pull-off area.

"Asshole!" she said in that shrill voice she could not control when upset. Even after forcing calmness, tears she tried to suppress poured from her eyes. She wiped them away with her shaking fingers. This is too much. A perfect ending for a horrible day marked with verbal assaults between her mother and grandmother against Sylvie and Pilar, and the inevitable condescending and patronizing attitude she had to take from them. How much longer she could take it, she did not know, but something had to change. And soon before she did something desperate, such as slaughter Virginia like the pig. One way or another, she would not wait forever for that old woman to die.

CHAPTER 5

September 24, 2006
Phoenix, Arizona

Sylvie checked her watch as she pulled the Tahoe into her garage. Seeing the time was after seven thirty, she hurried inside to find her three small children in pajamas, huddled on the sofa around their father, Rod Folsom, with a large quilt pulled around them. All eyes were on the television, absorbed in the latest Disney movie. Sylvie smiled to herself as she admired her husband from his prematurely gray streaked hair to his tanned, trim physique. Sometimes, she could not believe he loved her, but there he was, a loving father but also the romantic, attentive lover. Forget the romantic stuff, she admitted. It was the great sex. She loved his earthy smell, the feel of his rough face on her skin at the end of the day, and the way his body fit into hers. She could not imagine life with any other man.

Cerise, the youngest, saw Sylvie out of the corner of her eye and smiled. The rest of the group turned as one to greet her.

"Come in and have a seat, young lady," Rod said.

Sylvie stayed in the kitchen and said, "In a minute. First, there's something I have to tell you."

She watched the muscles in his face relax to an impassive expression. Rising from the sofa while disentangling himself from the children's embraces, he joined her in the kitchen. Towering over her, she looked up into his now hardened face, but he was not looking at her. He had fixed his gaze on the indefinite, abstract design on the punched tin facing of the kitchen cabinet doors behind her. He had the removed and detached look that scared her.

"What now?" he said in a flat tone, still staring beyond her.

"I lost it today at your grandmother's place. You know what they're like when you're not with me. Today was worse. With Pilar coming to town, I suggested she meet all of them while I was with her. You know how they are. It was uglier than I could have imagined. They gave Pilar an emotional beating first, and then when I tried to stand up for her, they let me have it."

Rod crossed his arms, an action Sylvie believed was how he prevented himself from hitting her. Sylvie stepped away, occupying her hands by wiping up water spots from the faucet, and tried not to notice his anger.

"Of course, they weren't happy that I came alone to visit, even though I explained you and the kids were still recovering from the flu and couldn't handle the drive. I gave Virginia the birthday gifts, told them how the kids had handmade theirs. Do you know that not once did anyone ask how any of you were doing, but set the gifts aside and made comments about what a lousy birthday this was turning out to be?" Sylvie paused for effect, but Rod still stood arms crossed, glaring at her. She looked back down into the empty sink for something to wash.

"I said I was sorry you missed coming, but at least I was able to deliver the gifts the kids worked hard to make. Madera said that she'd hold onto the gifts until the children came to present them to Virginia properly, *in person*.

"That's about the time I noticed Pilar's car out front. I went outside to invite her in and introduce her to everyone. They were so cold and mean that I was sorry for her. Virginia accused her of getting in touch because she wanted money. I was so embarrassed and poor Pilar looked devastated. When I stood up for her, well, that's when they really turned it on me.

"I was trying to stay calm long enough to get the visit over with, but when they started hammering at me and criticizing me for wasting *your* money to pay for Mom's care attendant, I blew. I mean, they were attacking my mother for being alive after all the free babysitting she did for the kids when they were couldn't be bothered. Not to mention all the times she drove up there to help that old woman when her own two children were either too busy or not even around. I told them it would be a cold day in hell before I let those people around my children again. I told them to go rot in hell." Sylvie finished, out of breath, waiting for the worst, not looking at Rod or moving.

After several endless minutes, Rod looked her over, seeming to study her for recognition. "I'm sure you'll be their favorite in-law from now on," he said. "Don't worry, Hon. I know how they are. I'm sorry for the way they treat you. And before you say it, I know it isn't my job to apologize for them. I guess I ignore their behavior to keep what's left of us intact as a family. Considering how Tasha abandoned them, I feel a responsibility."

"That's because you're a good person," Sylvie said. "Better than me."

Rod hesitated, drew a deep sigh, and stared out into that faraway place again, as if a solution to this mess were somewhere trying to reach him if he looked long enough. After a few minutes, he said, "I'm not *blind*. I feel the undercurrents when we're there and the backhanded remarks they think I don't notice because I don't acknowledge them. I guess I hoped it would work out eventually. Understand, their behavior doesn't have anything to do with who you are. Any woman would be treated the same."

"I don't know if that makes me feel better," Sylvie said.

"I can't change who they are. For the sake of our kids, and you, let's stop this ridiculous driving to Flagstaff every week. I'll take the kids over to my folks' place. That'll keep those lines of communication open. I'll go up to Gran's by myself and do the fix-ups she needs. She loves having me to herself when I go up during the week to take care of the property."

"They'll have a fit," Sylvie said.

"To be honest, they won't take it lightly, but nothing will make them happy until we're divorced. Then it will be something else they don't like. More important, you need to remember Gran promised me the Flagstaff house when she dies. I know I sound no better than the rest of the family, but that has been a dream of mine since I was a boy. You have to control your temper. I don't want to lose that dream over your harsh words."

"I'm sorry, Rod."

"I'm the one who's sorry for asking you to put up with this family drama. Gran is an old woman who probably won't live much longer. Be patient. It's only a matter of time."

"Oh, Rod," Sylvie said in a trembling voice. The day's events had put her on automatic, with the drive back and forth, the emotional scene, and the worry of Rod's reactions. Now the dam was breaking loose and the tears came in a steady trickling of salty streams down her face.

"I'm sorry, Sylvie." Rod put his arms around her. "I wish I could stay here with you, but I've got to go to work tonight."

"I know. It's okay. Just knowing I can count on you is all I need right now."

They were quiet for a few minutes in each other's arms until her sobbing quieted to whimpers. Sylvie thought of the future without her in-laws. Her face hidden in Rod's shirt, she started to smile. About damn time, she thought. All she had to wait for now was for the old woman to die.

CHAPTER 6

September 24, 2006
Charlie Bismark's Condo, Phoenix, Arizona

Charlie Bismarck drew the twisted end of the joint to his mouth and thought about the unfair world. He closed his eyes, pursed his lips, and drew in a breath, forcing the smoke over his tongue, down his throat, and into his lungs. He held his breath as long as he could. After repeating his ritual three times, he leaned back onto the sofa pillows, raised his gangly legs onto the mirrored coffee table, and let euphoria overtake him.

"Good shit," he said, and set the joint in an ashtray near his right elbow. This is what he needed to end this crummy day. He kept replaying the scene in his head, feeling the face-burning, stomach-churning humiliation of getting the sack. The more he thought about it, the more sobering the reality.

He picked up the roach clip, inserted the remains of the joint, and then fired up the gold-plated table lighter from the coffee table. Leaning forward between spread legs, he took the lighter in his right hand and engulfed the joint end in flames. Smoke swirled above the smoldering embers and he used his nose to vacuum and capture the smoke. Within minutes, his worries of the day drifted further away until he fell asleep.

When he woke up, he heard the comforting and familiar sounds of Allegra in the kitchen. He could hear the timer ticking, water running in the sink, and smelled pesto and sausage. He also noticed she had opened the patio door and turned on the kitchen fans giving the place freshness and light. His next realization was that Allegra must have seen the ashtray and smelled the sweet woodsy smell that made it obvious what he had been doing.

Shit. After all my lecturing her on drugs, she catches me doing it. He had to find a way to present this before she knew he had woken up, which could be any minute. He had come to believe that she read his mind and would know if he were asleep.

He jumped when she called out, "You didn't forget I was coming, did you?"

"Uh, no. I had a bad morning. I may as well tell you. The truth is … they fired me this morning." He still had not sat up. He was ashamed of himself in front of her. She thought so much of him and he was letting her down on all fronts.

"What happened?" she asked, rushing over to sit next to him.

As he looked over at her, seeing the earnest expression on her face, he thought how beautiful she was with her long black hair pulled up on her head, her electrifying blue eyes, light Latina skin, her frailty, and tenderness, more than he ever deserved. His anger from the morning evaporated. She said once that there was something about looking into the eyes of someone who loved you that forced you to be honest with yourself. He was about to find out if that were true.

"I've screwed up everything. The mistakes I've made the last year caught up with me. They called me into the boardroom and told me to go. All I could think to do was get high. I'm sorry I've let you down." He looked away from her concerned gaze.

"Listen," she said. "Everyone makes mistakes. You'll get another job. Or even start your own business. You've talked about that before. *And* you're not letting me down. As long as we're together and I know I can count on you, that's what matters to me. I haven't had someone on my side since my dad died."

"I'll always be there for you, I promise," he said.

"Swear? Even if I wanted to murder someone?"

He reared back and searched her face for the ticklish smile she gave when delivering one of her scandalous punch lines. Startled that her face showed seriousness instead, he said, "Swear. Even if you wanted to murder someone."

"Good. Dinner's ready," Allegra said, kissing him before going back to the kitchen.

Charlie watched her walk away, her hips moving sensually side to side with every step. He pursed his lips to blow out a silent whistle. How strange, he thought, that she would think of murder as a test of his love and loyalty.

CHAPTER 7

September 25, 2006
Flagstaff, Arizona

Norma considered her advantage as she peered out of her kitchen window. As the lead member of the Neighborhood Watch, she was on constant alert for unusual activity on her corner, which is why she woke up. Her bedside clock read two thirty when she heard someone stumble on the piled up boxes next door. She looked out into the dimness of the yard between her house and the Rodchenko's corner lot. She saw the skulking figure moving toward the basement door. Despite Virginia's quarrelsome nature, Norma considered her watchfulness a public duty. She reached for her late husband's blackjack. With no time to wait for the police, she glided down the back stairs to her basement door and moved into the cool night air. She figured if she could prevent this man, or was that a woman, from entering the house, then she could get back to call 911.

With blackjack held high over her head, she tiptoed across the lawn. The figure looked vague against the darkness of the shadows. She saw movement and crept closer. Her heartbeat pulsing in her neck, she tightened her grip on her weapon, and prepared to swing at the head of the intruder. Her heart skipped a beat when the face turned toward her.

"Oh my goodness!" Norma said. "You scared me to death. I thought you were a criminal. What on this blessed earth are you doing creeping around in the dark? I could've given you a concussion with this thing," she said, still poised to strike with the black jack."

"Did you call the police?"

"No, actually I was going to call after I knocked you out. "

"Good."

As Norma squinted toward the darkness into the void left from the Rodchenko's open basement door, the blow against her head stunned her before dropping her to the ground.

♦ ♦ ♦

Out of breath from lugging the dead woman back to her own rear porch, the lithe figure slipped through Virginia's basement door, and listened for sounds. Quiet, maybe too quiet, but this had to be the night. Taking the basement stairs to the top floor, crisscrossing to miss the squeaking boards, caught a lucky break that the door to the kitchen was unlocked. Pushing it open by inches until the slender figure could squeeze through, the difficulty was just ahead. The den, converted into her bedroom since age and infirmity had not allowed her to take the stairs to the master bedroom, had a door with a lock that Virginia often forgot to latch.

Taking strategic steps toward the door, the gloved hand reached out to clasp the knob and turned. Unlocked, the hand squeezed the knob and pushed the door into the room. Finding no resistance and hearing no creaking sounds, entry into the room was effortless. The darkness, veil-like due to the shadows caused from gentle wind moving through the trees outside, the lone figure tiptoed with so little movement that breathing seemed to be an impossible action. Reaching for the decorative pillow placed on the easy chair at night, both hands clasped its sides and moved toward the bed.

Virginia's breathing sounded faint but steady with the comforting rhythm of sleep. Raising the pillow over Virginia's head, the hands lowered the pillow within two inches of the old woman's face before applying the violent pressure that would smother the life out of her. There was no compulsion for Virginia to see her attacker; there was only the conviction that she had to die tonight. After an attempt to wrestle the pillow from her face, Virginia stopped resisting. Leaning over another five minutes with the pillow pressed hard against her face, there was no doubt that she was dead.

Lifting the pillow off her face, the figure moved backward with caution and replaced the pillow on the chair. Still in reverse motion, moved through the doorway, and then dashed to the basement door, and descended the stairs. Locking the door, checking the entrance for signs of struggle with the neighbor, the figure moved to the back of the house, off the property, then disappeared to the waiting vehicle two streets away out of sight behind the vacant drugstore.

CHAPTER 8

September 25, 2006
Phoenix, Arizona

Madera Folsom sipped her morning coffee and used her toast to sop up the last of her fried eggs. She could not shake the hollowness inside. She kept thinking about Rod who had not called after yesterday's blowout. In recent weeks, Madera had heard an edge in her son's voice whenever they spoke. Even worse than hostile, he had an even and impersonal tone she found disturbing.

"Why can't they stay like they were as babies, obedient and needy? And why can't that old woman just *die*?" Madera said aloud, embarrassed by the sound of her voice.

At that moment, Bert came through the front door and headed for the coffeemaker at the end of the counter. "Just stopping for coffee on my way to an inspection."

No doubt ready to stuff his face again, she thought, still tearful. Bert answered as if he had heard her thoughts. "No, don't bother making anything for me. I have my lunch in the truck." When he saw her face, his smile dropped and he asked, "What's the matter? Are you all right?"

"No I'm not *all right*, dumb ass. I'm sitting here wondering how I'm going to get my son back and get him away from his witch of a wife."

"Madera, you know plans like that will backfire. Why don't you call him and tell him you want to patch things up. No one says you have to love Sylvie, but I think you're blowing her character way out of proportion to what it is. She's a good wife and good mother to their children. What is it you want her to do anyway? Is there anything anyone can do to make you and your mother happy?"

"How dare you," Madera said. "Who do you think you are telling me how to feel? She's taken my son away from me. As for Mom, she does what she thinks is best for everyone, and if she says Sylvie needs to go, she needs to go. My mother is a wonderful, selfless person and I won't stand for some reject from the white trash brigade commenting on her character." Madera was crying again, but this time her face had turned beet red, looking strangled and breathless.

Madera saw more amusement than insult in Bert's tightened face. She hated that expression of him holding back a laugh. He was the one person who recognized when she was rattling off poppycock for the benefit of others. If her mother was selfless, she was Mary Magdalene. He knew that as much as she did and that infuriated her.

"Madera, calm yourself. You know your blood pressure. Do what you want. Say what you want regardless of what I say."

After a few minutes, Madera had settled down enough to say, "Sure you don't want a chicken salad sandwich?"

"Maybe later. Now why don't you tell me what brought on all these tears?"

"I'll make you one to go, anyway." While reaching for the chicken salad, the lettuce, and the bread, Madera spoke in a relaxed voice. She had recovered herself but she was still not happy. "I'm upset because I haven't heard from Rod. I was sure he'd call me to apologize."

"He'll get in touch. I just don't believe he's the one that should apologize. I don't blame him if he *is* mad. The whole scene was unnecessary. Why couldn't you and your mother say thank you for her birthday gifts and let it go? I don't see the point."

As Madera was readying herself to give him a piece of her mind, they both turned toward knocking at the kitchen door.

"Anybody home?" Rod turned the knob as he peered through the windows of the closed Dutch door.

"Come on in, son," Bert said. "It's not locked."

As Rod turned the knob on the lower door, Madera saw Bert glance over at her and her face reddened.

"I'm glad I caught both of you here. I guess you know I want to talk about yesterday," he said after hugging Madera and shaking hands with Bert.

"It was an unfortunate thing to happen," Bert said. "How's Sylvie?"

"Naturally, she's upset about the whole thing. Mom, you know I've been a good son to you and Dad. I don't want to hurt you, but things have to change. I can't have my wife attacked by my own family any time I'm not present. That's not right. What you and Gran don't seem to understand is when you attack her, you're attacking our children and me, too. You're not giving her the respect she deserves and I can't allow this to go on."

The fear that trickled down the front of Madera like ice water was something she had not experienced before. For the first time, she could not speak out to defend herself, maybe, she thought, because she knew he was right. Instead, she said nothing.

"Here's how it's going to work from now on. We're not making those trips to Flagstaff on Sundays. I'll go see Gran and take care of the repairs she needs done to the house when I can fit it in during the week. The kids have their sports activities and their own friends on the weekends. Why take them away from that so they watch all the drama? They don't need to see their mother belittled and put down either. You're both welcome to come over any time to have a civilized dinner and be with your grandchildren, if you want."

"If we want," Madera said.

"I know you don't like Sylvie, so what's the point trying to pretend we're one big happy family when there's all this tension and backbiting. It's not good for the children to be in that environment. It makes them aggressive."

"I bet Sylvie's putting you up to this."

"No, Mom. This is my decision, not hers."

"Yeah, I bet."

"Listen, I don't want to argue. I've made the decision. I came over here in person because I don't want you to feel like I'm abandoning you like Tasha did, but you need to learn to have more respect for my ability to run my own life."

"It doesn't seem to me you know what you're doing."

Letting out a frustrated sigh, Rod ignored her remark and gave her another hug. "I have to go. I still have to talk to Gran, so I'm driving up since it's my day off."

After a nod to Bert, Rod left the way he entered.

Unable to look at Bert's self-righteous expression, the one he gave her when he knew, or thought, he was right, Madera moved to her chair at the table and sat down. The strain was almost too much, overwhelmed by the multitude of thoughts, plots, and emotions with nothing to show but more drama.

"Madera, you've got to stop trying to control everyone. Leave people alone to take care of their own affairs. It is not your job in this world to run their lives as if your children were still in diapers. Anyway, I don't know why you worry about Rod, who's always been hard working and responsible, when you don't worry about your daughters. Lenore at least talks to you, although I can't imagine why the way you treat her."

"What do you mean? I'm a good mother to Lenore. Don't I loan her money when I can? Haven't I run over there any time of the day or night when she's having one of her neurotic episodes about her job or Allegra? Wasn't I there taking care of the house when Richard died and she was all alone with that bastard daughter and needed a mother to look after things? What else can I do, I ask you?"

"Allegra is not a bastard. And those things you're so proud of doing for her don't require any affection or communication. You don't show any interest in her as a person. You don't even show any concern for her feelings, except for intolerance when she disagrees with you. Anymore, she sits there and agrees with whatever you say because she knows you're not listening anyway."

"I ... well, what difference does it make?" Madera stared down at the twisted dishtowel. "I know she's my daughter, but she's always been a disappointment. My friends beam with pride about their daughters who have university degrees and run businesses. I have a daughter whose biggest claim to fame is the huge amount of anti-depressants she needs to get her through life."

Madera's agitation returned, so she took a deep breath. "Even knowing how she feels, it's better to have a shallow relationship with Lenore than to have none at all. I guess I can't help letting my feelings out when I'm not thinking. Rod's the one child that acts as if he loves me. At least he did until now." Madera started to tear up again, but this time Bert went over and put his arms around her until she stopped crying.

"Maddie, being around this family is too much for one man alone to handle," Bert said, and kissed the top of her head.

"I'm sorry. I shouldn't have said that. Everything will work itself out one way or another."

"You mean when the old woman is gone."

"God forgive me, but that can't be too soon for me," Bert said, as the ringing of the telephone cut into the mental image of Virginia in a coffin.

CHAPTER 9

September 25, 2006
Phoenix, Arizona

Pilar stepped onto the Phoenix pavement for the first time, surprised at the contrast between the wintry humidity in Cincinnati and the balmy aridness in Phoenix. Wearing the turtleneck sweater and scarf she had needed during her drive from Flagstaff, the stream of uncomfortable wetness had begun in her armpits, so she looked around for a place to change. No need to arrive to meet Sylvie's family wilted and smelling bad, she thought as she pulled the car into a Squeaky Pete's Burger Barn parking lot.

From her first encounter in Arizona, she noticed warmth in the people, friendliness so opposite the cautious cordiality toward strangers back home. This was a good sign that she might have made the right choice in coming. Two vicious elderly women should not taint her view of the entire population. After she had calmed down yesterday, she had time to reevaluate her motives. The drama that these people thrived on was nothing to do with her, and probably nothing to do with anyone else outside their immediate family.

Smiling to herself while standing in line, she looked around to meet the vacant stares of her companions. Negotiating her tote bag with the large coffee and sausage roll, she made her way back to the car and ate in comfortable contemplation as she looked out at the spiky greens and browns of the landscape. On her way back from dumping her trash, she watched a mother Roadrunner leading about a dozen small chicks across the desert beyond the parking lot, when she heard her cell phone ringing. She rushed to her car, reached in to grab and pressed the green button.   "Hello."

"Good. I'm glad I caught you." Sylvie's voice sounded strange, high-pitched, and quivering. "Where are you?"

"I'm in a place called Anthem. I'm not too far from you. What's up?"

"I'm afraid I have some bad news. Virginia passed away last night."

"Oh, no. I'm sorry to hear that," she said. The words echoed inside like the time when she had heard of Pete's death. She gulped to suppress her spiraling emotions. "What happened?"

"She died in her sleep. Probably a stroke or her heart just stopped, who knows. I think the doctor said heart failure. We wouldn't have heard about it so soon if a jogger hadn't found her neighbor, Norma, dead outside on her back porch still in her nightgown. The police went to Virginia's to check on her and find out if she'd seen anything. That's when they found her. They had to break the door in to get inside when there was no answer. Virginia's family is well-known up there and everyone tried to keep an eye on her with her being so old."

"How shocking," Pilar said.

"Anyway, Rod's going straight up there. I'm staying here with the kids. I've got to get some sleep. You're still welcome to stay here, but I wanted to warn you beforehand. Rod's parents are coming here with Lenore, so you might find yourself in awkward company."

"Listen, I'll find a hotel room. We can talk tomorrow. Please send my condolences to everyone."

"Thank you for understanding. What a way to welcome you to Phoenix. Good thing Virginia made her funeral arrangements in advance. We can get that done without too much aggravation."

Even with the scene from the other day, Sylvie's crudeness caught Pilar off guard. "Well, that's something anyway, isn't it?"

"With Rod's job keeping him up all night, he doesn't have much time for additional obligations. Now that he'll be inheriting the Flagstaff house, he'll be busier than ever juggling his schedule."

"I'm happy for you. I didn't get to see much of it the other day. Is it a nice place?"

"The house needs work but it has good bones. The real value is that the house sits on a full acre with some other buildings and plenty of large trees. His great-grandparents built the house. Your grandfather grew up there."

"Nice. I hope I get an invitation under more pleasant circumstances."

"Of course. That's a great place for talking about family history. Listen, I need to go. I'll call you later."

The line went silent and Pilar looked down at her phone. Virginia dead, gone. *Well, that takes care of getting stories about Pete.* While searching the travel book for a hotel, she considered whether to leave Phoenix altogether and forget about her plans to connect with family.

At the hotel, Pilar stretched out across the bed to nurture a growing sadness. The drive had not been long, but she was somewhere between wired and exhausted. What she needed was a healing late morning nap, but sleep did not come.

Virginia's death stirred up a renewed craving for her family history. She got up to review what she knew so far. Copies of birth certificates, land deeds, census pages, marriage licenses, and death certificates looked up at her. All from the beginnings in Arizona, but Pilar wanted more about their lives in Mexico before and during the Revolution. With the last living relative with firsthand information gone, she wondered if that part of her— the part connected to the past— was gone forever.

CHAPTER 10

September 28 2006
Funeral Home, Flagstaff, Arizona

Looking down at Virginia in her coffin gave Madera the overwhelming pleasure that comes from the knowledge that she will never have to experience that particular unpleasantness again. Funny, she thought, she had no fear of the corpse as she had imagined. Nor was there pity, remorse, or kindness in her heart as she studied the face in the casket that had tortured her for so long. A face now in eternal contentment relaxed and satisfied with the life she had led. Madera stood there, amazed at how easy it had been for her to sneak out of this life without retribution. All anyone could hope for now was life hereafter to punish her for her sins.

"Mom is gone! Oh, God! Mom is gone!" Her voice rising to a hysterical pitch, she placed her hand over dry eyes to peer through her fingers at a group of older women across the aisle. "Bless her soul. Have mercy on us all."

Tugging her arm, Bert, red-faced, directed her to one of the front pews. "For God's sake, shut up. You don't have to engage the histrionics for the benefit of this crowd. You were the best daughter you could be considering how she treated you."

"Was I?" Madera said, feeling more like a child at that moment than a middle-aged woman. "I wonder if she thought so."

"I'm sure none of us will ever know. She was a sharp, hard woman, like a sack of nails." Bert placed a muscular arm around her and pressed her head on his shoulder. "Holidays will never be the same, I'm glad to say."

◆ ◆ ◆

During the drive home from the funeral, Bert said, "Do you have a copy of your mother's will? I know there's no question about the money, but there are the formalities."

Sighing, Madera said, "I guess it's with the attorney she always used. He didn't even show up for the funeral. I would think that with all the money she paid him during her lifetime, he could've made an appearance. Well, as soon as I'm in control, he's out, I'll tell you."

Bert took a sidelong glance at his wife. He had been anxious for what was to come in the next few weeks, and had made plans when he heard the old woman was dead. Timing his exit when Madera occupied herself with the excitement of her acquired wealth was essential. Leaving her at the strategic point was akin to placing a grenade in her hand and hoping he could convince her not to believe it was explosive until he could get far away. In the end, she would be angrier that he caught her off guard than she would be concerned about his absence.

As ever, her fretting about the opinions of the women at church drove most of her behavior. Knowing Madera for thirty-seven years as he did, he knew she would dump his blue-collar butt like a lead weight once she had her hands on her mother's money.

"I think the first thing we'll do is move to Flagstaff and redecorate that place," Madera said. "Get rid of all that old furniture. Paint everything, reface the cabinets, put in new sinks, new carpet, make it modern. Let me see, who is the best decorator? I must use the best or no one at all." Madera looked

over at Bert, and said, "Oh, sorry, I forgot who I was talking to."
  "I didn't," Bert said, leaving Madera looking puzzled.

CHAPTER 11

September 28, 2006
Funeral Home, Flagstaff, Arizona

Pilar whispered to no one in particular, weaving through the procession of viewers, "Death is ominous and eternal. The dread within us even when we're laughing." She tried to be brave as she entered the reception room. Thankful that the coffin had been closed earlier, Pilar found comfort that came from the implication that Virginia might not be inside. She had no desire to see the corpse. After all, she barely knew this woman and after her brief encounter, she was sure she would not have cared to know more of her.

Remaining in Arizona long enough to attend the funeral had been the right thing to do, and gave her the opportunity to look around Flagstaff before she returned home. While she had not yet met Rod, she had lost her optimism that he would be different. After spending the day before at the public library downtown, pleasantly surprised at the extensive Mexican history displayed, she estimated a few more days for the research she wanted to accomplish. After that, she had promised herself a sightseeing trip to the Grand Canyon before leaving for home. All she wanted to do was to get this funeral behind her.

Familial duty to pay her respects aside, she attended this funeral more because of what Aunt Marian would say if she did not. Lost inside her thoughts, she did not notice Sylvie enter and walk toward her. Startled at first, she took a double take when she realized someone stood beside her.

"Hi," Sylvie said. "Sorry about the abrupt phone call, but as you can imagine, all plans stalled when we heard about Virginia's death. We still want you to stay with us while you're here. Rod's interested in his great uncle and wants to hear about the family history you've collected."

"Where's Rod?"

"He took our children to a sitter. We had reservations about bringing them, and decided they were too young. It's not easy for parents to know which decision will have the lasting effect of either corrupting a sound mind or making it stronger." Sylvie smiled, her manner more in keeping with a cocktail party than a funeral.

"I plan to leave. I'm staying at Little America. To be honest, my reception here has not been what I expected. My intention is to leave after playing the tourist and then put all of this behind me."

"Rod and I are not like that, really. One or two children turn out to be normal in a family of freaks. I consider myself lucky to have Rod as my husband and I think you'll find him to be a good human being. Please say you'll come. We have a guest room ready for you and our children want to meet you too."

Looking into Sylvie's pleading eyes, Pilar smiled and nodded. "Okay."

At that moment, Pilar's eyes wandered as she was speaking when she noticed Madera and Lenore were glaring at her from across the room. Pilar sat, stunned at the antagonistic attention. A wave of anxiety seized her. Averting her eyes, she said, "Is there something wrong with Madera and Lenore. They're staring at me like they want to cut my heart out for the sacrifice."

Sylvie took a deep breath. "My opinion, for what it's worth. They're miserable, bitter old witches. They resent everyone, including each other. What they have is never enough and what everyone else has is always more than they deserve. They've treated me like someone who drinks out of the toilet from the first time Rod brought me home to meet them. I can't tell you how many times I left their house in tears. I could care less now what they think. In fact, I'm feeling crazy happy. Virginia is one down. One down, two to go."

Pilar watched Sylvie's face flushed, excited, and wondered for a second if being around this family was toxic.

"So, what did Pete tell you about all of us?" Sylvie put her arm around Pilar's shoulders as she spoke to guide her to the entrance where Rod was entering.

"Not much, really. He never talked about his family, only how much he loved and admired his mother. I thought there had been an argument that was never patched up due to living so far apart."

At that moment, Pilar and Sylvie stopped in front of a man Pilar knew could not be anyone but a relative of Peter Paralelos. Younger and suited, this man had the same dark almond-shaped blue eyes, and the same black eyelashes that had given Pete a distinct and debonair attractiveness. She guessed Rod was about the same 6'1" with slender features and muscular build.

"It's incredible how much you look like Pete," Pilar said. "Wow, I would know you anywhere."

"It's too bad I never met him. Welcome." Rod extended a long, lanky hand out to clasp her fingers.

Sylvie turned an ironic glance to the other side of the room and said, "They're giving her the treatment. They're outright staring at her. You can always count of them to make a newcomer feel just dreadful. Perfect for a funeral."

"Don't give them any attention," Rod said blushing. "If I weren't showing respect for my grandmother, I'd have words with them."

"I haven't seen Allegra," Sylvie said. "She's always in tow like the family puppy. Too bad Tasha didn't show up. You'd think she'd get over her issues long enough to say goodbye to her grandmother." Sylvie looked away from Rod, and rolled her eyes in Pilar's direction.

"I'm sure Gran left Tasha out of her will and that's more than she deserves," Rod said, who had been studying the casket as he spoke.

Smiling again, Sylvie said, "Let's forget about these people and move on. Pilar agreed to come and stay with us while she's here. I insisted she get to know us so we can prove we're nothing like them."

Rod looked at Pilar, then met Sylvie's eyes, "Yes, we're interested to hear all you know about the family."

Pilar shivered from a wave of coldness that passed through her. She could not decide if the chill was a product of the funeral atmosphere or a psychic barometer reading her company.

CHAPTER 12

September 28, 2006
Phoenix, Arizona

Allegra stood in front of Lenore's medicine cabinet reading the labels of the various prescription bottles that took up two of the four shelves. Familiar with ones similar to her own, she winced looking at this display of pharmacopeia enough to kill a herd of buffalo. If her mother was not the monster she is, Allegra thought she might pity her. From the usual over-the-counter allergy and pain tablets to the hardcore hydrocodone and oxycodone, she had no doubt the reason Lenore believed she needed the anti-depressants. If she were typical of the kids her age that she knew from the clubs, she would have handfuls of pills stuffed in her pockets right now. But she was not typical. She had a mission to substitute, not steal.

"Hurry up in there. This is making me nervous," Charlie said from the hallway.

"Don't be such a little girl. I have it," Allegra said, reaching for the brown glass bottle and closing the door on the cabinet. "She's at the funeral. She and Gran will stay long enough for everyone to watch them grieve. We've got time."

"God, I hope so. I don't like this."

"Don't judge me. You don't know what it's like, the way I've had to survive. Would you rather I was the one about to die? Because that's what will happen if she carried out her threat to have me put in a mental institution."

"Of course I don't, but I'm nervous about killing someone? I've done a lot of things, but never murder."

"Look at it as self-defense instead of murder. I've thought about this a long time. It's not so much about my trust as it is about having the freedom to live my life. If you have a better solution, tell me."

Allegra held out her open hand to him, and said, "Give it to me."

Charlie reached into the deep pocket of his jacket and handed her three small packets. Allegra took them and pulled out the cling wrap, stretched it over a chopping board she brought from the kitchen. She took the black and green capsules from the bottle and opened each capsule, pouring the powdery contents into the sink. After repeating the process ten times, she refilled the capsules with a combination of the three powders. She twisted the capsules back together, wiping each with a tissue, before dropping them back into the bottle.

"See. All done," she said, raising her head to look up at him. "Now, I just need to clean this up. We can start a fire out back in the pit and burn the gloves and the packets." Allegra returned the bottle to its place after wiping it down with her shirt, and grabbed her debris before following him outside. "Ok. Let's start the fire. I don't expect her, but it won't hurt to be outside if she comes back before we leave."

"Starting a fire is one thing I can do with confidence."

Allegra followed Charlie down the hallway, pausing to pull two sodas from the refrigerator before joining him to the backyard. She stared into the dark void of the fire pit as he built a pyramid of kindling and newspapers. He lit the edges of the paper and went to stand next to her. The crackling wood yielding to the fire and the tiny flames popping out from between the logs brought her back to the moment. She tossed the trash into the flames before she sat next to him on the bench.

"With the way she eats that stuff, we should only have to wait a day or two," Allegra said, still staring into the fire.

"You're sure you want to do this? There's time to stop it."

Allegra moved closer to him, rested her head on his shoulder, and said, "Dead sure."

CHAPTER 13

September 28, 2006
Glendale, Arizona

Pilar followed the Folsom's sedan to their home in Glendale. Off the Interstate, driving west for several miles, they turned up a winding road and pulled into the driveway of a large two-story stucco home that butted against the mountain. Lush desert fragrances soothed Pilar as she walked through the yard to the front entrance of their home.

Inside, following the spacious foyer into the great room and kitchen, the unoccupied space full of toys, primary reading books, and videos made it apparent children lived here. The entire back of the great room featured ceiling to floor windows providing a spectacular view to the backyard pool and more desert plants. Sylvie took Pilar's suitcase and led her to a guest room.

"Make yourself comfortable," Sylvie said, setting Pilar's suitcase on the bed.

A door slammed in the distance and in an instant, the house filled with small voices speaking on top of the other, a dog's guttural barking, and many unidentifiable scrapes and thuds. "You're in for commotion now. Come out when you're ready. I'm heating up leftovers for dinner."

After setting up her personal items in the bathroom, Pilar entered the great room to find three chattering children dumping out the contents of a bag and squealing about which game they would play first while an older woman stood next to Sylvie in the kitchen. When they noticed her presence, they stopped and looked up at Pilar.

From her station at the sink, Sylvie called out, "Pilar is a cousin of your dad's. Introduce yourselves."

They each blinked, smiled, and said their names.

Pilar said, "I'm happy to meet you," before they resumed their chatter over the game. Pilar sidled up to the island and said, "Beautiful children."

"Thank you," Sylvie said grinning. "They're my pride and joy. This is my mother's care attendant, Aggie. Aggie, this is Pilar, the relative of Rod's I was telling you about."

Aggie reached out her hand to Pilar, smiling. "Nice to meet you," she said and then turned to Sylvie. "I'd better get back to your mother. She enjoyed the children today but she might be tired."

"Thanks for helping out."

"Anytime. We enjoy having them around," Aggie said, before closing the front door behind her.

"This is a beautiful home you have here," Pilar said, her eyes sweeping over the great room and the formal rooms across the foyer.

"I like living in a brand new home even if it is far from town," Sylvie said, letting out a sigh. "It's going to be fun to hear about another side of the family. Being an only child, I had looked forward to having sisters-in-law. You know, shopping, sharing family outings. I envisioned having great holiday parties and all of our children playing together. That never happened, of course. One of the great disappointments, but in the end, it's their loss."

"My situation is similar but for different reasons," Pilar said. "My brothers were killed in the same accident that killed my parents, leaving me no chance for family relationships, good or bad. I still have relatives, but it's not the same."

"I know. I'm sorry," she said, giving a quick squeeze to Pilar's resting hand. Sylvie was quiet for a couple of minutes while she set the food on the table. Then she called Rod and the children to the table and the tone turned upbeat and congenial. After the meal, Sylvie, Pilar, and Rod went to the living room while the children moved the dishes to the counter next to the dishwasher.

"Now," Rod said. "Tell me about Pete. You know that he and my Gran were children of immigrants. The Paralelos were from Mexico. Then Gran married into the Rodchenkos who were from Russia."

"Yeah, he talked about that but not in detail. I always thought he didn't know or remember much about his parent's history, but he also said the past was the past and should be left alone."

Rod laughed. "I think they might have been secretive about their lives in other countries back in those days. Foreigners worked hard to fit in and not stand out. That meant leaving your past and your culture behind. They call it mainstreaming these days. They didn't see it as wrong either, more future forward. I used to ask Gran about her early childhood. Wow, that was like pulling teeth. She'd say, 'Why you so obsessed with the past. It's over.' I would tell her that there is an industry called genealogy full of other people as interested in their families' past as I am."

"What would she say to that?" Pilar said.

"She'd waive her hand and say, 'They're fools. You can't live your life with your thumb stuck up your ass,' and send me off to work on chores." As he laughed, Pilar could see him reliving the memories with a tinge of sadness. "Tell me," he continued. "What do you know of our family history?"

"It's odd. Not much, so I began researching Mexican history. I know more about the history of León than I do about specifics about our family. After Pancho Villa lost to the Obregón army in 1916, the family left León and escaped the death warrants by crossing into the US at Laredo. Ricardo's brother, Tomas, made a deal for his life and his family, but his family still had to leave. The army mistook him to be Ricardo because of their resemblance and decided to make sure by going after both men." Pilar took a quick breath to keep her momentum, while Rod and Sylvie watched her with blank stares.

"Imagine," Pilar said. "Both families travelled on foot, including six-year old Virginia and eight-year old Pete, carrying all their possessions with them. I'm not sure why, but they kept moving until they settled in Flagstaff. I think they must have saved money because they were able to buy property there. I'm vague on that part. My understanding is the revolution was about the poverty."

Rod shifted, glancing over at Sylvie as Pilar looked into her coffee cup before taking a sip, "You have some of the facts wrong about their origins," he said. "Tomas became a *Villista* because he believed in the cause, but Ricardo was a loyal *haciendado* until he lost the family home to Villa during his campaign to give land to the *Mestizos*. Our family escaped because revolution took everything from them, except money they had in US banks. It was my grandfather, Ricardo, who was bitter against his brother Tomas for getting all of the family involved."

"Oh, I see," Pilar, said, trying to hide her confusion. "Well, what about the Russian side of the family? I understand they escaped Russia during their Revolution."

"Yes, but with the distance, it's difficult to learn those details. Grandpa Ralph never talked about his family either. Maybe they were too young to remember much. He was a quiet man, sensitive. Gran said not to bother him with questions, because he had a hard time losing everyone. Both families ended up in Flagstaff about the same time and became friends. As far as I'm concerned, that's when our family history began."

Pilar paused. She understood that, finding her own memories of childhood dominated by interactions with her family more than current events of the period. "I wish these questions occurred to me when I was younger. Times I could have asked Pete when we took walks or went fishing. Later, it was about what was happening in the present, school, friends, careers, and boys. I feel a great loss now and regret that I didn't take more interest in his past when he was alive. I could've asked him everything. That's the way it goes, I guess."

Sylvie stood up and motioned at her coffee cup, "More coffee?"

"It's good for you that I know enough of their lives in Flagstaff. We spent weeks at a time up there when we were kids. Gran would tell us stories about what Flagstaff was like in those days."

"Wonderful," Pilar said. "I'd enjoy hearing those stories. I suppose it was typical of the old west towns I've read about."

"Not at all. Flagstaff had industry, affluence, and a business class who enjoyed culture and sophistication. Stop by to look at the Riordan Mansion when you get up there. It's something to see and unexpected when all you've ever heard of are Arizona mining towns."

"I'd no idea. Sounds like little Peter and Virginia had it good growing up. What was the family business?"

After a brief pause, Rod said, "Merchants. I guess they did well for themselves. I think they had a general store or something like that."

"From what I could learn, they came from León where the industry was shoemaking. I guessed they arrived in Flagstaff and set up a shop doing what they knew. "

"León. Right. Yes, it was something like that."

Pilar noticed an unusual mood shift. Was it in her imagination that he paused as if he needed time to find the answer? Was he guarded and evasive all of a sudden? What difference did it make after all this time, anyway? Maybe they did something embarrassing like ran a brothel. She decided to ignore this and move on to another subject.

"Tell me about the Rodchenkos. Is there a connection between your first name and that name?"

"Yes, it's a long name so I've always gone by Rod. Let's see. The Rodchenkos came here from Russia in 1914, after the Revolution in 1905. Russian assassins killed Nicolai and Natasha one evening while they walked home from the theatre. The Paralelos took in their two children, Rudolf and Varvara. Virginia married their son, Rudolf, or Ralph, as they called him here. As far as I've ever heard, Varvara, who went by English equivalent Barbara, moved back to Russia to fight after the Bolshevik Revolution in 1917. No one heard of her again. The rumor was Lenin's Cheka executed her when she returned to Leningrad. No confirmation or proof, of course. Like I said, before, it happened a long time ago."

"How sad that Ralph lost everyone like I did," Pilar said. Feeling the onset of tears rising behind her eyes, she swallowed and took a deep breath to control her emotions. Those involuntary rushes of emotions had always made her vulnerable. She cursed at herself as she took another deep breath.

"It was a wild time in history." Rod said. "Russia and Mexico had their revolutions happening at the same time, and then other countries, like Germany, supplying money and guns to the rebels to further their own agenda. Marxist ideology spread across the world like a lightning bolt, encouraging people to declare an end to their poverty and poor living conditions under oppressive rulers."

"Only to find that they replaced one dictator with another," Pilar said.

"You know your history," Rod said, in a tone more like an accusation than a compliment.

Pilar said, "Our families came to the United States and decided to settle in Flagstaff. What do you think made them choose that town?"

"I'm not sure," Rod said. "Maybe to get farther away from the border."

Pilar was beginning to wonder if Rod knew as much as he let on about the family. "I guess we might never know why some things happened."

Noticing the conversation was growing forced, Pilar said she was tired and needed to go to bed.

Rod brightened. "Yes, we've all had a long day. We'll talk more later. If you're interested in more history of those times, I have several books in your room. Tomorrow, I'll get out the old pictures. It's amazing to see them as they were when they were young."

"I'm looking forward to that. Thanks again for your hospitality, by the way. I hope this isn't an imposition."

"Not at all. I'm looking forward to learning about your side of the family, too, so don't forget. See you tomorrow." With that, Rod rose from his seat and headed toward the bedrooms.

After settling in, Pilar tried to calm down, but her active mind started a replay of the dinner conversation. Rod's attitude seemed off. As pleasant as he was, Pilar could not understand what made her uneasy. He was right that this had been a long day, as well as emotional and draining. Adding that to her long drive, the unpleasant experience in Flagstaff, followed by Virginia's unexpected death, anxiety was not a leap to situational depression. Setting aside her qualms, she pulled a book from a shelf, tucked in under covers, and fell into a fitful sleep with dusty visions of the Mexican Revolution.

CHAPTER 14

October 1, 2006
Phoenix, Arizona

Bert had listened all morning to Madera talk about the changes her mother's money was about to make in their lives. She insisted he quit his job as Construction Superintendent to make time to hone his social skills for all the events they would be attending. Oblivious, Bert still could not understand how Madera tuned out anything outside her own thoughts. He doubted she noticed that he had not spoken all morning, no more than she had not acknowledged his protests during the last few days.

"Madera, I have a document I want you to sign."

"Oh? What is it?"

"I was concerned about the inheritance, so I saw an attorney. He says this post-nuptial agreement will protect us both in the future."

Eyes squinting she fixed a stare on the paper, then back to Bert and said, "Why would you do that?"

"Because I knew you have a lot of other things on your mind and someone has to be thinking about practicalities. The document states that I hold no claim to your inheritance and you won't claim my paychecks and my retirement as community property. In case anything happened to you, you would want your inheritance to go straight to the kids, right?"

"I'll say I don't need your paychecks anymore. Give me that paper. I'll sign it," she said and grabbed the paper from Bert's hand.

"Wait a minute," Bert said. "We need a notary."

"Right. The neighbor's daughter-in-law is a notary. I saw her car a little while ago. I'll pop next door and get her."

Madera returned minutes later with a ruffled woman, notary book in hand. The signing and notarizing finished, Madera rushed the stunned woman back out the door with a profusion of thanks.

Bert smiled and took a deep breath. Tomorrow, after he moved his things out while she was at the decorator's, he would tell her he intended to file for divorce.

CHAPTER 15

October 3, 2006
Phoenix, Arizona

It had been two days since Bert left, and Madera decided she was fine about it. That creep sneaking that document in like that. Well, who cares anyway with the money I am about to get, she thought. She smiled into the mirror at her middle-aged face with sunspots, heavy folds around her eyes, overgrown gray brows, and stiff gray hair. She considered the plastic surgery she could now afford to turn back the clock for another chance to be happy. She might even meet a man worthy of her this time with his own money and they would live in casual luxury for the rest of their lives. With an uncharacteristic smile, she allowed her eyes to meet in the mirror as she applied her pink lipstick.

♦ ♦ ♦

Alfred Whitney sat across the table and regarded Madera. Typical older woman trying to disguise a lifetime of neglect behind heavy makeup and clothes meant for a much younger woman. Not all the money in the world can buy class and good taste, he mused as he motioned her to the chair. He reached out to shake her hand, and watched as she plopped into the chair across from him.

"I know this is a formality, but I understand you have to read the Will to me."

"Uh, yes," he said, confused. "I don't need to read the Will word for word. You have a copy here to take with you. I asked you to come today because I've received a few telephone calls yesterday and I need to clarify the situation in person."

"Oh, I'm sorry about the calls, but here's the thing. I want to start redecorating the Flagstaff house, but the furniture companies want more of a down payment than I have. I told them to call you, so you could tell them I'll be able to more than afford the bill."

"Well, Madera. That's the problem."

"What d'you mean? Is it unethical to disclose my financial position to trades people?"

Mr. Whitney shifted his tight frame in the wooden chair. He was going to devastate this pathetic woman. Even though this was not his fault, she would make an emotional scene as if it were.

"The truth is I don't know anything about your financial position."

"Of course you do. I've inherited my mother's considerable estate. I mean, you of all people must know what that's worth."

Proceed with caution, he thought as he reached over to offer her a copy of Virginia's will. Without considering it, she looked at him for a response.

"You see, Madera, your mother had a new Will, one she revised about six months before she died. The previous intent wasn't much different, except that in the latest document she included all her grandchildren. Therefore, you are one of several beneficiaries. After mementos and small bequests to the grandchildren, she left you a monthly allowance for life. She left the remainder of her estate to your brother Nikolas. I was under the impression you knew. It's set up in trust to pass down to his children after his death. She said she owed a certain obligation to him and that you would understand having benefited from her generosity all these years. I regret I'm the one to tell you."

Watching Madera, he was sure she was going to faint. He saw the muscles in her face turn to jelly, heard her stomach rumble, watched her hands tremble, and speculated that her throat was closing up by the beet redness of her skin, but she steadied herself. He hoped she would save the drama for later. He had never been good with hysterical women.

Still trembling, she said, "I don't understand. I've taken care of her for years while my brother has not shown his face in Arizona *once*. Week after week of driving to Flagstaff, listening to her insults, eating her crappy food, and all this time she was laughing at me. She told me I was going to get everything. How could she do this to me? How could she do this to my children? There's got to be a mistake."

"I'm sorry, but there's no mistake. She came here in person to give instructions and sign."

"Well, I'm going to contest this Will. This is a farce. My husband heard her tell me I got everything."

"You can contest the Will, of course, but written documents prevail over verbal contracts. Listen, I'm sorry that you're not getting what you expected but she did not exclude you. Your mother set you up with an allowance of two thousand dollars per month for the rest of your life. That is considerable."

"You don't understand. That's not enough for all my plans. I guess *he* gets the house, as well?"

"I'm afraid not. The house is not part of her estate because it was not hers to bequeath. It reverted to her brother, Peter, and his descendants. She knew he died a couple of years ago, but she said that her parents obligated her to return the deed to Peter. Apparently, the house was originally his and he deeded it over to her a long time ago when he moved away. You see, in their parents' will, there was a stipulation that the house would go to the male heir in each generation. Their parents left the house to him assuming he would make his permanent home in Flagstaff. When Virginia married, he had already moved to the east, so he signed the deed over to her for her use for life, but without the right to sell it. There was an arrangement to keep the property within the family, so if she had decided to move, the house would have reverted back to him immediately."

"What? She never told us. At least Nikolas will be able to afford to come here now," she said, her voice struggling to be audible. "She's mocking me from the grave."

CHAPTER 16

October 3, 2006
Phoenix, Arizona

Rod had been nurturing his hostility toward Madera since she called this morning for him to get to her house *on the double*.

"What's so important?" Rod said when Madera opened the door.

"Is that any way to talk to your mother? At least come in and sit down. I've had a great shock about your grandmother's will."

He saw Lenore sitting on the sofa looking bleaker than usual and Dad sitting in his favorite chair by the television. Neither acknowledged him, yet seemed locked in an argumentative stance. This could not be good, he thought while finding his familiar seat on the other end of the sofa. "So, what's going on?"

"The lawyer gave me a copy of the Will yesterday. I'm upset and I don't know how to fix this. There's got to be something that can be done."

Sighing deeply, Rod said, "What are you talking about?"

"We've been *had* by your grandmother. She left most of her

money to that asshole Nikolas."

"What! She always said he wouldn't get a dime after leaving town like that," Rod said.

"I know what she said. She always promised me the Flagstaff house too, but I found out it wasn't hers to leave. It belongs to Pete's family, which I guess is that Pilar person whose ass you're kissing."

"Gran always promised *me* the house!" Rod said.

"Don't be ridiculous. Why would she skip her children and give you alone such a valuable asset?"

"For all the time I did repairs and helped to maintain it. That's why," Rod said, hearing his ten-year-old voice speaking.

From between the raised voices, Lenore spoke up calmly and said, "She obviously lied to us to get us to wait on her hand and foot. The question is how are we going to fix this?"

"I'm not sure," Madera said. "We'll have to take the Will to another attorney to find out if we can contest it. No telling how much that will cost." Madera had the document in her hand, waving it as she spoke, until Rod grabbed it away and started reading it.

"I see you're the only one getting a monthly allowance. Tasha, Lenore, and I get a thousand dollars each. Why is Tasha even mentioned?" Rod's voice had grown huskier and deeper, a bellow that echoed throughout the small house.

"That's nice for you, isn't it, Mom. You'll take it. Forget that I'm going to have to fend for myself," Lenore said.

"What are you complaining about? Allegra's trust is more than enough to take care of you. Once you have her committed, it's all yours. I don't see you wanting to share that with the rest of us."

Sitting off to the side, Bert turned toward the three and said, "This is what all of you deserve for letting her bully you all these years. For whatever reason the sadistic old battleax decided to screw her family, it's over now. It will cost more to hire attorneys to fight than it will benefit you. She knew how all of you would feel and probably has a clause in there disinheriting anyone who disputes it. It's time for the three of you to accept the situation and move on with your lives."

Madera, almost unable to speak, yelled at Bert with a voice more like a croak, "Why don't you just get the hell out of here? I should have known you'd be useless. I'm sorry I asked you to come."

"I'm happy to leave," he said rising from the chair and crossing the room.

"Get out and don't come back. Ever!"

"My pleasure," he said. For the next few minutes, the three watched him walk to his car and drive away.

"So what should we do now?" Rod said.

Looking at Rod, Madera said, "I don't know yet. I thought you'd have some idea. Does Pilar know yet?"

"If she does, she hasn't said anything. What difference does that make? "

"Not much, I guess," Madera said.

"Face it," Lenore said. "We're screwed. I just want to forget about it. You two do whatever you want. The house is a money pit and it's not like there's a buried treasure to make it worth fighting over. I agree that cash would have been nice, but we'll have to make do without it." Lenore stood up and took her sunglasses and keys from her purse, and then walked to the door. "Let me know if anything changes."

She shot one last furtive look at Rod, turned and left.

Madera turned to Rod and said, "So, Mr. Big Shot. What are you going to do about this?"

"Go hunt for buried treasure." He laughed deep and loud, and walked out leaving Madera speechless.

CHAPTER 17

October 4, 2006
Phoenix, Arizona

Inside Charlie's master bathroom, he studied Allegra as she looked at herself in the mirror. On the outside, he saw an alluring woman, kindness emanating from within, her soft features hinting at inexhaustible compassion and empathy. His familiarity with his own demons had taught him how disparate the face the world sees is to the inner individual that is always taming a primal need to have what it wants at any cost. Understanding that in himself, he believed anyone could commit crimes. Not crimes of the moment brought about by the need for self-preservation or out of angry impulses, but premeditated crimes committed purely for profit or revenge. When he looked at Allegra, he knew that she had summoned her inner demon in the attempt to free herself from circumstances she saw as insurmountable and hopeless.

"Isn't it ironic," Allegra said, jarring him from his thoughts.

"What."

"That a murderer would become the murder victim."

"You don't have any proof that she killed your dad."

"I saw the detective's report on Claire, didn't I? Mom knew about his affair before he died, but never let on. You know how insecure she is. She must've been sure he was going to leave her. What she didn't count on was the trust. And she didn't count on me getting into the safe and finding that envelope buried underneath everything else."

"You're right about that. I don't think she counted on you being strong enough to open your own eyes. I'm sorry to say it, but the women in your family are the types that give all women a bad name, present company excluded."

They both laughed, making eye contact in the mirror's reflection.

"The time they spent manipulating other people, they could have had brilliant careers curing cancer or AIDS, for heaven sake. Think of the brainpower it takes to keep track of the machinations, keeping the truth away from certain people. I'm going to do whatever it takes in my life not to become one of them. They make me ashamed."

Looking at her as she combed out her dark hair, he said, "How long do you think it will take before she takes them? With the meth and heroin, it won't take too many to get the job done."

"Any time now."

"Listen, Allie. I'm not sure this is the best solution to the problem. You know the risk you're taking? I'm behind you whatever you decide. You know that, so don't give me that look, but both of us know a day won't pass that we won't wonder if we really got away with it."

"Don't worry. We won't get caught. When they find the drugs in her system, they'll assume she was like all the other prescription junkies, mixing legit drugs with street drugs in the mistaken belief they knew what they were doing. Tragic and sad, like those dumbass celebrities who have everything and still think they need drugs to be happy. I'd like them to have my life in this family for a day. They'd really have a reason then."

"How different the situation could have been if Lenore had been a good mother," he said more to himself than to her.

HERE LIES BURIED

"Maybe, but she made a mistake that Gran didn't make. Getting diagnosed," Allegra said, looking at him as if she were trying to read his mind. "What the average person doesn't get is that once they advertise they have a mental disorder, real or imagined, others view you as different. They expect you to fall apart with the least bit of provocation. My mother thinks the people around her at church and at work are rooting for her because they say all the right things about how well she's doing. The truth is that they're walking on eggshells, afraid to be the one to push her off the edge. I can't blame them."

"You're starting to sound sympathetic. It's not too late to change your mind, you know."

"Listen, I don't enjoy the idea of killing my own mother; but what choice do I have. I can't find another way. As if enduring the humiliation and abuse by Mom wasn't enough, Grandma and Great-Gran were as bent on controlling my life as her. Trying to find ways to take over the Dad's money. Good luck for me, Great Gran went on her own with no assistance from any of her tortured victims, but Grandma and Mom still threatens to have me committed."

"Why don't you approach the bank trustee?"

"No, he would never take me seriously. Then what if he told her? That would set her off in a frenzy to have me committed as soon as she could drive me there. If she had any inkling I was taking back my power, she'd have prevented me being with you. No, I can't see a way out while she's still alive. She'll overdose and go out with a real bang."

"I know I'm a worrier, but I can't help thinking you missed something. A fingerprint in the wrong place, a trace of drugs on a piece of your clothing, one little thing, and you're nailed. We're nailed," he said. "Everyone misses something." Charlie stopped to take a deep breath, and then said, "If you're bent on going through with this, you need to keep your normal routine. Go back to your mother's house today. I worry about you when you're not with me, but it might look suspicious if you stay away."

Watching her pull on her T-shirt and jeans and apply lip stain and gloss to her lips, he grew fascinated by the fact a woman in midstream of committing murder turned him on. What was the scarier part: That she was capable of it, or that killing someone evil did not bother him?

She turned to face him and reached around his waist to pull him close. She smeared her lip color across the side of his neck and let her tongue glide slowly up his neck to his ear. Her breath on his ear, she whispered, "You're still going to love me when I'm a murderer, aren't you? You know, if you told me to stop it, I would."

Charlie struggled to concentrate against the stirring sensations she brought out in him. Commonsense won out. He leaned forward, backed her onto the vanity, and took her face in his hands. "I would still love you but I want you to stop it now. I can't say the woman doesn't deserve it, but we can find another way. A legal way that won't have us looking over our shoulders the rest of our lives."

He saw the innocence come back to her face and relaxed. Unable to hold back a nervous laugh of relief, he hugged her as tight as he could and said, "Go back. Find a way to get rid of that bottle, even if you have to bring it with you."

"Okay. I'll grab a taxi when I get downstairs and have him wait while I'm inside. I'll be back soon."

"I'll be waiting," he said, brushing her hair back into place and kissing her on the forehead.

After she had gone, the tension left his body for the first time since this had started. He wondered what he had been thinking, but he had to admit that when it came to Allegra, he would do anything that she asked him to do. Including being her accomplice to murder.

CHAPTER 18

October 4, 2006
Phoenix, Arizona

The sound of the closing door woke Lenore out of her semi-conscious dream state. Sitting up in a jerky motion, she looked around but saw no one, heard no one. Funny, she thought, as she started going room to room, that you do as those idiots do in movies. First, she looked in the kitchen, then the bathroom, the dining room, and the three bedrooms. Here, she thought, is an intruder in the house but she was willing to face the unknown without even a baseball bat for protection.

When she got to the last door, Allegra's bedroom, she heard a rustling sound and opened the door. There she was in all her splendor, almost naked, in the process of changing her clothes. Allegra's round sultry eyes went from the dress now lying on the bed to her mother in the doorway.

With a start, she said, "Oh. I didn't hear you open the door," she said as she slipped into a sweater dress and boots.

"Where've you been?" Lenore leaned forward, hands on hips. "You were supposed to be here days ago. Then, you don't show up for the funeral, but you do come back for a change of clothes. How do you suppose that looked to everyone? This is not Hotel Lenore. You're going to be home by midnight, every night, not just drop in when you feel like it. You know, I could've reported you missing to the police after two days, you know."

"You didn't call the police because I'm eighteen years old and an adult. Just because you don't know where I am doesn't mean I'm missing. I can come and go as I please. If you don't like, I'll move out."

"That's what you think. This is my house and you'll do as I say. I'm your mother and responsible for you. Remember, you're not competent to make your own decisions. If you keep staying out like this, I'm going to have to have you put somewhere where you can't leave."

"You'd like that, wouldn't you? Go ahead. Try it. See how far you get. I'm tired of your threats. Boy, if others could see the real you. Why is it, I wonder, that you only have the guts to pick on someone you think is defenseless. You're a miserable coward who hasn't the nerve to stand up to anyone. I'm not going to be your victim anymore. I'm moving out and you'll be lucky to get the correct time from me."

"You couldn't stand on your own two feet five minutes without me and you know it. Within a week, you will be crawling back on your knees begging for my help. You're a weak, sniveling brat who hasn't the least idea of how to make it on your own. Go ahead. Get out. See what it's like. See how far you get."

"If I'm weak and sniveling, it's because you're a screwed-up parent."

"If I had a decent human being to work with maybe I would've done better."

"You made me, so you should know."

"It wasn't my genes that made you like this. It was your bastard father's fault."

Allegra took three steps toward the door and slapped Lenore across the face so hard that Allegra's hand stung. Allegra leaned back, ready for a return assault. Lenore stunned, frozen in place, held her face. She looked at Allegra with glassy eyes.

Glancing across the room to the dresser mirror, she saw the pastiness of her complexion, exaggerated by the red mark left by Allegra's handprint. Perspiration dampened her permed hair until it was in wiry lumps against her head.

They both stood mute and still, until Lenore said, "Get out of my house, and never come back. I will get you for this if it's the last thing I do."

"Go for it, bitch." Grabbing her purse, Allegra shoved past Lenore through the door and hurried out to the waiting taxi.

Lenore watched as the taxi drove off down the street. It was time to put her plan into action. Sick to her stomach and her face still stinging, she jumped when the telephone rang. Allegra will not know what hit her when I call the doctor about having her committed for observation, she muttered while walking to the telephone table. When she saw the caller ID display read UNKNOWN CALLER, she changed her mind about ignoring it. She grabbed up the receiver and said, "Hello."

"Hi, Lenore. I was wondering if you had time to meet me downtown for coffee. I have a few things to discuss with you."

"Sure, I'd love to. Right now? It's kind of late to be going downtown, isn't it?"

"The bus station is open twenty-four hours. It's not like we'd be the only ones there."

"Okay, I'll be there in a half hour, about eight."

The fight with Allegra pushed behind her, a renewed excitement for the new changes happening in her life swept over her. Before she closed the door, she returned to the coffee table to pick up the letter she had written to her father.

A few blocks from her destination, she dropped the letter into a mailbox with a satisfied sense of accomplishment that her dad was not the only one to receive good news this week.

CHAPTER 19

October 5, 2006
Downtown Phoenix, Arizona

T he Phoenix downtown area was almost uninhabited at two o'clock in the morning. The homeless, the drunks, and the whores were you would find walking around the periphery of the bus depot that time of night.

Inside the station, lines formed for the outgoing departures and other sleepy, travel-ridden folks lumbered up to the food counters, wandered through the gift shops, or leaned back on a bench to watch for whatever bus they were waiting for. Officer Downley patrolled here every night between midnight and seven, forever expecting the worst, yet finding a comfort in the dreariness and apathy of the travelers. Except for an occasional drunk, nothing much happened and he looked forward to stopping by the all-night restaurants, having a quick sandwich, and chatting with the staff.

While the days were still warm, hovering around the nineties, the desert nights cooled down this time of the year. He appreciated how the clean freshness replaced the dusty heat of the summer nights, sometimes chilly in the mid to high sixties or a soothing brisk comfort in the seventies. He lowered the window of his cruiser to take in a breath of fresh air and listen to the relative quiet of the night.

A few rushes of soft sound came to him that he recognized as passing cars; even the wind was silent until he got nearer to the bus station. Getting close to the opened door, he heard the muted and anonymous voices inside. He could hear the announcements summoning travelers to the next bus leaving, big engines running in place amid a constant din of movement of bodies and machines inside the lobby. An atmosphere he found soothing and familiar.

When he pulled into the parking lot to look around, he was surprised to find a Toyota Camry parked in a dark corner by the dumpster. Out of all the strange things he expected to see, a conservative, late model, well-kept vehicle was not one of them. The aging yuppies he encountered sprang to mind. The ones no one suspected. The ones who indulged in high-risk behavior sacrificing their hard work and accomplishments for an easy escape from the lives they created. Expecting to surprise the occupant of the vehicle passed out at the wheel, he braced himself for a confrontation as he pulled over, turned off his car engine, and got out.

He reached the driver's side of the car. Adrenalin surged through his body that reminded him of taking hold of a refrigerator cord with wet hands when he was a kid. Moving by inches, teeth clenched, and his hand on his gun, his anticipation of trouble turned into a sort of morbid yet relaxed dread. By her awkward posture, slumped over the steering wheel, her face pressed into its hard surface as her arms dangled limp, his instinct told him she was dead, but he had learned that appearances could be tricky. She could be sick.

Apprehensive as he reached the car, he rapped on the window twice, waited, and tried again. No response. He tried the handle. It was unlocked and he pulled until the door gave way from release of the internal vacuum. He touched her dangling arm with his left hand and pressed two fingers on her neck to check her for a pulse and found none. Her skin was cool and stiff, but not cold, and rigor had already started. He estimated she had been dead over three hours, but the medical examiner would determine time of death. He grabbed the radio from his belt and called for his patrol supervisor.

As he waited for the detectives, the crime scene unit and the medical examiner, he secured the area by stringing up crime scene tape around the perimeter of the vehicle. He was glad not to see the crowd there would have been here if this happened in the daytime.

He allowed his thoughts to wander. The scene made him think of his daughter, who at ten, was beginning to resent his overprotective meddling. Without traumatizing her with real crime scenes and dead bodies of kids from overdose or murder, he had trouble convincing her of the dangerous world we live in. Seeing the woman who had looked to be his wife's age, he experienced that recurring panic that he had to protect his wife and daughter from the ugliness he saw in his job every day.

He sighed as he looked down at the dead woman and shook his head. In a voice not much louder than a whisper, he said, "Not the best way to be remembered by your family."

CHAPTER 20

October 5, 2006
Phoenix, Arizona

Madera woke up startled. She opened her eyes long enough to look at the illuminated dial that read three o'clock. The telephone beside her bed rang in her ear, merging with her dream about an unwanted caller so that she considered ignoring the call. By the fourth ring, awake but disoriented, she realized this was not part of a dream, and reached over to answer.

"Hello."

"Are you Madera Folsom?"

"Who else would be at my house this time of the morning?" Madera felt angry, positive this was a prank call.

"Do you know Lenore Santos?"

"Yes, she's my daughter. What *is* this?"

"An officer is on his way to speak with you. We needed to confirm your relationship first. Is she married?"

"No, she's a widow. What's this all about?"

"The officer will explain. He's already in the vicinity."

"This better be good," Madera said. She slammed down the

receiver and considered lying back down. Imagine the police coming here in the middle of the night. What could Lenore possibly have done? This must have something to do with Allegra.

Madera reached for her robe and slipped into her house slippers. She decided this required coffee, so she started a pot and waited in the kitchen.

Before she had time to sit, she heard the doorbell. A nervous chill rippled through her. She walked to the door, peered out through the peephole, and let them in when she saw a badge. She turned the deadbolt and let them in.

"Mrs. Folsom, I'm Officer Petrey. This is Mr. Angleside. I'm afraid we have some bad news. Can we sit down?"

After they sat down in the living room, the officer said, "First, can you confirm this woman is your daughter?" He held out his cell phone to show her Lenore's driver's license photo.

"Yes, that's my daughter," Madera said. "What are you doing with that?" She looked into his face for an answer, and knew the worst by his discomfort.

"Your daughter was found in her car this morning. I'm sorry to tell you she has passed away."

Madera could not control the buzzing in her head or the sweating. She heard the other man say, "Are you alright, Mrs. Folsom? Can I get you anything or call someone to be with you?"

"What? No, I'm all right. It's just a shock. Was she robbed?"

Madera saw the two men exchange uncomfortable looks. What could be worse? She must have been raped.

"The investigation is in the preliminary stages," the officer said. "An officer found your daughter in her car downtown by the bus station. We won't know the cause of death until an autopsy, but we're treating this as suspicious. We will be questioning her family, social acquaintances, fellow workers, or anyone who might have information about her recent activities."

"You suspect she killed herself? She's had a depression problem, but I didn't think she couldn't deal with it," Madera said. The full implication hit her. Just another example of

Lenore's total lack of consideration for how her actions affected other people.

"We don't know at this time. Do you know if anything unusual happened? Are you aware of any drug abuse?"

Madera watched them looking at her, and winced. They were judging her already, just as the women at church would when they learned about Lenore. She had gone from shock to indignation, and she no longer wanted to be a part of this discussion. "I don't know anything about what she's been doing. I would like to be alone now. Is there anything else?"

The two men glanced at each other before standing. "Here is my card if you need to talk to anyone," said the second man. "This must be a difficult time for you."

Madera took the card and shoved it in her robe pocket, but did not speak. She remained sitting even after she watched them leave and listened to their retreating vehicle. Who cares what they think, she thought. She surprised herself that the shocking aspect of this news had more to do with the public opinion more than the loss of a child.

After going back to bed but not able to sleep, by nine that morning she still had trouble processing the news. Sitting now at her kitchen table looking with vacant eyes through the open door, Madera could do nothing but hold her fingers up to her mouth as if to stop the screaming.

Of course, she knew it was suicide. What more could anyone expect from someone weak like Lenore. How they would talk behind her back now, the ones who never liked her anyway. They would say things like, 'It's always the mother's fault,' or 'If she had been a better mother, Lenore wouldn't have felt she had no choice.' She knew because she had said the same thing about a woman last year. With everything else going on with her mother's will and Bert's leaving, she had reached her wit's end. What else could go wrong?

Madera blinked hard several times. She had to tell Bert, Tasha, and Rod. More unpleasantness, more questions. She reached for the telephone hanging on the wall, and pressed the speed dial key for Tasha's cell and waited.

"Yes," said a voice that sounded remote and unfamiliar.

"It's your mother. I'm afraid I have bad news. Your sister's dead," Madera said, without emotion and to the point.

"What do you mean?"

"How much clearer can I get? Lenore is dead. The police found her last night. I'm sure it was suicide."

"She wouldn't," Tasha said. "I know she'd never consider that as an option." After a short hesitation, Tasha inhaled deeply and Madera realized Tasha was staving off the tears. "I can't believe she would do that intentionally. Even if she were depressed, it was only because she wanted more out of life, not to escape life. What does Dad think?"

"Your dad doesn't live here anymore. Hasn't since after Gran's funeral. We expected to see you there."

Tasha inhaled again before speaking, "I couldn't. A funeral is for the ones who feel a loss. I would have been out of place. Would you like me to come over? It can't be easy to be alone right now."

"That would be nice, if you can."

"I'll explain to my boss. I should be able to get there in few hours," Tasha said.

Madera heard sympathy and duty in Tasha's voice, which normally she would have rejected but today she found she was losing her combativeness as well as her pride.

"I'll see you then. Goodbye."

The next two calls were easy. She left messages for Bert and Rod. Getting that type of news from voicemail was cold, she thought, but she had no more energy.

Speaking with Tasha again, Madera realized how much she missed Tasha's bright optimism, so unlike Lenore's dark pessimistic attitude toward the world.

As a child, Lenore was quiet, mild-mannered, but never an attractive girl. That fact was difficult to explain since the girls were identical in appearance. Where Tasha was charming, Lenore was stiff and off-putting, like a block of ice surrounding her. Lenore was cold, impenetrable, a person difficult to touch.

She jumped out of her daydream at the ringing telephone.

She stood up, pushing on the seat of her chair, and reached out to answer the telephone.

"Madera, Glenna speaking. You know, Lenore's neighbor. I thought you would want to know that a woman in a fancy car arrived and is in Lenore's house with the police. Bert is there, too. I was surprised not to see *you* there." She let her last statement hang as a question, but Madera ignored it.

"I appreciate the call. I'll come right over," Madera said. Glenna was fishing for gossip and she was not going to take the bait.

"I thought you would want to know. Just before they arrived, I heard the news on the radio. What a tragedy for you. If there's anything I can do, please call on me."

"Thanks for the call, Glenna," Madera said while reaching for her keys. She'd call Tasha on the way about the change in plans. As she put the key into the ignition, she thought there was no time like the present to establish her authority over Lenore's home *and* Allegra's trust.

CHAPTER 21

October 5, 2006
Phoenix, Arizona

Madera wasted no time driving to Lenore's house. When she arrived, she recognized Sylvie's white BMW SUV. Sylvie had been in the living room talking to a plainclothes detective, and rushed over and hugged Madera when she entered the room.

"Madera, I'm sorry about Lenore," she whispered through tearful gasps.

"What're you doing here," Madera said, extricating herself from Sylvie's embrace.

"The police found Rod's information as an alternate emergency contact and called to ask a few questions. Rod said he couldn't leave work, so sent me to see if I could help. I thought you and Allegra would need some support."

"Is she here?"

"No."

"What do the police want to know that they thought *you* could tell them, anyway? I don't see why you feel the need to stick your nose into our business."

Ignoring her last comment, Sylvie said, "According to Detective Macy, they're speculating the cause of death accidental overdose. They're trying to establish her prescription medications to what they found on the floor of the car. The brand names of these drugs are Valium, Prozac, and Ritalin. All I know is she took Prozac for her depression, but I told him I did not know anything about the others." Sylvie looked to Madera.

Instead of addressing the question, she aimed her eyes up at Sylvie with as much hatred as she could muster. Thinking how she could care less and wanted this to be over, she said, "I don't know anything about what you're describing. You should not be telling the police anything to give the impression my daughter needed to take drugs."

Sylvie rolled her eyes. "Madera, we need to discuss this because there's going to be an autopsy and an investigation. It's not as if the police can't figure out how to call the pharmacy. If we clam up and hide things, they'll pry even deeper."

Madera's eyes grew round and bright. "What do you mean by an investigation? She mixed up her medications. Why drag all her dirty laundry into it?"

"As I understand it, the police always investigate suspicious or unusual deaths. I'm sure there's nothing in it. Did you know she was taking all those medications?"

"I knew about the Prozac, but that doesn't mean anything. I'm sure she did lots of stupid things without telling anyone." Madera looked around the room for a distraction, any reason to end this conversation.

"I wonder if one doctor would prescribe all those medications together. Seems odd, doesn't it? Anyway, we need to be more concerned with the living at this point. Where's Allegra?"

Madera shrugged, "I have no idea. I don't even know if she knows her mother is dead yet."

"What?" Sylvie said. "How can she not know with all that's been happening here? Do you mean she hasn't been home?"

"I've no idea where she is, where she's been or what she's been doing, but don't you worry about her. She's none of *your* business. We don't need you." Madera brushed past Sylvie and walked into the kitchen. "You heard me. Brush off. Beat it. Get lost."

Madera's voice had risen to a high shrill, but she stopped short when a police officer, with Bert at his heels, burst from the kitchen entrance.

"Is there a problem here?" the officer said, with the authority of someone used to defusing volatile domestic situations. Bert stood behind him as if his appearance was a beacon of normality.

"I asked her about Allegra, Lenore's daughter, and she freaked out." Sylvie raised her eyebrows in mock defeat. Madera glared as if icicle daggers shooting from her eyes could freeze and silence Sylvie.

"Ma'am, we're going to have to find her to get her statement," the officer said. "Is she eighteen?"

"Yes." Madera said, resigned to the presence of authority.

"When was the last time you saw your granddaughter?"

"About a week ago. Her mother brought her over for dinner."

"Did Lenore appear to be different in any way?"

"Lenore and Allegra were arguing, as usual."

"What do you mean, Ma'am?"

"They picked at each other all the time. Sometimes I couldn't stand either of them when they were together. Nothing major. Just mother-daughter stuff."

"Does your granddaughter live here with her mother or is she on her own?"

"She lives here. I don't know why she's not here, but then it wasn't up to me to keep track of her *before*."

Detective Macy entered the room, and stopped next to the officer. He looked at her at least a whole minute before saying, "Where does she work? Maybe we can contact her that way."

"Work?" her grandmother said, "She's never worked. My daughter applied for her to receive disability because of her emotional problems. She took the death of her father hard, couldn't get past it. Lenore had her in therapy since she was thirteen, but the thing that helped to make her halfway normal was the Ritalin. I blame her father, even if he is dead. Defective genes."

"Don't you ever think before you open your mouth," Sylvie said, shaking her head. Madera saw Sylvie give Bert a sympathetic grin. He, in turn, nodded back to her, as if this explained everything. Traitors, both of them. Why was everyone against her?

Detective Macy said, "Officer, did you check her bathroom for prescriptions?"

"Nothing but over-the-counter allergy and headache meds. I bagged them anyway. No prescriptions."

He looked at Madera. "I thought you said she took Prozac. Have you any idea where she would have kept something like that?"

"That's where she always kept medications, including ones for Allegra when she was little to keep them locked up. Maybe she was out. Can I look?" Madera, followed by Detective Macy, Bert, and Sylvie, walked to the master bedroom bathroom. The room smelled of bleach and window cleaner and she sniffed at the odorous combination. She looked inside the open cabinet and saw a gaping void where Lenore had stored all her medications. "Everything is gone. I don't understand."

"Can one of you give me her doctor's name and the name of her pharmacy? We'll have to figure out what's missing. Might not be important, but we have to check."

"Madera can help you with that," Sylvie said, enjoying watching Madera's deflated demeanor.

"Do you have a photo of your granddaughter? If you don't hear from her soon, we might have reason to be concerned."

Detective Macy took a physical description of Allegra while Madera found a recent snapshot in her room. Madera gave him the number and address for Tasha, along with hers. Sylvie and Bert offered their information, as well. Bert nodded to Sylvie and left without acknowledging Madera.

"I'm staying," Madera said. "Allegra might show up and someone will have to break the news to her." Lifting her cell phone from her bag to call Tasha about the change in plans, she heard Sylvie say,

"Do you want me to make the calls to tell everyone what happened?"

Madera shrugged. "Go ahead, but I can't imagine who'd care about a hermit like her."

◆　◆　◆

Once inside her car, Sylvie pulled out her mobile and called Pilar. "You're not going to believe this, but Lenore's dead."

"What? How? When?"

"The police found her in her car last night somewhere downtown. The police called Rod when they found his name in her address book. Since he couldn't leave work, he told me to try to take care of things. Gosh, I'm still shaking from being in that house."

"You must be upset, losing a sister-in-law like that, so sudden and disturbing."

"That's not why I'm upset. Madera showed up and made a scene. Instead of a simple accidental overdose, she's making suggestions to the cops about Allegra, implying she killed her mother. She just can't keep her mouth shut. She always wants to act as if she's in charge of everything. I swear I could kill her sometimes."

"Is there any reason to believe this was suspicious? I mean, was she in the habit of going out at night alone?"

"Who knows?"

Pilar was not sure what to say to Sylvie. Maybe the woman had an odd way of seeing the world, but her reactions to death were inconsistent with the loving and nurturing woman she was around her children. Best to leave psychoanalysis to the professionals.

"Listen, Sylvie. What can I do for you today? I'm happy to cook, clean, run errands, whatever you need."

"That's sweet of you. The hell with cleaning, but cooking dinner would be wonderful. I don't know what to expect the rest of the day, but we'll need to eat. I'm leaving Lenore's place now. I have a few errands I have to take care of now, but then I'll be home. Don't say anything about this in front of the kids.

"Naturally, I'll be here if you need me," Pilar said.

Sylvie disconnected the call, and stared out beyond the windshield.

"Dammit to Hell," Sylvie said. She turned on the car engine and moved into the traffic. "This is turning into a fucking mess."

CHAPTER 22

October 7, 2006
Phoenix, Arizona

Allegra woke up next to Charlie Saturday morning. Her eyes moved to the clock on the nightstand and she groaned when she read six-thirty. Her puffy eyes, itching from yesterday's mascara, and her chalky tongue amplified the pounding in her head. She sighed and looked through the window at the gray sky. The absence of the usual sunshine cast eerie shadows over the décor of industrial steels, glass, and wood that exaggerated her morose mood.

She crept out of the bedroom on tiptoes. She was halfway down the hall when she jumped at the sound of a soft thud as the concierge dropped the newspaper outside the door. She started the coffee, and then reached outside for the bundle on the doormat. Comfortable on a stool, she poured a cup, and spread the paper across the counter.

She leaned in, sipping the coffee, while her eyes followed the large lettering across the front page. The headline screamed at her. IDENTITY RELEASED OF WOMAN FOUND DEAD IN DT PHOENIX. When she read the first line in the story and saw her mother's name, her legs buckled underneath her causing her foot to lose its grip on the bottom rung. She stumbled to the bathroom with little time to spare before leaning over the toilet to throw up.

Her body still trembled and her empty stomach ached after she returned to the kitchen. She managed a few sips of coffee with a piece of toast before she returned to the article. Even without details, she guessed that Lenore had taken the doctored pills. All she could think of was how she would have to live knowing this was her fault.

◆ ◆ ◆

Pilar woke up exhausted like someone who had been awake all night. She turned away from the window and pulled the sheet and comforter over her head. In the darkness, she tried to sort out what happened from the dreaminess of a disturbed sleep. Lenore dead. She remembered the last time she had seen Lenore at Virginia's funeral, glaring at her with hatefulness in her eyes. The image chilled her. Pilar found the idea of suicide doubtful. She thought Lenore capable of evil against someone else, but not the self-destructive type. Sylvie had disagreed with her, and being one who had known the family most of her life, she might be right. After all, Pilar thought, she had arrived only in the last week.

Pilar sat up. An explosion of thoughts overtook her speculating whether Lenore was a victim or a persecutor. The contradictions sent her back into the past again, recounting the opposing theories of the family's background. Genealogy has a way of uncovering embarrassing family secrets and patterns. Rod's claims that their Mexican ancestors were *haciendados*, versus her grandfather's view of them as political refugees fleeing from persecution, she wondered which story was right or if the truth was buried in yet another story. Pilar wrapped the covers around her and fell back into a disturbed sleep of dusty landscapes and the thunder of approaching hoof steps bearing down on her.

CHAPTER 23

October 7, 2006
Glendale, Arizona

Opening her eyes slowly, Pilar dared to look at the time because she wanted it to be early so she could stay in bed for another hour. When she saw it was seven-fifteen, her internal dialogue started as it did every morning with the question of whether to get up and enjoy another glorious day, or was it better to get more rest to fortify herself for the unknown future events. She had not made her decision when she heard a gentle knock on the door.

"Pilar," Sylvie said. "Are you awake?'

"I'm awake. Just taking it slow."

"Rod brought a letter from the lawyer for you. I think you'll want to read it as soon as possible."

"Okay," Pilar said. "I'll be right out."

Pulling on her sweat pants with matching sweatshirt, Pilar pulled up her long hair into a ponytail and stepped into her slippers.

When she arrived at the kitchen bar, Sylvie already had a mug of coffee waiting next to the attorney's embossed envelope.

Anything from an attorney's office frightened Pilar, reminders of the legal correspondence after her parents' deaths. Settling onto the counter stool, she shifted a little more before she blew on her coffee, and reached over to inspect the letter. Sylvie watched her as if to say 'get on with it,' so she tore off the end and pulled out the papers.

Knowing Sylvie's eyes were on her, she started to read carefully. First a frown, then a gradual grin turned into a giddy laugh. A prickling on her neck gave her a chill. She bet Sylvie knew the contents and might not be happy about her turn good fortune.

"Is this for real? The Flagstaff house is mine?"

"Sure is. Rod found out about it earlier, but thought he shouldn't say anything until the attorney made the formal notification. After all, it's not official until you get it from the lawyers."

"Strange that Pete never told us about this. He talked like he had no interest in coming out here again."

"That's irrelevant now, isn't it? The house is yours," Sylvie said. Pilar heard the forced enthusiasm in her voice. She made no secret that Rod thought he was getting the house, and after all the work he did to the property with that goal in mind, he must be angry and resentful at his grandmother's betrayed.

"I feel bad about this, Sylvie. I had no idea. Both of you must hate me right now."

"It's a money-pit anyway. We're better off." Sylvia said the words with kindness, but her eyes told Pilar she was pissed.

Pilar decided to let Sylvie have her jabs. Even with the age of the house, it was a treasure. It was not as if she did not have a good reason to be resentful. Looking down at the paperwork, she saw a key taped to the back of one blank sheet. Pulling it from the tape, she slipped it into her pocket, and put the papers back in the envelope. The lawyer could wait until later today.

"This way, you can stay in Arizona and we'll see you often," Sylvie said. Lightening her mood, Sylvie brought out pastries and refilled their coffee mugs.

"I admit that I'm beyond delirious owning a house like that, but I can understand your disappointment. I feel that Virginia intentionally withheld the facts for her own benefit."

"That's nothing to do with you. We'll get over the shock. Right now, let's focus on Lenore's death."

Pilar was glad to change the subject.

"Allegra's father died five years ago and left his money and business holdings in a trust for her when she turns twenty-five. Bert's concerned Madera's trying to get her grubby paws on Allegra's money. Rod and I suspect Lenore was attempting to tap into the money on the grounds Allegra is quote-unquote unstable, so Madera might try the same thing. Bert saw an attorney yesterday in case she tries. Since no one has seen Allegra, he hasn't had the chance to let her know he has her back."

"Wow," Pilar said. "No one's seen Allegra? You don't think something's happened to her?"

Leaning forward, Sylvie gave Pilar a sly glance and said, "Got to be a guy. If it weren't for Lenore's death, I wouldn't worry about it, but it looks bad that she hasn't come home. The story's in the papers this morning, so it's not like it's a secret."

Pilar thought about that possibility. She inhaled and she took a drink of cooled coffee and said, "What can we do? What do we *need* to do? I think I'm confused about something. Are you suggesting that someone killed Lenore and that the police will suspect Allegra?"

"Maybe," Sylvie said. "I still think she killed herself, but if it turns out to be murder, Allegra's the best suspect. You know, it would help if you could you stick around a little longer. I need to have someone to talk to and feel like I have some support. Allegra needs help, too. They could build up with a case against her the way Madera runs her mouth. What do you say?"

Pilar tightened her lips over her teeth by habit while she considered the request. These people are my relatives after all and she had inherited a house in Arizona. Besides, she would hate to see an injustice happen because someone was falsely accused based on circumstances."

"Okay. I'll do what I can to help."

Sylvie smiled. "Good. Now, let's get started by finding Allegra. Go over to the house and check around. Allegra might have been there without anyone knowing or there might be a clue about why she was downtown. Any snips of information that suggests she was into something that got her killed."

"How do I get in? Are you sure this is ok?"

"I'm giving you permission. Lenore kept a spare key at the back door tucked behind the doorjamb on the right. Weird, I know. Let yourself in and look at her computer. There must be a clue somewhere. If you leave now, you'll miss rush hour."

"All right," Pilar said, as a chilling thought rushed over her. Was it so smart to search the house of a murder victim?

CHAPTER 24

October 7, 2006
Phoenix, Arizona

Pilar smiled as she tapped the top of the GPS on the car dash as it announced that she had arrived at her destination. Pulling into Lenore's driveway gave her the creeps, like she were grave robbing, or at the least, breaking and entering. Maybe she was committing a crime. Sylvie is the one who gave permission, not Allegra. Sylvie had told her where to find the key and assured her it was okay.

She kept her body moving forward out of the car, self-doubts in check. Around the back to the kitchen door, she used her short fingernails to pinch out the old key from behind the jamb, unlock the door, and enter a small country-style kitchen.

Except for daylight trying to make its way through the curtains and blinds, the house was dark. For the time of day, Pilar expected the house to be brighter. Upon closer inspection, she saw that the darkness was intentional. Blackout drapes in the living room and dining room to keep the house cooler in defense of the desert sun created a dismal pall.

Pilar looked for an office or a computer as she moved

through the house and was surprised to find a safe in the dining room. When she found the combination taped to its side, she paused to speculate about the mental processes of some people and their inability to make logical connections. But then, Lenore did not strike her as an intellectual.

She looked inside the safe to find a plethora of loose papers and yellowed envelopes. Frustrated by the disorganization, she carefully lifted them out in their current order and set them on the top of the dining room table.

Going on the assumption that the police had already gone through the mess, she did not expect to find anything of earthshattering significance. Still, maybe they had no reason at the time to do a full search, even given that Sylvie had offered to let them. Just in case the police had not been through this, she figured she should keep the papers in order.

Not far into her search, she understood why Lenore was not worried about security. She had no cash, no checkbooks, nothing of intrinsic value. Instead, Lenore had collected information. Some of the loose papers were interesting, Pilar thought while reading about century-old Arizona robberies, early twentieth century revolutions, cemetery markers, and even a reference to coin collecting.

Opening each envelope, taking a quick look inside before going on to the next, Pilar started to see that Lenore had been one of those motivated loners who found projects to encompass her time instead of seeking human companionship. She had assigned herself the task of research into hundred-year old unsolved crimes. Pilar could not make a connection to any of the stories, either with the family or one another. If for no other reason, Pilar found them entertaining and a good read for a quiet afternoon.

When she came to the last envelope that looked older than the rest with its worn corners and withered gummed flaps, a nervous chill ran down her back. Peering around the dining room, as small as it was, the hairs on her neck stiffened. Still light outside, the dimness in the house cast a greyness that started to unnerve her. Turning her back to the wall, she sat down on a chair and began to read the report from a private detective.

After she read it, she put the papers back in the envelope and stuffed it into her purse. Positive the police had not seen this report, her first instinct told her to get it out of the house before someone showed up. This was what would convince the police that Allegra had a motive. As for the other papers, she placed them in an empty stationary box abandoned on a shelf and tucked them inside until it was bursting, then secured it with several rubber bands. She looked around for somewhere to stash them, and ended up in the kitchen pantry where she found a partially exposed wall cavity, an unfinished repair job she guessed. Stuffing the box inside the wall, she propped up the matching drywall section against it, and shoved storage bins in front to secure it in place.

Often as a child, she hid things that she thought were important. None of the items had been of any value but had been important to her, as if a piece of paper held a clue to an important memory she did not want to forget. That idiosyncrasy had been annoying to her family, but she was not able to kick the habit. At this moment, as she stood back regarding the hidden space, she thought how useful childhood habits could be.

Standing in the pantry doorway, a foreboding crept over her. Something was wrong that she either could not remember or was not understanding, something important. It was not in her character to believe in ethereal messages from the dead or to believe anyone's soul lingers on after death to take care of unfinished business, but at this moment, she would have admitted she could be wrong. She knew she was the only person in the small house, but her senses told her she was not alone. Not only in the house, but also in the room where she stood.

She embraced the moment rather than run from it, and took her time to look around the tiny room. Except for the package she hid a moment ago, nothing of any importance jumped out at her. The pitiful remains of a small life were all that she saw; cans of stew and peeled tomatoes, rice, cornmeal, sugar, flour canister, cutlery, and picnic dishes. She shook her head and backed out of the pantry, shutting the door behind her with more eagerness than necessary. With the shadows from the trees casting shadows on the house, the rooms grew darker. She wanted to look around more, but thought her nerves needed a chance to settle. Checking out the computer would have to be for another day.

Leaving the way she came in, she heard the deadbolt engage when she closed the door. She squeezed the key back in its hiding place and started to walk around the house. As she rounded the corner, she almost collided with Glenna.

CHAPTER 25

October 7, 2006
Phoenix, Arizona

The two women swayed left to right in the narrow space between Lenore's house and the shrubbery along the property line. For several seconds, they stared at the other, neither deciding who was at fault for the near collision.

"Excuse me," Pilar said. "I didn't expect to see anyone there. That could have been an embarrassing accident."

Glenna creased her brow and said, "I don't recognize you. Who are you and what are you doing in that house?"

"It's alright. I'm a relative. Pilar Sagasta. Virginia's brother, Peter Paralelos, was my grandfather. Sylvie asked me to come over to check on Allegra. Are you a neighbor?"

"Yes. I've lived across the street since before they moved here," she said pointing across the street with her thumb.

"Quite a tragedy, isn't it," Pilar said, feeling the older woman's scrutiny.

"But not a surprise. Ever since that poor man died, the husband, I knew it was just a matter of time. Things were never right with that woman. And that poor little girl, so gentle and waif-like, I don't know how she survived having a mother like that."

"I haven't met Allegra yet. Sounds like a sad situation. You say it was different when the husband was alive?"

"Oh, yeah. It was a happy home," Glenna said, perking up at the chance to be heard. "I remember that awful night when he died. There was so much commotion. The whole neighborhood was out here. Lenore ran out of the house like a banshee, screaming for someone to call an ambulance. My first thought was, why she didn't call before she ran out of the house. I don't go in for theatrics."

Pilar gasped picturing the scene, while Glenna paused to enjoy the effect.

"By this time, we're coming out of our houses to find out what's going on. She runs back inside. I followed her inside and saw her giving him CPR. It was all a little weird, but we thought she had to be in shock. The paramedics came, did their work on him, knowing it was too late. The frightening and grotesque way his chest heaved upward from the pull of the electrical stimulation made all of us weak in the knees. All the time this is going on, that poor little girl is standing to the side crying. After the ambulance took him away, she ran to her mother for comfort and guess what she did?"

Captivated by the story, Pilar started when Glenna asked a direct question. "What?"

"She pushed her away so hard, the poor thing fell into the bushes. These here," she pointed at the Pyracantha bushes bordering the neighbor's property. "I couldn't stand it and ran over to pick her up. She held onto me for over two hours, whimpering and shaking. I've never seen anything so horrible in my life. Some people should not be allowed to have children."

"Gosh, that's horrible. Was there a question about whether it was a natural death? I mean, with Lenore acting so weird."

"Not that I heard, but I thought something was off. Robert Santos was a healthy man. And they had been fighting a lot just before he died. Mainly about Allegra. It was too convenient, if you ask me."

"My God," Pilar said. "Didn't the police ask questions or anything?"

"Nothing. I figured they did an autopsy and didn't find anything but natural causes. The way I see it, if Lenore killed Allegra's father, that would give Allegra a strong motive for killing her mother."

"For Heaven's sake, don't tell this to the police. There's no reason to get someone into trouble when you're not positive about the circumstances of her father's death."

"Don't worry, I'm not volunteering crap. They had their chance before. Besides, that woman deserved killing after the way she treated her daughter. The hand of God," Glenna said, giving a nod of finality before returning to her own home.

Pilar watched Glenna leave, then made her way to her car. She drove down the street and let the shock sink in of this new knowledge. She wondered how to figure in this new information, if it fit anywhere in the current situation. Without hesitation, this was a second strong motive for Allegra to kill her mother. Glenna's story about an abusive situation and the detective's report about a cheating husband.

"Where the hell are you, Allegra," she said as she made her way back to the Folsom's home.

CHAPTER 26

October 8, 2006
Phoenix, Arizona

Allegra had decided to stay at Charlie's another day. The idea of facing the police was too much, trying to explain what her life had been like and what had gone wrong since her father died. The fear that the police believed she was mentally unstable enough to kill and would put her in jail, had sent her into hysterics last night. The problem was she had been willing to kill. Maybe she was crazy and they would detect that as soon as they questioned her.

"Charlie, wake up." She poked his shoulder with her index finger.

"Yeah, what is it?" he said in a groggy, half-awake voice.

"I have to get back to my mother's house."

Awake now, he said, "Oh shit. I wonder if the cops noticed the missing bottle already. Yesterday, the news said it was being investigated as a suspicious death."

"Oh, no! I didn't think of that. Damn, what am I going to do? Should I still go back there and check?" She had to get rid of the bottle without admitting to Charlie that she had missed her chance to get into Lenore's bathroom and had to leave it there.

Propping himself up now with pillows against the teak headboard, he considered what to do. "I bet they wouldn't assume *you* did it. You never threatened her. You saw an attorney who gave you a way to get out from under her. *And* you moved in with me, even if we did that on the sly. Her death is motiveless as far as you're concerned. We'll both go as a couple to handle the arrangements. We'll say we were in all day Saturday and hadn't bothered to read the paper until today. As soon as we found out, we rushed right over."

"That sounds good, Charlie. I can't believe how simple it sounds when you say it."

"Yeah, I'm a real genius," he said.

CHAPTER 27

October 8, 2006
Phoenix, Arizona

Allegra was glad Charlie still had the Mercedes. Thinking it made a good impression on anyone who might be there, she told him to park in the driveway. When she saw her grandmother's station wagon parked around the back, she thought she was going to lose her nerve.

Charlie took her hand and gave it a tight squeeze.

"I'm with you, sweetie. Don't let anyone intimidate you. We're going in to see what needs to be done, talk to anyone we have to and leave. We should call the police to tell them we're here."

"What? Why?"

"Don't worry. The strategy is to call them before they have to track you down. Listen, I'll call *before* we go in. That'll eliminate too much time alone with your grandmother."

After several transfers between operators, desk sergeants and two other officers, Charlie got through to the detective in charge of the case. "I told him we'd wait for him inside. He said he'd be there in fifteen minutes or less since he's already in the field and close by. Okay. Let's go in."

Before Allegra had time to turn the front door handle, the door flung open with such force it slammed against the back wall, followed by the muffled crunch when the knob thrust through the drywall. Several small trinkets tinkled on the wall shelves.

"Where the *hell* have you been?" Madera said. "Have you any idea of what has happened here? The police have been here asking all kinds of invasive questions and asking where you are. I can't believe the extent of your inconsideration and irresponsibility. Get in here before the neighbors see you."

Madera grabbed Allegra's arm, using her fingernails as hooks that penetrated Allegra's skin. She squealed in pain as Madera's nails dug deep enough to draw blood. As Madera braced herself to hurl Allegra into the living room, Charlie grabbed Madera's free arm and twisted it behind her.

"That's enough, old woman. Settle down before I call a cop."

Madera released her hold on Allegra to try to defend herself but could not get a good angle to swing, leaving Allegra to stumble backward.

"Get out of here, whoever the hell you are. This is a matter between me and my granddaughter and you're trespassing."

"Listen, lady, I'm not the one who's trespassing. This is Allegra's house now, not yours, and she says who comes and goes. Either watch your mouth or get out."

"Allegra," Madera's voice was shrill, angry, and menacing. "Tell this asshole to let go of me and leave, right now. I'm warning you."

"Listen, Grandma, you're not warning me of anything, not anymore. I don't intend to let you continue to abuse me like you and Mom did in the past. I'd think you'd have the decency to mourn instead of being here searching for valuables." Allegra's recovered composure made her voice smooth and calm, but inside, her heart was racing and her knees were shaking.

"I'll leave since you have this brute here to attack me, but this isn't the end. You're not competent to handle your own affairs and I'm going to see to it you are dealt with on a permanent basis." Madera's face was tight and red with rage, her voice choking out forced spurts of air.

"Are you threatening me," Allegra asked. "If you are, I'll remind you that I have a witness this time."

Taken back by the authoritative tone in Allegra's voice, Madera hesitated but stood her ground, unwilling to yield her position.

Charlie stood firm as if he had planted his feet into the padding under the carpet. "Listen, Allegra is home and taking charge of this house. There's no need for you to stay here. Please leave before we have to call the police to have you removed." Charlie turned to the open doorway to guide her out and found a towering bulky man blocking his way. Charlie wondered how long he had been there.

Madera, seeing his appearance as an opportunity, leapt forward, and said, "Officer, this man threatened me. Arrest him. I also believe he's been keeping my granddaughter against her will. Considering her emotional maturity, I also believe he's trying to …."

The detective raised his hand flat as a stop signal before she could go on. His large hands were startling, but suited to his strong, square face, piercing eyes, and military haircut. Allegra, comparing him to Charlie's sullen features and thin build, found that she had to deny herself the urge to scrutinize his attractiveness by remembering that he might arrest her soon.

"Ma'am, why don't you go home? I think I can handle the situation from here. If you want to press charges against this man, that's your business, but to let you know, I saw a good deal as I drove up and heard the rest as I walked up. I witnessed your attack on your granddaughter. He pulled you off her. He did not attack you. I have questions for both of them and it's my strong suggestion that you go home. If we need you, we'll call you." His quiet voice had an unexpected strength and authoritative air.

Madera was speechless; her mouth gaped open but no sounds escaped except for intakes of breath. Her eyes moved from one to the other while her complexion turned from angry red to surrender white as if someone pulled a plug to let the rage drain out. She grabbed her coat and purse, and left through the front door without another word. After a couple of silent minutes, she started her car engine. They listened as the wheels rolled over the grass to pass Charlie's car in the driveway, and drove away.

Still, no one spoke. Charlie opened his arms and Allegra moved to him. She relaxed her defenses and started to cry. Charlie smoothed back her hair as her face rested in his cashmere sweater. The bulky man, Detective Macy reached over to close the door. Before the door met the doorframe, the chilly desert air washed over the momentary frieze.

"I'm Detective Macy. Are you okay, ma'am?"

"I'm fine. It's a shock, that's all. I've been out of this for a while and it's like reliving a bad dream. Living around normal people and doing normal things, I forgot how horrible she is. I'm all right. This is Charlie, Charlie Bismarck. We're, uh, I moved in with him a few days ago, but we've known each other for a while."

Charlie nodded and pointed to the sofa in the front room. "Let's sit over there. Allegra needs to calm down." He looked at the wounds on her arm and said, "Maybe tetanus shot, too."

CHAPTER 28

October 8, 2006
Phoenix, Arizona

Reaching inside his jacket for his leather identification case, he held it up and said, "I'm Detective Steve Macy from the Phoenix Police Homicide Unit assigned to this investigation. I guess you know about your mother. I'm sorry for your loss, but I have to ask you some questions. It's important to get on these situations at the earliest point." He reached inside his jacket again for a notebook and pen. "I'm sure you know that we're looking at this as a suspicious death and investigating it as a homicide. We have to look at all the possibilities, like whether suicide is an option. We need to get at all the pertinent facts about your mother and her habits. The sooner we get the big picture of her life, and particularly her last days, the sooner we can eliminate certain theories."

"What do you need to know," Allegra asked.

"Did your mother have any stressful problems, like work, boyfriend, church, or friends?"

Allegra gave out a laugh, seeming to catch Detective Macy by surprise. "Boyfriend! I haven't known her to date once since my father died. I wish she had gone out and left me alone once in a while." She regretted the words as soon as they were out of her mouth.

"Nothing unusual was going on that you remember?"

"The only unusual thing was a big fight between my Aunt Sylvie and everyone else at my grandmother's house last Sunday. I remember because Gran died that same night. I wasn't there, but my mother left me a voice message about how Sylvie told them all off and walked out."

"Other than family arguments, anything different in her habits in the weeks before her death?"

"Nothing that I know about, except that new girl, Pilar, came to town. She's related through Gran Virginia. She was there during the fight. Mom said she was the cause of it, too."

"Ok, we'll talk about her later. I need to establish a few facts. First, where were both of you between eight Friday evening to three Saturday morning?"

Charlie spoke up and said, "We went out for a bit. Had dinner at the Biltmore, hopped a few clubs in the neighborhood, and went home. We had an early night. We must've been home by eleven thirty. I didn't pay much attention after that, but I'm sure I can vouch for Allegra being at our place all night. I would've woken up if she were gone."

"Is that your recollection?" Macy said.

Allegra looked distracted for a minute before she answered, "Yes, but I don't know the specific time we went home. I do know we were together the whole evening and night. And the next morning, too. That I'm sure of."

"Okay. Now, I have to ask if you are still taking the Ritalin and Prozac."

"Absolutely not," Allegra said proudly. "Last month, Charlie said I should stop all of it and I did. I've never been happier or healthier in my life."

"What did you do with what you had left?"

"Flushed them, I think. Although, now that you mention it, I don't remember. Does it matter?"

"Well, your mother died from an overdose and we found two of the medications prescribed to you on the floor of her car. We don't have the toxicology results yet to know what specific drugs killed her, so we're interested in a surplus of any medications she might have taken or had available."

"I see, but I still don't remember if I got rid of them. I only remember stopping."

He took a business card from his pocket and handed it to her. "Think about it. Call me and let me know. Now, did your mother have any money of her own that she would leave to anyone?"

"That's a big N-O. That was her problem these last years since my father died. He left an insurance policy with me as the sole beneficiary with the proceeds to go into a trust he established when I was a baby."

"What did he leave your mother?"

"Not much, according to her. My father believed everyone, including women, should stand on their own two feet. He used to tell me how he built his businesses from the ground up when he was in his twenties, before he was married. He said that he expected me to build my own empire, no matter what he might have to leave me." Allegra stopped and swallowed. When she started speaking again, she averted her watery eyes from both men.

"I have no idea why he cut her out. I know she was pissed. She argued with the insurance company to change the policy so she got half. She tried to break into the trust, but she didn't get anywhere. I mean, she was wild about the whole thing. She received Social Security checks for me, but nothing else. At least, that's what she told me. I wouldn't be surprised to learn he left her a lot of money but she spent it, and then wanted mine."

"As a matter of fact," interrupted Charlie, "her mother was still trying to get her money."

"Yes, which is why Charlie suggested I see a lawyer. I had an appointment last week."

"I see. I'll need your lawyer's name. Can you think of any reason anyone would want to kill your mother?"

"She bullied me, but to everyone else she was a lamb. I can't think of anyone who would want to kill her. She didn't have enemies, but she didn't have friends either. I can't think of anyone."

"Do the two of you have any plans to get married?"

"At the moment, Detective, I'm out of a job and wouldn't ask a woman to marry me under that condition."

"Making no judgments, sir. It's the obvious question that I need to ask in a situation that involves a suspicious death and a large amount of money. Will you be staying here?"

"No way," Allegra said. "I want to get rid of this place as soon as I can. This house holds too many bad memories."

"Do we have permission to enter the premises to look around?" Detective Macy said." In your absence, your grandfather and aunt gave us permission to check on the medications. We can get a warrant, but if we have your permission, it's easier."

"Fine with me."

"Good. Some advice. I suggest calling the police if you have any other confrontations with your grandmother. Trying to handle a volatile situation on your own can lead to bigger problems."

"Thank you, I will. It feels like I have people on my side at last. No one believed me before when I tried to tell about how I was treated."

Detective Macy nodded. "The relationship with your mother must have made you angry and frustrated." He looked at them both for a few seconds longer, studying them. He rose to leave without asking more questions.

"I'd appreciate a call if any ideas occur to either of you."

"Yes, of course," they both said in unison. Charlie walked the detective to the door and locked it. The two sat on the sofa, not speaking until they saw him drive away.

"Sweetie, I need a drink," Charlie said.

CHAPTER 29

October 9, 2006
Carefree, Arizona

In the sunny breakfast area of Claire Spenser's kitchen, Pilar sipped coffee and observed the woman seated across from her. She could not get over the disparity between Claire and Lenore. To the unknowing observer, Claire Spenser looked unapproachable. An alluring green-eyed blonde, talented as both a performing actor and a visual artist, Pilar bet most women hated her whether or not they knew her despite her self-deprecating demeanor. Pilar also bet Claire did not care what other women thought.

Pilar took another sip of coffee, looked up, and said, "I'm grateful you would see me. I admit that I was shocked to find the file on you in Lenore's safe. I'm hoping you have some information no one has considered before," Pilar said. She went on to explain the dilemma with the police and that they considered Lenore's death suspicious.

Smiling, Claire said, "It doesn't surprise me someone killed her. I thought about killing her many times over the years."

Pilar said nothing and waited.

"You see, I believe she killed Richard. He'd decided to

divorce her and take custody of Allegra. The next week, he was dead. She claimed he had a heart attack, but he didn't have a heart problem in the five years I knew him. I don't know how, but I know she did something. When I heard Richard left an insurance policy with me as the sole beneficiary, I knew she would find out, but she never contacted me. Why? Because she had taken care of the problem and knew that confronting me might reveal she had a motive to kill him. The only consolation is that he made sure she would not get his money."

A low sobbing broke into her words like hiccups. Feeling inadequate to console her, Pilar looked down into her coffee cup. So much pain, she thought. Claire could not prove any of this, but Pilar believed the woman's story based on her short time around Lenore and Madera. It filled in another missing piece to this dysfunctional family puzzle. She thought how tragic the unnecessary misery these people inflicted on one other.

"I appreciate you sharing these memories that must be difficult to relive."

"There's not a day that goes by I don't think of Richard. My friends say I live too much in his memory, so I guess you can say the memories are not difficult to relive. If Richard were here now, he would want you to protect Allegra. Even if she killed her mother, Lenore had it coming."

"I can tell you that I don't believe she did it and Sylvie feels the same way. We'll figure this out. I promise."

Claire laughed, "That's a big promise for such a little girl."

"You're right, but I'm a very determined little girl." Pilar regretted that Claire's laughter lasted less than a minute.

"It was a pleasure to meet you," Pilar said, really meaning the words. "I hope the next time we meet, I have good news."

Pilar left Claire's house imprinted with her sorrow. The picture of Claire would not leave her, sitting at that table, alone, and bitter, a woman trapped by the memories of her past.

CHAPTER 30

October 9, 2006
Phoenix, Arizona

Once the Medical Examiner released Lenore's body, Pilar learned from Sylvie that Allegra left the funeral planning to Madera. Lenore had not left specific requests, so Allegra had allowed her grandmother to make the arrangements. Madera appeared to bask in the spotlight believing that Allegra remained dependent on her. Pilar suspected that, to the contrary, Allegra had no interest in the details of her mother's send-off and was glad not to be bothered.

Unlike the well-attended funeral party for Virginia, Lenore had a quiet funeral service attended by the fragmented family, no friends, coworkers, or acquaintances. Watching the pastor of Lenore's church beginning the sermon with the 23rd Psalm, Pilar noted the way the family had splintered off making their alliances clear. Pilar sat in the front pew next to Allegra, then Charlie. Bert sat alone behind them. Across the aisle, Madera and Tasha sat in the front row, with Sylvie and Rod behind them. All of them made a point to avoid eye contact.

Thinking the attendance was not much better than no one, Pilar looked behind her when the door opened. She saw a man walk in and sit down at the furthest row back. Aware that he was scrutinizing them, Pilar felt a chill rush through her adding to the already bleak atmosphere. No one acknowledged him, but returned their eyes back to the pastor as he continued his interrupted monologue.

Pilar had made the choice to sit with Allegra and Charlie when it became obvious her relatives were disregarding Allegra for an unclear reason. Pilar observed how family traits passed through the generations from Virginia to Lenore, but how different Allegra appeared. Pilar decided that by making Allegra an outsider to their little group, Allegra had rejected them and embraced her late father's gentler nature.

Pilar reached over and squeezed Allegra's hand for comfort. Allegra looked over to Pilar for a brief second to smile. Even upset, Pilar saw Allegra's expression, a hidden strength in that said she was used to suffering and would survive. Her dark eyes showed no signs of sadness or loss that made Pilar hesitate for a moment on the likelihood she could have murdered her mother. Setting aside those macabre thoughts, she returned her attention to the pastor as he wrapped up the service, saying,

"Dear Heavenly Father, we thank you for the gift of Lenore's life. Even though she was taken from us at a young age, her time on this earth was filled with charitable acts and loving devotion to others. We pray that you will comfort her family and friends in their time of mourning and remind them that she is now in peace. May we all be reminded of the frailty of life - for it is in your Son's precious Name that we pray. Amen."

"Amen," the group said in harmony.

If there were any place that hypocrisy was acceptable that was at a funeral, thought Pilar. Not knowing this pastor, she wondered if he meant any of the words he had just uttered in praise of Lenore. He must have an inkling of her true character, because no one offered to speak. When Pilar's own family died in the accident, so many friends had gotten up to speak about their kindness and involvement in the community that the service took twice as long as had been expected. Remembering how many of them came to her, held her, reassured her, and lamented on the loss being personal for them as well, she knew they were sincere. The contrast here was not only glaring, but also depressing.

"I'll ride with you to the cemetery if you'd like," Pilar said, when they all rose.

"I'd like that," Allegra said.

Following behind them, Pilar leaned over to Sylvie and Rod and said, "I'm going to ride with them, if you don't mind."

"That will work out since Madera and Tasha are riding with us," Sylvie said, rolling her eyes out of Rod's view.

Doing her best to hide the smile, she turned away and returned to Allegra.

"Granddad is riding with us, too," Allegra said.

"I'm so glad," said Pilar. Turning to Bert, she said, "I'm sorry about Lenore."

"Thank you," Bert said.

For the first time, Pilar thought she saw genuine sadness in someone over Lenore's death. A troubled man, he was also a man whose posture spoke of someone waiting for the next devastating blow in a life full of disappointments. On impulse, she reached her arm through his as they walked from the church. What the others thought at that moment was not something that worried her.

Once they reached the car, Allegra pulled Pilar to the side.

"I have to talk with you for a minute," Allegra said.

"Sure, what is it?"

Looking around before speaking, she said, "I know you found the report on Claire. I don't care about that, but I want you to know that I found it a long time ago, but I never told my mom. Claire didn't let on when you visited her, but she called me to tell me you visited her. You see, I got in touch with her when I found out about her because I wanted to know about my Dad. We both knew it would have made things bad for both of us if my mother ever found out, so we've kept our friendship a secret from everyone. Even her friends don't know. I want you to know because I know how it looks. Like I took revenge for my father's death, but I didn't. I swear."

After taking in this new information, Pilar said, "Let's keep this between us. I don't believe you killed your mother, but you're right about how it would look to the police. Thanks for telling me, though."

Giving Allegra a gentle nudge to get into the car, she followed her into the back seat while Bert rode in the front with Charlie. During the drive, Pilar found it comfortable that no one attempted conversation, giving her time to think. This was a new spin on the family drama, but did this have anything to do with Lenore's death, Pilar wondered as the desert landscape passed by her eyes in a blur.

◆ ◆ ◆

During the ride from the cemetery to the restaurant, the mood was lighter and relaxed giving Pilar the opportunity to observe the other three passengers. Allegra continued to be a contradiction of types: she was an innocent child in a sea of sharks and a wise temptress with the world at her command. Pilar had never known someone who was two extreme opposites within one personality.

On the other hand, she had not made up her mind about Charlie. Her impression of him was like the colloquial expression "no stranger to the streets." Expensive clothes, well-groomed appearance, and luxury car should speak of someone highborn, sophisticated, and successful or a combination. Instead, Pilar noticed that he tried too hard to fit the image, as if he were an actor portraying a character he did not fully understand. Then again, what she saw could be the characteristic that distinguished the *nouveau riche* from upper-crust society; that ostentatious display of expensive purchases combined with a lack of social graces.

Her third companion, Bert, was another character that might be more complex than the others. He had lived a tenuous life avoiding land mines within that family, but did so either out of loyalty or out of responsibility. Who knew? He seemed to resist the intoxication of his new freedom, still living a simple, humble life. Pilar believed he was the only person experiencing the loss of his daughter, which spoke of a man with deeper emotions than she would have imagined from her previous encounters.

"Allegra," Bert said. "I've contacted a lawyer for you about the trust. Don't worry about your grandmother and those threats to have you committed."

"Thanks, Grandpa. I didn't mention it before but I saw a lawyer a few weeks ago."

"Thank heavens for that," Bert said. Pilar noticed some of the tension left his body with that remark. "She wasn't like she is now, when I first met her. Maybe I didn't notice or maybe she changed over the years. One thing for sure is she is one miserable person who needs to butt out and stop worrying about everyone's money."

"As long as she leaves me alone, I'm fine, but after all the abuse, I don't think I could take much more without striking back."

"You don't have to worry about her anymore," Charlie said. "We're all here to support you and to protect you."

Pilar saw Allegra wincing to conceal watery eyes, so she changed the subject by suggesting they go out for dinner. The idea of food lightened the mood inside the car, Charlie choosing his favorite Puerto Rican restaurant off the Camelback Corridor Bypass.

By the time the waiter had seated them and they had ordered, Pilar thought she had to start her personality analyses over. Behind the sociable conversation, she looked on between her own participation, observing an antithesis of personalities in her companions. The extent of what she had seen before in the three of them had been situational, she realized as she studied them from behind her wine glass.

The day had been exhausting, so after a quiet meal and small talk, Charlie dropped her and Bert at their cars, and they went their separate ways. When Pilar laid her head against her pillow at last, she was still asking herself how well she could know any of them. A bigger question was whether she was smart enough to avoid being manipulated, and street-wise enough to recognize a con by Allegra and Charlie.

CHAPTER 31

October 9, 2006
Phoenix, Arizona

Charlie threw his long body into a side chair, and groaned. "Today has got to count as the second worse day of my life. The number one worst day was only last week," Charlie said. "And with the life I've lived, that's saying a lot."

"If that's the worst you've been through, you're lucky," Allegra said.

"I should qualify that by adding, without drugs."

"What about the other day?"

"I'd had a great shock and needed to settle my nerves," Charlie raised his arm over his forehead and performed his best woman-in-distress shrill.

"You better watch it or Gran will want to lock you up, too." They both laughed at that. "So you're trying to find a way to tell me you're going to see a friend?"

"I believe the uterus gives women mind reading abilities. Yes, I confess."

"The mind reading gig's a secret. Who told you?"

"That's need to know. Seriously, are you disappointed?"

"No, there're times we all need something. But I've had drugs crammed down my throat for a long time, and that makes me not want anything to do with them. I'm going to take a shower and go to bed early. Try to get the stink of this day out of my system."

"I won't be long. Make sure you keep the door locked. Your grandmother freaks me out. I thought grannies were supposed to be sweet creatures baking cookies and keeping gardens."

"You live in a lost decade, old man. Now get going and hurry back." Before he stood up, Allegra reached over to kiss him with one of her long, deep kisses. She moved her tongue slow across his top lip, around the bottom, and inside across his teeth.

When she leaned in closer, he pushed her back, and said, "I'll be back before you know it. Just let me get out of here without needing to change my pants."

Still smiling during the drive into South Phoenix, his stereo blaring, he pulled into the driveway of a white plantation-style home on a large lot. In the distance behind the property, Charlie hesitated to view the mountain range that extended in both directions in the distant south. The contrast between the brown mountains and the green leaves of the orange grove pleased him. When he shut off the car, two Dobermans ran out from the side of the house. Charlie knew the dogs and they recognized him, but the sight of them running toward him, dirt swirling on the unpaved driveway, made his heart leap.

The dogs sniffed his pants, looking up at him for what, approval, acceptance, raw meat, he never knew. He reached the front door, and stepped onto the weathered wooden floor of the covered porch. Up close, he could see signs of age, the need for repairs that someone stoned missed unless pointed out to him. He pressed the doorbell and listened as the soft ringing echoed from the upstairs windows.

Ironic that Den was from Cincinnati like Pilar but lived worlds apart. Den lived in a Cincinnati characterized by the fight for survival in an environment full of crime, imminent danger, and high-risk relationships. Den had told him those stories long before he knew Allegra. Nothing like the upper-middle class lifestyle Pilar and her family enjoyed in Amberly Village situated inside the I-275 Circle with one-acre lots and open green landscaping. He had listened as she told them about it after the funeral. He wondered if she knew how elitist she sounded.

The underbelly of most cities was alike, he figured, even in sleepy Phoenix, a small town that had put on its big town pants. Two separate worlds existing parallel to the other. One side is mainstream, middle-class America where everyone's children grew up to go to college, get good jobs, buy homes, get married and start a family. The other world, the counter-culture where bourgeois misfits and the hoi polloi coexist in a desperate environment. Within their own communities with a separate set of social rules, they live day to day to protect their families and hope to make enough money from their minimum-wage jobs to keep them in their homes one more month. No one who has not lived that life would understand. Charlie understood.

He knocked on the door hard, frustrated that no one had come to let him in yet. Hearing high heels approaching, a wave of disappointment overtook him recognizing that no matter how far you go in life, you always end up back where you started.

Charlie surveyed the girl who swung open the door, cute but underage, he suspected. She welcomed him inside with a nod of her blonde floppy curls and painted red nails, motioning him to come in. He followed her into the shotgun style house, deep and narrow, its hallway leading the length of the house to the back door, all rooms on the left side of the hallway. She stopped short and pointed him to a middle room.

"Den's coming. He said to help yourself to a drink from the fridge," she said, spun around on a heel and left.

"Hey," Den said as he entered the room moments later. Looking like the characterization of Satan himself with his dark eyes, black hair smoothed back into a tight ponytail that ended at the middle of his back, his pursed lips, high cheek bones and pale skin packaged in black leather pants and sleeveless black wool vest.

"Hey, man. What's happening?" Charlie said, reaching his hand out to Den's.

"Not much. Had a visit last night from a dealer in Tucson you may want to meet."

"Me. Why?"

"He brought in a shipment of hydro, good grade, the stuff you like. You know I don't mess with that shit. Brings too much heat."

"Okay. How do I get in touch?"

"I've got an address, but you need to go down there in the next two days. After that, he'll have moved the operation to a new location. Likes to keep on the move. Interesting guy. Name is Nick. Has a wife and daughter. Works at Cinetel Electronics."

"So why should I care about his happy home life," Charlie said. Another poser, he thought.

"He makes his connections in Phoenix, but does his trade in Tucson. I think he gets a kick out of socializing with Mr. White-Collar Conservative while all the time selling dope to his kids. Smart, dangerous, cold-blooded bastard."

"I know the type." Charlie frowned. "You're giving me too much information. What're you're trying to tell me?"

Den had been watching Charlie as he spoke, but relaxed back in his over-sized leather chair at the question. Still watching Charlie as if to size him up, he said, "Let's say that I want to stay in Phoenix operating my little business. Ay? Let's say that I know something about an *associate* who has a connection to one of my customers. What I might think is that it might be a matter of time before this associate is exposed. If my customer is involved, the cops could connect me between these two people. It would be to my best advantage to expose him in such a way that doesn't expose me. Are you following me?"

Charlie was frowning now. "I think I'm going to need a hint."

"You're not a subtle guy, are you Charlie?" Den got up and shut the door to the hallway. Sitting down again, he continued, "Nick's been around for a couple of years, but we'd never met. It happened that a mutual friend suggested we might be able to do a deal, and brought him over the other day. Dig this. I recognized him."

"From where?" Charlie asked in eager anticipation.

"Remember when you brought your girl over and she was showing me photos of her relatives?"

"Sure, I remember."

"Well Nick was in one of the photos, but she called him her Uncle Rod." Den delivered his bombshell, and leaned back with the satisfaction of one who knows he has placed a lit firecracker in someone's palm.

"What the...! Are you saying that Rod is living a double-life? How could he get away with that?"

"Man, I don't know. Don't care. What I care about is avoiding jail. I like my life just the way it is and I want to keep it that way. I've read the papers the last couple of days. I know what happened to your girl's mother. Do you think she found out and he had to get rid of her?"

Charlie's mind was reeling trying to process all of this. It was as if his brain needed to reboot. Stuck on one piece of data that was not compatible with the current programming. "I don't know what to say. Anything's possible, but if everything you say is true, I don't see how Lenore would have found out anything about her brother. They weren't that close and she didn't have much of a social life that would put her anywhere she might learn anything. What are you suggesting *I* should do?"

"Bigamy is a crime. If the cops expose him for that, the rest will come out with it. Once the press gets a hold of a sensational story about a local, they will keep digging along with the police. Like, how does he support two households and when does he get the opportunity to go to Tucson? It would be better for us if the cops busted him for the murder with a connection to his family, not dealing drugs. The cops might not find out about the second wife and all the rest."

"How do you propose I do all of this? Like, how am I supposed to know this on my own?"

"Charlie, my man. You're unemployed now. You'll have plenty of time to figure it out."

Charlie looked over at Den with a smile between sarcasm and irritation and said, "You're as bad as a woman with your cryptic comments."

Den laughed, causing him to look more satanic than before.

"Listen, find a way to link him to his sister's murder, and find a motive unrelated to Tucson. He had to have something to do with it anyway. He's the cat among the pigeons. Do this, and you're fixed for life with me."

As he looked at Den's dark features, Charlie's mind was already calculating his moves.

"Do we have a deal?" Den said.

Charlie's face took on its own devious smile, and he said, "I'll see what I can do, mate."

CHAPTER 32

October 10, 2006
Glendale, Arizona

The desert winter was much like this group of people, Pilar reflected as she sat back in the comfortable recliner in Sylvie's family room the next day. With a steaming mug of coffee, she stared out onto the back yard where the desert garden soaked up the rays of the morning sun. From inside, one could believe it was summer looking at the sparkling pool, the blooming Radiant Lantana, the green Chilean Mesquite trees glistening from the spray of the cycling sprinkler, and the welcoming warmth of the intense vibrant blue sky.

Once she walked outside, however, the cool sixty-degree breeze nipped at her exposed skin giving her an unexpected shock about the deceptiveness of the desert winter. In comparison, this family gave her a *trompe l'oeil* feeling. From the outside, they used optical illusions to create a forced perspective of their respectability, successfully tricking everyone as long as no one securitized them too closely. Their façade shattered when someone came too near the harshness of their personalities. She closed her arms around her and shivered.

Sipping on her coffee, Pilar allowed her thoughts and recent impressions from the last few days to absorb her attention. Still not recovered from the darkness of her meeting with Claire, Pilar wondered where this knowledge would take her and if it mattered to anyone other than Claire and Allegra. No doubt, Lenore had a hand in her husband's death, but that revelation could give the police a stronger motive for Allegra, if they learned about it. Still, Sylvie had portrayed Lenore as someone who never let the past go and who held grudges longer than most of them. More than anything, Pilar worried there could be more bad news to come. Dark secrets never stay in the shadows forever.

How *did* Rod fit in? He was the good son. His family regarded him as a victim of a bad marriage. Sylvie saw him as a good husband and father from an unfortunate family. Pilar speculated on the impact of Sylvie's influence on him and how that must have angered Virginia and Madera. It was odd that he did not seem anymore affected by Lenore's death than by Virginia's death. Rod, the good man, who exemplified the virtues of family over all else, did not act that way when she placed him in context.

Pilar turned her critical lens on all the family. She could not understand this group of individuals who had every reason to be happy, but instead spent their energies on being hateful and miserable. What did that say about the parenting skills of the parents, as well as the influences of the past generations on the younger? Her side of the family was loving and supportive, unfailing and constant. She could not imagine growing up under Virginia's rule.

She wished she had never come here. Tammy was right, as usual. Trying to sift through the relationship mire, Pilar grew fatigued, then depressed. As soon as she had the chance, she would go back home. The sooner she left this mess to the police, the better. She had to think about how to keep the family mud from sticking to her.

CHAPTER 33

October 10, 2006
Phoenix, Arizona

During the afternoon, Bert had picked up his mail at the new Post Store mailbox. He had not checked for mail since he opened the box, knowing from life experience that they were all bills. He had opened the bundle and pulled out the envelopes, looking but not seeing a particular letter. Seated now in his recliner with a can of beer at his elbow, he began to sort his mail. He winced at how his debt was piling up since he moved out from Madera. That was to be expected, he guessed, shaking his head as he had reached the bottom of the pile. In the habit of always stacking his mail by size, he had ignored the large envelope postmarked October 4, 2006. A sudden overbearing anxiety seized him when he recognized the writing on the label.

Lenore's script was distinctive since she was not able to grasp the art of joined-up handwriting, making it notable for its erratic unfinished loops and stabbing marks signifying an end to the sentence or exaggeration of mood. This writing looked less pronounced, but Bert knew she had written it. He dreaded speculating what the envelope contained.

He gently opened the large envelope by disturbing the gummed flap with his forefinger and releasing the metal clasp. His fingers shook when he pulled out the letter written in longhand and began to read:

October 4, 2006
Dear Dad,

I decided to write this letter because I don't know if I can tell you to your face. For years, I have avoided being close to you because I had been afraid of Mom and her jealousy, but after that last visit to Grandma's before she died, I decided to Hell with her. I can't take it anymore. What I don't want is for you to think this is about you. You will always be welcome in my home as long as I live, under any circumstances.

The hard part of this letter is to tell you a couple of things that happened a long time ago. The first thing I have to tell you is about when I was at Grandma's one summer exploring the basement while Tasha was sleeping and Rod was playing softball with the neighbor boys. I noticed a loose brick behind the furnace when I was trying to figure out how the furnace worked. I wiggled it out of its space and looked in. At first, I couldn't see anything, but after I aimed the flashlight into it, I found a small tin box. When I took it out, I saw there was no lock on it except for a small metal hook, so I opened it. Inside were three old keys and a pocket watch. The pocket watch had a small opening in its back. I decided the watch must have been broken, but someone's keepsake. Anyway, after thinking about it for a while, I took the keys out but left the watch inside the box, and put the box back in the hole and put the brick back. I even smeared dirt from the under the furnace in the cracks. I hid the keys in a plastic baggie and kept them until the next summer.

That is when I found a false wall in the basement. It was narrow, but I could get in. I found that the keys fit into locks of boxes sticking into the wall. Inside each box were gold bars, eight all together, along with various gold and silver coins in the other two boxes. Now the entire contents are in a safe deposit box at Phoenix World Bank in downtown Phoenix. They have sat there since I was eighteen when I was old enough to get a box on my own.

For years, I intended to have them appraised but never had the time or the nerve. Enclosed here is the key. Yesterday, I notified the bank that I authorized you to have access to the box with the proper ID, of course. Please don't tell anyone, especially Mom. If she found out where the gold came from, she would claim them, but I don't believe even Grandma Virginia knew about them. Otherwise, she would have put them in a safe deposit box herself.

I always hoped Mom would die before you so you could have a little peace, but it seems circumstances worked out for you anyway. As far as I am concerned, you have suffered much more than I have and deserve some enjoyment. Please sell everything and enjoy the money. I know there is a fortune there but I expect to be getting control of Allegra's trust soon so it's not as if I will need it anyway.

The second thing I want to tell you is more difficult because it happened long ago and is vulgar and mean. When I was seven and had the room in the attic on Culver, there was a time, I believe Mom was drugging us kids. You were working the night shift at the factory and we all had to go to bed by eight o'clock. For a long time, I would wake up and feel funny, like I was sick, every day. I noticed the other kids acted the same way. Mom would always say it was allergies and tell us to have a cup of tea in the morning. I started to get the feeling Mom was lying to us. For one thing, she would insist we have our "milky drink" before bed every night. Not just me, but even the babies.

One night, I pretended to drink it but poured it in the sink. Mom would not watch us drink, she just made sure the glasses were empty when she came back. She put us to bed and turned off the lights. When the hall clock in the hall rang at nine o'clock, I heard a knock on the back door. I looked out and saw a man standing at the doorstep until Mom let him in. I was afraid to leave my room but I opened the door a crack to listen. I could hear Mom talking to the man, and then they would laugh. I could hear them changing the record player and opening beer cans. Then I heard all kinds of groaning sounds, which I realized when I was older, were the sound of them having sex right in the living room.

Since Mom was confident she was safe, she never suspected I never drank one of her "milky drinks" again. Every night you worked, this man came over at the back door at nine o'clock. The first time I found out it was spring and it went on until Halloween. I remember because he wasn't coming over anymore and afterward, she was meaner to all of us kids. She yelled at us while we were trick-or-treating and saying how awful it was to have to babysit children. I was afraid but I didn't know what to do. I thought if I told you, you would leave us alone with her and that would have been worse. After that was when she went into the hospital and you took care of us for a long time by yourself.

I'm telling you this now so you know you were never at fault. As an adult, I don't understand how you could have stood her even not knowing about that man.

Believe me when I tell you, I love you and I have always been proud to have you as my father. Let's get together soon.

Love, Lenore.
P.S. I researched the gold I found and it came from old stagecoach robberies. Exciting!

After reading the letter several times, Bert knew he had to make a decision. Should he take it to the police? He would have to produce the letter that would expose the story about the gold, and the humiliating fact that his wife had made a fool out of him. In fact, if Madera got the opportunity to read the letter and found out about the gold, no one would ever see either again. Bert conjectured Lenore would feel the same. After all, she had held on to that terrible experience all these years and had to feel more bitterness toward her mother than he does. If Lenore wanted her mother to have the gold, she would have sent this letter to her.

Reaching inside the envelope, he grabbed the key, and after finding nothing else, tossed the envelope into the sink and set it on fire. Deciding what to do about the letter was more difficult. Destroying it could be a mistake, but hiding it here could also be a problem. At his age, he could drop dead of a heart attack. Thinking about it, he had a brilliant idea. When he went to the bank tomorrow to check out the box, he would leave the letter inside, keeping it available and away from snooping eyes.

He figured gold bars and coins were undoubtedly worth a fortune. Placing the letter and the key in his wallet, he placed the wallet in the pocket of his pajama bottoms and went to bed feeling better than he had since before marrying Madera.

CHAPTER 34

October 10, 2006
Glendale Arizona

Pilar jumped at the unexpected telephone call. She had nestled on the comfortable chair in the family room to read the *Oxford History of Mexico*, and found it a sanctuary from recent chaotic events. The demanding peal kept nudging her like the alarm snooze in the morning. She resisted the urge to answer until she grasped that Sylvie might be the caller. Sylvie knew Pilar was in and might think something was wrong if she did not pick up.

"Hi, Pilar. It's Allegra. Can you come over to Charlie's place? I have something I want--, no, I *need* to talk to you about."

"Sure, why not." Pilar was curious to get a look at Allegra after digesting all she had learned at the funeral.

"I'm relieved. I'll make lunch, so don't eat. How about noon?"

"That's good for me," Pilar said.

♦ ♦ ♦

Charlie's Condo

Pilar stepped from the elevator into the broad hallway of the Biltmore Towers. She took a few moments to capture the elegance of the building décor in her mind before she looked for Charlie's unit number. She had been impressed with the valet service and travertine floor in the lobby entrance with its lavish seating, crystal chandelier, and antiques strewn throughout. More upmarket than she expected. Maybe she was wrong about her assumption that Charlie needed Allegra's money.

Allegra surprised her by standing next to a half opened oak entry door of a height that suggested an expansive interior. "The doorman called to let me know you were on your way up," Allegra said answering Pilar's questioning look.

After a quiet hug, Allegra ushered Pilar inside and over to a breakfast bar. Pilar noticed that Allegra provided no explanation for the opulence, and offered it without apology. A glass coffee pot and platter of small sandwiches next to two place settings looked inadequate in the expansive kitchen. Pilar seated herself on one of the high-backed stools and watched Allegra wave to Charlie, who nodded in her direction before going out to the balcony.

Pilar studied him while he sat on one of the lounge sofas, and picked up a newspaper. Neither lived up to preconceived images, each time she met them they were a contradiction of who they were before. She picked up a sandwich and turned her attention back to Allegra.

"Thanks for coming. I don't know who else to turn to. Charlie supports me, but he's too close. The police think he would lie for me because he's after my money. Grandpa's kind, but he wouldn't understand what I have to tell you." Allegra's voice quivered and her eyes moistened. She took a deep breath to control her emotions and went on.

"I'm afraid the police think I killed my mother!" Allegra blurted out as Pilar tried to swallow a mouthful of sandwich.

"What do you mean? Who said that?"

"No one yet, but I know the police will. Mom and I had a terrible fight. The same night she died. Isn't it too obvious I had something to do with it?"

Pilar said, "I hope this doesn't sound patronizing, but children fight with their parents without murdering them. They would need more than an argument to charge you with murder. Like evidence."

"I had access to the house. She wasn't afraid of me so it would have been easy to poison her. Then there's my trust."

When she did not elaborate, Pilar said, "What trust?"

"The one my father set up for me. When I turn twenty-five, I will be worth somewhere near thirty-five million dollars. My dad was very good in business."

Allegra stopped talking and sipped her tea, giving Pilar the seconds she needed to process this new information. Not only about Allegra, but also about Charlie. She had believed Allegra was a hanger-on, a social parasite benefiting from his generosity and emotional support. In reality, Charlie, now unemployed from his highly paid executive position, has a stronger reason to be with Allegra than love, and an even stronger reason to remove her controlling mother from the picture.

"I worried you'd start to judge us once you knew. I see in your face that I was right. Believe me, there's more to our relationship than outside appearances. But that's between Charlie and me, and not the real problem. I have something else to tell you."

"Go on," Pilar said.

"I spiked her anti-anxiety meds about a week before she died."

"You did what? Are you out of your mind?"

"You have no idea what my life has been like since my dad died. She threatened to have me put in an institution. She sabotaged everything I tried to do, from sports, acting class, boyfriends, and especially girlfriends. She had me on every drug from Ritalin to Prozac that her quacks prescribed. If it weren't for Charlie, I don't know where I would be right now. I'd changed my mind and tried to get them back but she was home.

That's when we had the big argument and I slapped her. I ended up leaving, figuring I could go back later when I knew she was at work. That was the afternoon of the day she died."

"So that's how she was poisoned. You say you didn't get back in to take the spiked pills, but they were gone when the police looked in her cabinet. Sylvie was there and saw Madera open the cabinet. No prescriptions of any kind. The only other bottles were the ones in the car with her."

"No, I didn't go back. And the bottles they found in her car aren't right. Those weren't mine, but you see how bad this looks. I'm afraid that any minute, they'll find the capsules that I tampered with. They might think if I did that, I, oh, I don't know, decided to use something else. I was the only person who could've done that."

"No doubt," Pilar said. Her sarcasm did little to conceal her contempt for Allegra at this moment. "Exactly what do you expect *me* to do? If you think I am going to help you cover up, you're delusional."

"I didn't ask you over for that. I want help to find out who really did kill her. Just because I tried to do something bad, I shouldn't be punished while the guilty person gets away with it."

"Who else could it be? From what I've heard, she didn't have any friends or even go out much. Aside from you, did she have arguments with anyone else? Or maybe a long-standing feud of some kind?"

"She never stood up for herself with anyone that I ever saw. She talked to Aunt Tasha recently. She might have an idea."

"Sylvie didn't mention the sisters were on speaking terms."

"That's because they kept it a secret from Grandma Madera. Rod was so harsh about Tasha separating from the family, Mom didn't tell him either. This family does not confide in one another. Neither Tasha nor Mom would tell Sylvie the temperature. Even if they liked her enough to include her, they'd know she'd run right to Rod and tell him."

"I believe that. I guess there was always friction between Sylvie and your family."

"They always claimed Sylvie didn't fit in. Said she thought

she was better than we were. I got tired of hearing about it. I don't know of anything Sylvie did to anyone. As far back as I remember, whenever Uncle Rod brought her around, they were horrible to her. I wouldn't have married him after meeting this family, but she did. She must be crazy."

"Or maybe she loves Rod very much."

Allegra rolled her eyes. "Whatever. Rod is not *that* great. If only he were as wonderful as he tells everyone he is."

"Let's get back to you." Pilar helped herself to more coffee. Not as angry as minutes before, she looked out into the empty sky beyond the balcony rail to ground her emotions. "Is there anything *else* you haven't told me?"

"I've told you everything I know."

"What about the family? My Gran used to say that we should not judge people because none of us knows how we will behave under the same conditions. Maybe you're not as bad as you sound to me. Maybe I would act out under the same pressure. But to find another motive, you have to think outside yourself and your own problems. Think of another motive someone might have to get Lenore out of way. Other than you, what does her death mean to the others?"

Allegra focused on a framed watercolor landscape across the room, her soft face tight showing furrowed eyebrows and squinting eyes. "There's Claire, but I don't believe she would kill anyone. The only one I don't trust is Rod. There's something I sense when I'm around him. A storm brewing under the surface. Like, he could explode any minute and beat you to death."

"Wow. Anyone else?"

"Sylvie. I only say that because she's married to Rod. I don't believe she keeps any secrets from him. I think she would do anything for him or anything to protect him."

"Not knowing them as you do, I can't say you're wrong, but Sylvie has her children. Would she risk losing them? With Rod, I can understand better. Besides that, Sylvie asked me to help figure this out to save you. I say we get together with her and talk about all of this."

"I guess, but I'm afraid of going to her house. What if she

came here?"

"You're right. That might be better." Pilar said. "I'll call her now, okay?"

"Sure. But please swear you won't tell her anything about Claire and the meds."

"Ok. That's a good idea anyway. The fewer people who know that, the lower the risk they would use that knowledge as leverage to protect themselves."

Reaching into her bag for her phone, Pilar pressed redial and sipped her coffee until Sylvie answered. After she explained they wanted to discuss Lenore and who might want her dead, Sylvie agreed to go to Charlie's place the following day at 1:00.

"Rod's working then, so I'll get Aggie to pick up the kids at school," Sylvie said. "Don't mention this to him this evening. He hates family gossip, and if he knew what we were up to, he'd hit the ceiling."

"No problem. See you later." Turning to Allegra, she said, "She'll be here at one o'clock. Before I leave, would you mind allowing me back into your house again?"

Allegra pulled a key ring from a bowl on the counter and handed it to her. "Here. What do you expect to find?"

"I don't know, but if you didn't kill her, there must be a clue about someone else in her personal things, specifically in her computer. I want to look around."

With the cups empty and the last sandwich eaten, Allegra and Pilar said their goodbyes at the door.

"Thank you for agreeing to help me." Allegra looked at Pilar with wide eyes and parted lips, looking relaxed and younger than she did when she arrived.

"I'll do what I can. I promise." Pilar reached over, hugged Allegra, and said, "Everything will be fine. Just don't do anything that stupid or ever tell me about it."

♦ ♦ ♦

Charlie hesitated when he came through the balcony door. Allegra's turned to face him when he said, "Is she gone?"

"She's gone," Allegra said, her voice weary. "I told her what I did to the medicine. I hope she doesn't believe I'm to blame. What a mess I've caused myself. Maybe I feel guilty because I know what I was *going* to do. Now that Mom's gone, it's as if I've woken up from a bad dream. The nightmare's not as frightening in the daylight and I feel foolish."

"I was listening. I heard what you said about Rod."

Now sitting next to him on the sofa, she looked off at the distance through the window and said, "Uncle Rod might appear to be a nice guy, but he makes me nervous. I get a bad feeling from him. At Grandma Virginia's place, he always came early to take care of anything she asked him to do. Like a creepy caretaker who didn't want me there. Oh, I don't know. Maybe it's my imagination, but I know deep down something is not right about him and I would rather avoid him."

"Who knows," Charlie said. "Maybe he's a ghoul underneath it all, like Dorian Gray." Charlie wanted to reassure her that she was justified and her instinct was right, but decided against it. He had to find a way to take care of this without involving her. She had been through enough and he did not want to think about what Rod might do to her because of a nervous slip of the tongue.

"Yeah, right," she continued. "No one would ever believe he was capable of smashing a cockroach. It doesn't matter now since I don't have to go up there to those depressing Sunday dinners." Smiling, she said, "If I went there now, it's Pilar's house. I wouldn't be nervous around her."

"Let's hope she can find out what happened before the police dig up something on us."

CHAPTER 35

October 10, 2006
Glendale, Arizona

With the hunt for clues at the front of her thoughts, Pilar speculated on the scenarios she thought had potential. By the time she was back at Sylvie's, she was excited to talk about her theories.

"What do we have so far?" Pilar began.

"Two dead women. Virginia's could have been a normal death, and Lenore's could end up declared be a suicide, but what if they were both murdered," Sylvie said. "The question is whether it was for revenge or money."

"Revenge or money?" repeated Pilar.

"That's what it all comes down to in the end. We know two things about both of them. First, Virginia was loaded from an inheritance from her parents. Lenore wasn't loaded, but she had plans to take the reins on that trust her late husband left for Allegra. Second, neither were nice people. There's a point when someone like that goes too far with the wrong person."

"Where did Virginia's parents get their money? Pete inherited but I never asked him the source of the money. We know their parents were immigrants seeking asylum after the fall of Pancho Villa. Rod said they were from Mexico's ousted aristocracy during the Revolution, but that didn't match the research. I still don't understand how they came to be so rich. Could they have made that kind of money running a shop?"

"I believe Rod knows what he's talking about more than your research," Sylvie said. "He got the stories from his grandmother whereas you only have internet search results. Besides, that all happened long ago. How could that matter now?"

Pilar rubbed her finger around the edge of her coffee mug, trying to figure out the root of Sylvie's resistance. "I don't know, I'm sure, but we've got to start somewhere. Except for Allegra's father, that's the last time anyone had money."

"Well, from what Rod says, his great grandparents came to this country with their money in gold coins and settled in Flagstaff. They had other immigrant friends, one Russian couple named Rodchenko. Virginia married their son. We heard something about a couple from Spain who died in a house fire, but I don't think Rod knows much about them. Anyway, the four were close friends. I believe it was a happy family at that time before it all went nasty," Sylvie said.

Pilar saw Sylvie's expression change briefly, causing her to wonder if Sylvie revealed details that she had not planned to tell.

"Peter, your grandfather, left for college in the east, and ended up staying back there. Now we know his parents left the house to him, but he chose to stay in the east and no longer wanted to live here. To keep it in the family, he let Ralph and Virginia live there. If you ignore the decorating, you will find she took good care of it." A bitter edge came into the last sentence. Pilar tried not to notice what she suspected was Sylvie's growing resentment about the property.

Sylvie shifted and continued. "Rod believed he would inherit the house when she died. She had said that was her intention because she hadn't spoken to her son Nikolas and his wife in years, and because he had worked all those years to help keep up the place after she was on her own. After all the promises, the house wasn't hers to leave anybody. Rod is not happy about that but won't say anything. I can tell he feels betrayed."

"What I don't understand," Pilar said, "is how much money was left to Virginia and Peter to start with. I mean, Virginia and Peter had enough money to live on throughout their entire adult lives. Doesn't that sound like a lot to you?"

"I guess it does when you put it like that. Does this have any relevance to the present, though?"

"Maybe not. If we look at public records and old newspapers, we could research their business interests. What if there are continuing business interests, like stocks or mineral rights. What do you think?"

"What d'ya mean," Sylvie said. "Like ask the search engine for how they earned the money? The Internet is amazing but it's not a physic channel. This is a waste of time. The answer is in the present. I'll do what I can, but don't expect much. We'd do better to ask about that trust of Allegra's. That was shabby of Richard to leave that policy to her instead of to Lenore. Maybe Lenore was getting ready to do something we don't know about yet, and Allegra or Charlie killed her."

"I'm no expert on trusts, but Lenore wouldn't be able to take over that trust, except to request money for Allegra's expenses. Lenore would have to be careful in case Allegra accused her of embezzlement. I'll check that out tomorrow."

The two women sat in silence for several minutes. Pilar thinking about the money, but she had the feeling Sylvie was thinking about the family.

"I've got it!" Pilar said.

"What?"

"I'll call my Gran Marian. She may know the story. It's too late today, but I'll call tomorrow when I know her sister and niece won't be there. You know, if we don't come up with a good reason for someone else to kill Lenore, Allegra's in for it."

CHAPTER 36

October 11, 2006
Amberly Village, Ohio

Marian was sitting at her kitchen table finishing her breakfast of white buttered toast and a large mug of coffee when Pilar called. Her aching sacrum was giving her more trouble this morning when she walked over to her chair to answer the telephone.

"Blessed be, girl," she said in a voice that belied her true weariness once she recognized Pilar's number and answered.

"Hi, Gran. How are you feeling today?"

"I'm fine. The bigger question is how you are today?"

"Well," Pilar hesitated. "I should have called you sooner about this but there have been two deaths since I've been here and one is being looked on by the police as suspicious. Sylvie and I are trying to help Allegra, but I'm at a loss because of all the things I don't understand."

"My goodness gracious. Who died?"

"First, Virginia, Pete's sister. As far as anyone knows, she died of natural causes in her sleep. Next, her granddaughter Lenore, Allegra's mother, died of an overdose in a car in the middle of the night at the bus station. That's the suspicious one, which I guess goes without saying." Pilar's voice started to give way to emotions of recent days and she paused to hold back the tears.

"Did it ever occur to you that there might be a reason Pete separated from them?" Marian said.

"I don't understand how two siblings can be so different, raised by the same two people," Pilar said, noticing the smile coming back in her expression.

"If we knew that answer, we could probably cure family dysfunction and make a million dollars. Seriously, Pilar, the easy answer is that each child looks to a different parent as a role model. If two people are so different in their characters, and if they don't bother to present a unified front to the children, well, all I can say is to remind you of the old expression, 'a house divided.' If you want a Biblical approach, think of Cain and Abel. No easy fix for a condition that's as old as time."

"Cain and Abel, of course," Pilar said. "Shows how long it's been since I've been to church not to catch the reference."

"No matter about that. We raised you with a strong moral foundation. Everything you need to know you learned before you were ten years old. Knowing right from wrong, and learning enough analogies to get you through whatever life serves you."

"I can't tell you how good you make me feel. All of this has been getting me down, but as usual, you get me back on track."

"You need to come home right now. I knew those people were nothing but trouble. Now, they're dragging you into their messes."

"They *are* family, Gran, and I've told Allegra that I would help her and they're not all bad. I'm staying with Rod, Lenore's brother, and his wife, Sylvie, who are wonderful people. In fact, Rod looks like a young version of Pete.

"I'm not convinced yet," Marian said.

"If you can help me, I can get out of here sooner," Pilar said.

"Anything to get you home. What do you want to know?"

"How did Pete's parents make their money? Weren't they considered rich?"

"To be frank, your mother and I never knew. Pete was always cagey about it, but we didn't think it was anything more than his feeling that it was none of our business. You know how men are. Well, at least back then. Women had no place in a man's business affairs."

"That's irritating to imagine. What about his parents' friends? Did he ever mention the Russian or Spanish couple?"

"That I do know. He told us the Russians, named Rodchenko, were their parents' close friends. Their children went to live with them after assassins shot down their parents in the street. Virginia married their son, Rudolf. His sister, Varvara, went back to Russia to help fight Stalin and the Bolsheviks. They assumed she died or went to the Gulag. Whatever happened, none of the family ever heard of her after she left Arizona."

"Rod told me about her before. What about a couple from Spain?"

"They were the Velasquez family. Pete said the whole family died in a house fire. Pete said Josefina never got over it. She was a strong woman with a sensitive constitution, but the tragedies took their toll on her. I met her once when they came for Pete's wedding. I thought she was so beautiful. She had large, sad dark eyes, dark hair pulled up on her head, a small frame but erect and proud. I thought it was too bad we couldn't have her visit, but that's what it was."

"I've seen her picture," Pilar said. "That's exactly how she looked. How sad. She must've missed her son. What else can you tell me about them?"

"Well, when we asked Pete about his parents visiting, he would say that he and his father did not agree on things and that it was his father who wouldn't allow his mother to visit without him. He didn't want to come and he didn't want her traveling alone. Sad."

"I wonder what his problem was."

"He never said. We let it go. After a while, we all had busy lives raising children and one thing or another and we didn't have time to think about the past anymore. That's the way of life, Pilar."

Pilar struggled against the impulse to cry. "Well, thanks for the information, Gran. By the way, I inherited the Flagstaff house, at least Pete's heirs did, and I'm it. I'm going up there to check it out tomorrow."

"That's exciting for you. Are you keeping it?"

"I don't know yet. It might be nice to have it for vacations. I don't have to make that decision right now."

"Drive safely, then. Call me tomorrow. I'm going to worry until you're back home."

"Sure, Gran. I'll call when I arrive and describe the place to you. And Gran, I love you," Pilar said.

"I love you too, sweetheart. I'll wait for your call," Marian said, hanging up. She knew that girl well enough to know she was holding back tears. Damn those people.

Marian placed the telephone back in its cradle, guilty about lying to Pilar. It was for her own good, after all. She hated lying to the child, but that was what Pete had wanted. The idea that she might learn about his parents' past had been a shame to him, and Lord knows she would never have done anything to hurt that kind old gentleman. How could any of them have dreamt Pilar or her brothers would be curious about generations that far back. Those poor boys were beyond worldly concerns now, which could be the reason Pilar had this itch to connect. Who could have known, she thought, feeling frustration at having to make this decision on her own. All she could imagine is what Pete would want her to do.

The answer was always to keep quiet. Let the past stay buried. She set finality to her thoughts, and decided that was exactly what she would continue to do. Let the past stay buried.

CHAPTER 37

October 11, 2006
Phoenix, Arizona

Allegra agreed to meet Pilar at Lenore's house instead of going alone. Pilar worried she would get spooked again. Now they sat in front of Lenore's computer watching the small screen run through its permutations until the desktop icons appeared. Images of program shortcuts and PDF articles littered the empty space of the beach scene. In her desktop favorites, they found links to historical news articles, book references, census images from the 1880s to 1930s, and notes about crimes for the same time span. After they had read everything, the two leaned back, studying the unkempt desk without speaking.

"Pilar, I don't know who these people are. I mean, I think this is supposed to be genealogy, but why would my mom bother with any of this? Maybe these are tangents that kept her busy."

"Who knows? I wish Sylvie hadn't cancelled. If Rod is such a so-all-about-the-family guy, Sylvie would know if this is important. I guess if you can't find a babysitter, that's that."

"That's what she said, but more than likely, she blabbed to Rod about what we're doing and he wouldn't let her come."

"Let's forget about them and move on. Look. Here's Virginia and Peter Paralelos, children of Josefina and Ricardo Paralelos in the 1920 Census. Others in the household were Varvara and Rudolf Rodchenko, so this had to be after their parents died."

"Were murdered," Allegra said, feeling the harshness of her own father's death.

"Right. Look at this," Pilar said. "Here's a record from the *Registro Civil*, listing the baptism of Doroteo Paralelos on 13 June 1892, Purisima de *Coecillo*, Guanajuato, Mexico. This must be Pete's grandfather."

"Why didn't she share this with anyone, especially me? Why the big secret?"

"That's strange," Pilar said. "And look at this in the same folder: Articles on a stagecoach holdup and train robberies. I wonder what she found interesting in those stories. The posses tracked down some of the thieves, all gringo names, and no mention of anyone I've heard of. Makes you wonder why she thought these details belonged in this folder."

Allegra said, laughing, "Maybe she thought we're descendants of outlaws."

"More than likely, she tucked those in with the family files because it was the same time period."

"That makes sense. Anything else?"

"Nothing obvious. I'll print out these stories and the newspaper articles. I'd like to find out more about the Velasquez family, too. While that's printing, let's look at her emails."

Pilar clicked on the Outlook Express icon and watched as new messages loaded. Her inbox was so full of saved messages, she groaned over the idea of sifting through so many without knowing what to look for. As with the folder contents, they read each message, finding most to be responses from website owners about their research into the old west unsolved crimes and details of Flagstaff society in the early 1900s. She gave up reading after a half hour.

"I'm printing these out so I can read the rest later," Pilar said. "I set up twenty or so to print. Let's take a break."

The west facing sun bore down on the windowpanes of the small room, and the air had grown stifling. Pilar could tell that Allegra welcomed the break as much as she did. Allegra poured them both white wine mixed with sparkling water, and followed Pilar to the back yard patio.

The strain was getting to Pilar. She looked over at the small pool, and the fire pit, surrounded by Queen Palms and Bermuda grass. The scene was so relaxing that she started to nod off until the cold drink started to drop from her hand. She came back with a jerk in time to prevent an accident, set her glass on the table next to her and rested her back into the soft cushion of the chair.

"You're tired, aren't you," Allegra said.

"I guess I am. I've had a rough week. But you have too."

"I hope you're not getting discouraged and decide to go home."

"That's crossed my mind, to be honest. A friend from back home warned me about getting involved with extended family. Except for you and Sylvie, I'm disillusioned. It's hard to believe my grandfather ever had a connection to Virginia. She was so mean. I wish you could've met Pete. Rod looks like him, but Pete was the type of man that made everyone comfortable."

"All I've got is Bert. He's okay, but a big wus."

"I just thought of something," Pilar said, springing upright. "Instead of tracking family history, why don't we look more at those crimes? I don't know why I didn't think of this before. What if they were involved and that's why Rod and Sylvie steer me away from their past before Flagstaff? That would account for the money they had when they came to Flagstaff. Maybe Rod is ashamed and that's why he doesn't want to talk about it. What do you think?"

"That's kind of awesome. How cool would that be? Like being part of Arizona history." They jumped up at the same time and headed back to Lenore's computer. Pilar stared at the screen, searching Lenore's icons.

"Yeah, but I don't see a connection to Mom's death yet," Allegra said. "Surely, no one would kill her over an awkward family history."

"Not unless she stumbled onto something else along the way."

"Good point. Like someone she emailed didn't like where she was going with her research. Her death might not have anything to do with this family."

Pilar started opening the desk drawers, and said, "Do you have any blank CDs around here?"

"She bought some she never used that she kept in the bottom drawer."

Pilar pulled out a CD and inserted it into the computer. "I'll make us each a copy, the emails, the address book, and all these research files. Later, I'm going to read everything from a different perspective, especially the details of the robberies. The answer has to be in these records. I'm sure of it."

"What should I do to help?"

"Can you go through the address book and see if you can account for all the names there. If you find anyone you don't know, we can start with them."

"You know, Pilar. For the first time since Mom died, I feel afraid. Not scared I'll be arrested for murder. Not even afraid of being spooked by her ghost. More like we're walking into whatever it is that got her killed."

Pilar stopped to look at Allegra. "I'm worried about that, too, but we can't stop. However mean-spirited she was, she didn't deserve killing."

"I hope her killer doesn't decide we rate the same treatment."

CHAPTER 38

October 11, 2006
Glendale, Arizona

When Pilar returned to Rod and Sylvie's house, she was ready for a long night's sleep. The burger, fries, and hot chocolate during her drive back slowed her mind and relaxed her body, but she continued to have a vague apprehension. Almost ten o'clock, the children would be asleep and Rod would be getting ready for work. She planned to slip in the front door and go straight to her room. Once there, she could close the door and watch television after a shower.

Tiptoeing after she entered the house, she was halfway down the hallway when Rod's deep voice coming from the direction of the bedrooms startled her.

"You're a real night owl, aren't you?" Rod said, walking forward until his tall frame loomed over her.

"You scared me," Pilar said. "I was trying to be quiet and not bother anyone. Are you working tonight?"

"As a matter of fact, I am. I'll be leaving in a few minutes. Since you're here, I'm interested in what you've found out about Lenore," Rod said, whose emergence from the shadows had given Pilar a creepy feeling she could not shake.

"Oh, Sylvie told you about that? Well, come on in and I'll show you," she said as she pointed to the family room. Still uneasy, she could not pinpoint why. His imposing silence did not alleviate her feelings, but made her self-conscious and awkward.

"We went through Lenore's emails to see what she might have been into that could get her into trouble. You know the type of thing, meeting someone online, agreeing to meet him, and it goes wrong. I printed them out, but there's not much there. It seems her main interest was in genealogy and Arizona history. None of that is helpful, but we're still confident we'll find something that will lead to a real suspect or a motive. There must be a reason a conservative woman like Lenore would meet a stranger downtown in the middle of the night."

"I want this intrusion in my family's business to stop" Rod said in a deep, menacing tone.

"Excuse me?"

"You heard me. I want this to stop. You have no business interfering in our affairs, asking questions, trying to dig up dirty laundry on my parents and grandparents. You know nothing about them, but you're willing to make them scapegoats to try to save that worthless piece of trash."

"Where's Sylvie? She'll tell you that it's nothing like that," Pilar said, her voice high and trembling.

"Don't worry about Sylvie. I've told her told not to talk to you anymore and she won't. I suggest you pack up and shove off right now. I want you gone before I leave for work."

He stood over her, and when she looked up, she thought he was going to strike her, but instead he crossed his arms and kept a cold stare on her. Her hands shook as she started to gather up the emails when he slammed his hand down and said, "Don't even think about it. You have no right to have them in the first place," he said, scooping up the papers and started ripping them into pieces.

Backing away, she hurried to her room to gather up her belongings. In the bathroom, she tossed her toiletries into a mesh bag and tucked it into her carrying bag. Picking up her suitcase, she grabbed her keys to leave. Her face was still hot, the threat of violence making her stomach queasy and her bladder weak as she passed him on her way out the front door.

Her nervous fingers fumbled with unlocking the car door before she was able to feel the key slide into the door lock. She tossed her bags into the passenger seat and started the engine. She heard the front door close and thought he had stayed inside, but when she looked back, Rod stood in front of the door watching her.

Driving was second nature to her, but she struggled to concentrate. Her heart still pounded, tears rolling down her face, her palms sweaty on the steering wheel. This must be how battered women feel and why they look paralyzed with inaction. Some things had to be experienced to be understood. Fear was one of them. She would not be able to hear another story from a battered woman again without reliving this moment.

Her next thought was of Sylvie. What had changed? Then she remembered Sylvie had said Rod did not like gossip. Sylvie must have talked about the meeting. It seemed an extreme reaction. What could Sylvie have told him to make him this angry? She wondered if Sylvie was all right, but she was worried more about herself at that moment.

Without too much more thought, she turned onto Interstate 17 for Flagstaff. With relief in sight, she was grateful she owned the house now and could stay there, no matter what anyone thought. Bless Mr. Whitney who had given her the keys when he sent the letter. All she had to do was get there in one piece.

Time and distance between her and Rod, she regained a grasp of her emotions. Whatever was going on in that house had nothing to do with her. She had barely arrived in town. What struck her the most was how Rod had changed. She thought of her grandfather again and how much alike they looked. She had judged Rod as having the same character and disposition as her grandfather solely on his appearance.

She judged Sylvie the same way, allowing her soft-spoken, feminine demeanor to lull her into the misguided notion of kindness. Driving through the middle of darkness, Pilar understood those two were as sinister as the rest of the family. Maybe worse.

Her rattled nerves kept her alert on the road, welcoming the darkness, as freeway lights grew fewer and less prominent the further she drove from the Phoenix metropolitan area. She enjoyed the chilling air of the desert night when she rolled down the window. Crisp biting wind blew past her face, dancing around the interior of the car like a ghost, quiet and secretive. She would remember this later as a favorite Arizona experience.

Away from the congested roadways and avenues of Phoenix, she drove into the rocky terrain of the barren mountains invisible until her headlights brought them into view. Into the towering pines of Northern Arizona with sleepy bedroom communities and rustic towns along Interstate 17, she drove until she reached Flagstaff.

Here, the night did not frighten her as it did back home, and in other major cities that she had visited. The odds were a lone woman broken down in the middle of the night would run into a bad guy looking for trouble. In Arizona, the odds were good you would see a coyote, an elk, a deer, or a nocturnal predator on the hunt more than a person. She grinned as she thought about how afraid she was of cows, but had no concept of the dangers of coyotes and javelinas. The same could be said for trusting estranged relatives who were more menacing than a serial killer hitchhiking on a lonely highway.

She listened as the GPS reminded her which turn to take off Route 66. She started her ascent up the hill, driving and watching for street numbers and a familiar landmark. When she arrived, she pulled up into the driveway this time, her jangled nerves on edge again. The absence of light behind the windows and in the surrounding property looked creepy and unwelcoming. In a moment of blind terror, she decided she could find a hotel. Instead, she weighed the fear she had felt from Rod and decided nothing could be scarier tonight. She took one last look at the house before getting out and walking up the porch stairs.

CHAPTER 39

October 12, 2006
Flagstaff, Arizona

After the two-hour drive to Flagstaff, followed by six hours of sound sleep, Pilar woke up on the sofa refreshed. After finding the coffee and brewing a pot in the old-fashioned percolator, she walked out to the front porch to look around. She had noticed the porte-cochère that first day, but had not seen beyond that.

Now she saw a design detail she appreciated in the way the architect had taken advantage of the downward slope to build out a full-size door into the basement. Beyond the sharp curve of the driveway leading from under the porte-cochère, she saw two large basement windows. At the back, wooden stairs led up to a small deck outside the kitchen door. She walked back to the front porch and took another appraising look. She contemplated her future here while she enjoyed a mug of coffee in the brisk morning air.

The old house had a melancholy air, a sadness speaking to her from the front parlor window. Not as malevolent as she had thought last night. The porch with its wicker furnishings, and brown-painted wood floor brought visions of respectable ladies from a distant era sipping tea, and discussing the events of a sunny afternoon. She doubted that ever happened here, though. Part of her loved the house already while a deeper part of her dreaded its memories and the secrets it held over the last hundred years.

She tried to tell herself she was not nervous, but she was. Last night, she had been terrified here alone. Rod's anger looped through her mind, casting a pall over the house, its contents, and the surrounding darkness. She had curled up on the living room sofa with a blanket she had found in the front closet. This morning, she woke up no longer terrified, but determined not to allow Rod or anyone else to intimidate her.

After washing up in the upstairs bathroom, she came down to look for something to eat. There was something welcoming about the old-fashioned coffee maker on the stove, so she made another pot. Eying the spacious farm-style kitchen with the percolator gurgling in the background, she decided she could see herself here for the long term. She clasped her hands around the coffee mug for warmth, resting her elbows on the large wooden kitchen table while she thought about the logistics of living here.

It did not take long before the situation in Phoenix interrupted her fantasies and pushed to the front of her mind. Facts swam through her head in a dizzying swirl. She had trouble zooming in on something meaningful that would pull the plot together. As if she were reading one of her favorite mystery novels, she assigned herself as the detective who had to sort out the truths from red herrings.

How should she figure Rod's behavior other than he acted like a man with something to hide? What about Allegra? A young woman in love and ready for her freedom. She had the strongest motives for murdering her mother. The most important question was how was she to recognize the red herrings in her mystery? Deciding what is important from the extraneous facts thrown into the story to muck up the plot.

Aside from Rod and Allegra, what about Charlie, an outsider who had a lot to gain from Allegra's trust? Then there was Tasha and Bert, who both claimed to be on good terms with Lenore before she died, but she only had their word on that. And what if Virginia was murdered? Madera had a strong motive to kill her own mother, assuming as Rod had done, that she was coming into a huge inheritance, but she had nothing to gain by killing her daughter. Madera could not assume she would control Allegra's trust with Lenore gone.

She looked into her mug and saw it was almost empty, took a refill, and decided to give herself a break from crime solving to investigate the rest of the house. She did not consider herself given to supernatural ideas, but she had to push out images of spirits and evil as she headed up to the second floor landing. The eeriness at Lenore's house still haunted her, adding to the close atmosphere upstairs. Coffee in her right hand, left hand on the banister, she cleared her head of spooky thoughts and started up the stairs.

While standing at the top of the stairs to consider which room to tackle first, she noticed the door to the attic at the end of the hallway. Its traditional paneled door was identical to the others up here except it was set on a step. The unlocked door swung toward her when she turned the knob.

She climbed the narrow stairwell to an open room that spanned the area half the size of the second floor. Windows situated on each wall, the cloudy panes allowed a filtered light that exposed the neglect and dust accumulated over the years. To her left, she saw old trunks, a few pieces of good quality furniture, set aside and long forgotten, she guessed. The tall items gave off a chilling vibe, hidden under sheets at the back of the room. She told herself it was best to keep them covered until she had better control of her nerves. The right side was sparse with a banker's desk with a coal-oil lamp on top and chair tucked inside its knee space.

The desk set aside from the other furniture looked curious, so Pilar went over to look. The top surface was clear except for pen and inkwell, blank writing paper and the lamp. Maybe someone was a closet writer, but who would want hang out up here to write? A light layer of powdery film told of relative recent cleaning compared to the other furniture covered in thick planes of compressed dust. She sat in the chair and started to open drawers. In the bottom left drawer, she found an old diary that dated back to the 1910s. An opportunity to read someone's intimate thoughts drove out her worries. She flipped through the delicate yellowed pages and began to scan pages at random.

Josefina wrote in detail about her friends lost in an accident and had written in the diary because she believed she had no one to confide in. She wrote of her misery, about other friends who she had lost in a tragic way, their children she and her husband would now raise as their own, and their fear now that they were alone.

Pilar was excited. This was her great grandmother. Through her words, Pilar experienced her grief, maybe more because she was no stranger to loss and could empathize.

The diary spanned a short space of time. Pilar guessed she was ahead of her time in using a diary as a means of therapy to get through emotional distress. Pilar wrapped the diary in a scarf she found flung across a trunk and set it on the desk to finish reading later.

Pilar started rummaging through the trunks, astounded to find old military uniforms. She had no idea how to distinguish which army or country they represented, but they were in good condition.

In two other trunks, she found rifles and ammunition. She closed the lids on the trunks and sat at the desk again. She considered the diary a few minutes before reading the entries again. Still, no reference to any other name except Josefina, but Pilar recognized them by descriptions and the way they died.

Pilar tried to remember what she had read in the book at Sylvie's place about the Mexican Revolution. Skimming through that book, she remembered some had considered the *Villistas* no more than *banditos*, especially when they attacked haciendas owned by Mexicans or by Americans. In the diary, Josefina had written of her memories of leaving their home in León, and everything they owned for safety to come to live here thanks to American friends. In her despair, Josefina wrote how they had never stopped hoping they could return, but by the time the revolution had seen the emergence and decline of Huerta, Carranza, and Obregón, they had realized the home they knew would never be the same even if they lived long enough to get there. Her husband decided they would be better off staying in Arizona.

Pilar decided to start at the beginning of the diary when the first entry started on December 31, 1910 and ended in 1920. As she went through one page after another, Pilar became aware of references to the two other couples still unnamed but certain to be the Rodchenko and the Velasquez families. In earlier entries, she mentioned them as the "Russian" couple and the "Spanish" couple. They had been working on something together, but had to stop. As Josefina had relaxed into her writing habit, she began to reveal more details, alluding to her distant past and personal relationships.

Pilar grinned, shaking her head as she read further. All this time, she thought, the motive was never about the people of today, but the people of the past. The more she read, the more she understood that Pete had been his mother's son, kind, and sensitive, realizing he was a part of something wrong. Even the innocent cannot escape the guilt. Virginia, on the other hand, embraced her father's avarice and took no particular care about harming others in order to get what she wanted.

Pilar could not explain her feelings, but she sensed that Josefina meant her to find this book. Josefina had written her shame for the life she had embraced. She only had to wait for Pilar's hands to pick it up and make things right. Maybe Josefina meant to give her clarity or perhaps to warn her, but either way Pilar believed now she knew the real motive to Lenore's killing.

CHAPTER 40

October 12, 2006
Flagstaff, Arizona

P ilar carried the diary with her and moved down to the master bedroom on the second floor. At a writing table by the window, she sat down, pulled out a pen and a pad of paper from the drawer, and began to jot down dates and locations referenced by Josefina. The more she wrote, the more she realized how strange that those immigrants who had left the bulk of their wealth behind them had so much affluence. The obvious answer documented in the diary made the most sense. It was spectacular that the law never caught or identified the most notorious gang in Arizona, but lived quietly among the very people whose valuables they stole.

The air was cool and the neighborhood quiet. She heard the whirr of ten-speed bikes out on the street and enjoyed her first sense of peace since arriving. Her eyes traveled outside the window to the tops of Ponderosa Pines and the distant mountains. Something soothing and regenerative about nature had renewed her sense of place and self. She could not lose herself in the eddy of broken people sucking her down into their sad lives. She had to stay removed and focused.

She stared down at the paper to review what she had written. She believed she had recorded everything Josefina had to tell her. Pilar conjured her image as she closed the diary, folded up her notes, and stuffed them into her jeans pocket. The penetrating cold of the wintry day had crept inside the house and she shivered. Her first thought was getting someone in here to check the windows for drafts and installing insulation. These old houses could be drafty, she thought as she tried to calculate the cost of replacing windows with funds she did not have.

She stood up from the desk, suddenly uneasy and apprehensive, a warning to listen to her instincts. Alert and guarded, she listened for sounds of a possible intruder, but heard nothing. She inched to the open doorway and listened. Again, nothing but silence. "Pull yourself together," she whispered, and walked into the hallway.

Once in the hallway, so wide it was a room in itself, she peeked inside the other three bedrooms and bathrooms, comforted not to find anything out the ordinary. At the top of the stairs, she held the banister as she descended one carpeted step at a time to the bottom. She kept listening for sounds, but when she still did not hear anything, she relaxed and went into the kitchen for more coffee.

She sensed something was different, but could not distinguish what. The coffee pot was still on the burner. She checked inside of the refrigerator and inside the pantry for something that might have fallen, and turned the back door knob to confirm she had locked it. Nothing looked out of place. Irritated, she believed the creakiness of an old house could convince anyone of an intruder or unearthly presence. This place needs a security system, she thought standing in the middle of the kitchen.

The little diary was still in her hand and she looked down as if she realized its existence for the first time. Now she had to find a hiding place. She ruled out her car in case of damage in an accident. Best to find a hiding spot here, she thought as she looked around and headed back upstairs.

Pilar took the last step before she reached the landing, when a cold chill whipped through her body. The nape of her neck tingled. Her lungs forgot to breathe. She thought she was having a seizure until she realized she could move. She turned her head, her torso twisting to follow until her entire body made a full circle, looking for a cause of her disturbance. The hall was quiet and empty. Was that her fear expressing itself? Or was something showing its fear to her?

CHAPTER 41

February 2, 1918
Flagstaff, Arizona

After the others had passed from their private basement door and out through the back yard, Josefina cleaned the dishes, and then sat down with her sewing in her favorite chair. Ricardo had stayed in the basement, saying he had repairs to take care of. With the children sleeping in their rooms, the house was tomblike to Josefina, who still had the premonition of evil that she could not shake. She had mentioned her feelings to Ricardo before, but he laughed it off and told her to stop letting her little female brain play tricks on her. She disliked him when he treated her like a child, so after a while, she stopped telling him. She wanted to believe these intuitions were imagination, but she had not been wrong before and that frightened her.

She worried about her friends, her children, and their friends' children. She feared what would happen if they would be exposed for the robberies and went to jail. Worse than that, be hanged for Ricardo killing that Deputy last year. A conscience is a bad thing in this business, she thought, and Ricardo had none she had observed over the years. She worried about his soul. He had told her they had too much behind them to start worrying about their souls now. With all of her worries and no one to tell them to, her eyes overflowed with tears. She brushed them away with her towel in case Ricardo should come in and see her.

♦ ♦ ♦

Ricardo worried about Josefina. She had too much heart, and one day she might tell an outsider, like the priest. He did what he could to keep her close and discourage her not to go out too often on her own. She was a good woman, a devoted wife and loving mother for his children, but she placed too much importance on the state of their souls. At other times, he saw her as a witch, unnerving him by knowing his plans beforehand with her intangible feelings. He was fearful enough of her ability to kill with any weapon at hand to know what she was capable of if she believed he had gone too far, like when he killed the Deputy. At least then, she only made him give their share of the gold to the man's family, anonymously. He would have to keep her away from his current plans. If Josefina ever found out, he was certain she would kill him before he had the chance to put up an argument.

♦ ♦ ♦

Josefina had a small book full of blank pages designed for a young girl to use as a diary. Picking it up at the General Store years ago, she had thought that one day she might use it for recipes. Now, if she had no one to talk to, she would tell it to God by writing it down. Setting aside her sewing, she retrieved the journal from the bookcase across the room and began to write about the times since she and Ricardo married and all the adventures until now. Once started, she did not find it easy to stop the flow of her frustrations and fears from the last few months. When she finished her first entry, she thought, I will do this every day. This will give me strength knowing I at least have one place to go with my worries.

♦ ♦ ♦

Ricardo thought about the past and the bonds he had formed with Velasquez and Rodchenko. They were as daring and fearless as he, not to mention intelligent. They had engineered some of the most successful robberies of their day, but they were becoming sentimental. Did any of them believe they were doing this for their homelands? Maybe that is how we all kept our women going along with it, he thought. At least he was not foolish enough to believe those lies they kept telling themselves. He did it for the money, not for Mexico.

Years before the Revolution, he crossed the US border to rob, and then returned to Mexico to live like a nobleman. The situation had changed through his close association and friendship with General Diaz, or maybe because of it, but he was no longer safe in Mexico. His home burned to the ground, Pancho Villa claimed his land and redistributed his property into *ejidos*. The *Mestizos* now occupied his land. He had kept his money but nothing else. He had secured his personal wealth in US banks, as well as the gains from the robberies hidden in stashes in various locations. He was happy where he was. The idea of returning to Mexico was ridiculous to him. It was not his home anymore nor was it *his* Mexico.

As for Velasquez and Rodchenko, what did they have to return to, anyway? Anarchists in Spain organizing under the Spanish National Confederation of Labour with the sole purpose to overthrow capitalism, to be replaced with a society ruled by workers and peasants, no doubt influenced by the revolution in Russia. Velasquez had been wise to take his family, and his wealth, out of Spain years ago.

Rodchenko, even with his well-placed brother, as a Menshevik of the Provisional government, his public disapproval of Lenin and the Bolsheviks had earned him a death warrant from the Lenin's Soviet regime. Going back was not an option. It was madness to consider it. As far as he was

168

concerned, he smirked to himself, the worker and peasant revolutionaries of Spain and Russia would have to lie in the beds they made for themselves, as would the *Mestizos* in Mexico.

♦ ♦ ♦

Josefina secured her diary away in a desk drawer in the attic, and a peace rushed over her. To write it out served her conscience for the moment. Confession would be best, but Ricardo was right. The priest was flesh and blood, and he would not be able to keep the knowledge to himself.

She hurried back downstairs before Ricardo realized she had been up there. If he noticed, she would need to give him a reason. He had become bitter, quick tempered, unhappy and dark. She would go to church and pray for him, pray for the return of the kind man she knew from years ago before they had the money and something to hide. For all she enjoyed of their wealth and position, she believed that the more they had, the less they had where it mattered. She belonged by her husband for better or for worse. Nowadays, she worried they were in for more "worse" than "better" on the way.

Flagstaff Courier, September 3, 1920

The entire Velasquez family burned alive by a kerosene fire in their home last night. Sheriff Reed told this reporter that it looked like an accident, although the fire burned hotter than what he had seen before. He said that he believes one of the children did not turn off his or her oil lamp before falling asleep and that it must have fallen over for some reason. The Volunteer Fire Brigade was on the scene almost at once but could not battle the intense blaze. Doc Reno said he did not find evidence of foul play when he examined the bodies and concurred with the Sheriff that this was a tragic accident.

Everyone will recall the Velasquez family as community-spirited and generous. A major contributor to the local schools, Borja and Magda Velasquez also gave their time and money to many community charities and causes. Although still young, the Velasquez children were following their parents' example. Both volunteered as ranch hands at the Two Widows Ranch. Margaret Bixby and Colleen Mayfield said the children were Godsends and they will be missed.

There will be a memorial service this Monday, September 6, 1920, at their church, Holy Redeemer Trinity. Anyone wishing to eulogize should see the Reverend Barrows.

Josefina sat with Natasha Rodchenko, both women sobbing into each other's embrace. Beyond her grief, Josefina knew Ricardo had set the fire. He had avoided her conversations and stayed in the basement alone the past week. She could not stand to look at him. With Natasha here, she had someone who was as immersed in their secret lives as deeply as she and Ricardo. Poor Magda. She grew physically ill to imagine the horrors of her last moments. She recounted the day and her suspicions in her diary, no longer caring if anyone found it. She believed that Natasha suspected, but kept it to herself. Nothing would ever be the same between the four of them again.

Before and after the funeral, both she and Ricardo remained distant. Peter and Virginia grieved for the loss of their close friends and contemporaries. The Paralelos household that at one time had been alive with singing and game playing, chilled her by its solemn quiet. All four operated mechanically through the day, each retiring to their bedrooms early. When she believed the clouds were starting to pass from her household, they were dealt another mortal blow.

Flagstaff Courier, September 25, 1920

An unknown assailant shot Nikolai and Natasha Rodchenko leaving a reception for a visiting Russian ex-patriot. The Sherriff believes they knew their attacker, observing that the shootings took place from no further than ten feet away. The police have no witnesses or evidence against anyone in town. Still further, there were no reports of strangers in town other than the Russians themselves who were inside with other guests. Rumors are spreading that one of the townspeople must have committed the crime. Another rumor that Bolsheviks assassinated them has sent fear throughout the community. The Sheriff announced this morning at an emergency town hall meeting that an unverified source satisfied the Sheriff and the townspeople that the danger was not from within their small community, citing a witness who claimed to have seen a stranger riding out of town last night.

Rudolf, (Ralph), and Varvara (Barbie) Rodchenko, now orphans, have the sympathy of the town. They are staying with close family friends, the Paralelos. Due to the fears of a Bolshevik assassin, most families are not sure that taking in the Russian children is a good idea, but Josefina Paralelos said it was the least she could do for her dear friends.

Nikolai Rodchenko, a prominent retired businessman, immigrated from Russia in 1914 after the start of the Revolution. The charming couple hosted charity events and established a scholarship fund at Northern Arizona University for children of immigrants and another for promising children who could not afford to go to college. The university and the local public schools will hold a brief memorial on Monday. The official memorial will be held on Tuesday at Holy Redeemer Trinity.

It must be noted that only three short weeks ago, the Paralelos, and Rodchenko families lost their close friends, the Velasquez family in a house fire. When asked about how they were holding up under the grief, Mr. and Mrs. Paralelos issued the following statement: "To have lost these close friends as we have done is a grief we will carry the rest of our lives. They were more than friends, but the families we no longer have since we immigrated to this country. In the spirit of family, we have told Rudolf and Varvara it is our intention to keep them with us for as long as they need us. It is the least we can do for our dear friends."

The people of Flagstaff extend their deepest condolences to Ralph and Varvara during their horrific loss.

"We're taking them in with us, Ricardo," Josefina said. "That is the end of it. I might only be your wife and I have always been obedient, but now I say that if you do not agree, I will never be happy again and neither will you."

Ricardo knew her threat was serious. Without saying the words aloud, this was her way of telling him she knew he murdered their friends. She would never leave him or turn him in, but she would do worse. Make his life a misery until the day he died. He hoped that she knew what she was doing. It had never occurred to him that she would feel this obligation. They were around the ages of their own children, young and familiar. Maybe it would work. Maybe they would never find any reason to suspect he had been the mysterious assassin and that the fortune he might bequeath to them as well as to his own children already belonged to them in their own rights.

Now with strangers in the house, Ricardo put the coins and gold bars back in the basement wall and slid the keys in a small leather pouch behind a brick behind the icebox. That will keep those Rodchenko kids from getting any ideas.

◆ ◆ ◆

As she continued to write in her diary for the next six months, detailing her daily routines with her observations of her husband, their children and their adopted children, the hollow inside her filled with the joy of parenting and the excitement of planning for their futures. She made one last entry describing the emotional scene when she took Peter and Virginia aside to explain.

November 16, 1920

I told the children about our shame today, the robberies, the killings, and the share of money Ricardo killed his friends for. Ricardo thinks it's a mistake, but they need to understand to protect themselves later. My handsome boy, Peter, so sensitive and kind-hearted wept with me. Later he said he could never forgive his father. He told me today he is going to a university in the east so he can put space between them and try to forgive him. I know I did the right thing, but my son will never be here as my son again. I don't believe he will come back to me.

Virginia, my sweet Ginny, showed no emotion. She did not cry or say she was angry with her father. She worries me, but she must have her father's cold heart. She asked if we had to give Ralph and

Varvara their parents' share. I looked into her eyes and saw evil. I had a chill run up my back. I will pray for her soul.

♦ ♦ ♦

May 21, 1957
Flagstaff Medical Center

Josefina contemplated meeting God, suffering from physical pain and a clarity she had not known in years. She remembered everything now, from her days riding on horseback with the other five, their robberies, fighting in the Revolution, and the deaths of so many before her. She remembered when she lost her sister Petra in 1916, bound with the other *Soldaderas* in groups of six, before the *Dorados* set them on fire to burn alive. Pancho Villa had his personal army execute all sixty women because one woman shot at him, even after all military support the Soldaderas had provided him. That was when she turned her back on Mexico and the *Villistas*. Her dear Petra consumed in flames with no more consideration than kindling. Just as the Velasquez family must have suffered.

She believed God punished her with her memories now so she could reflect on her failures to live up to His Word. She had prayed for forgiveness since those early days, but had stayed unrepentant in her actions. She knew that doing nothing to prevent sin is worse than committing sin. A moral person knowing what is right, but doing the opposite, is worse than the heathen that does wrong but does not know it is wrong. She had much to answer for before Him.

Between her physical pain and emotional distress, she did not want to go on another day. Her memories flooded her vision and she begged for mercy, until a sudden panic seized her. She remembered the long-forgotten diary hidden upstairs in the attic. Ricardo had predeceased her and no one else, except Peter and Virginia, knew their secrets. She knew that the knowledge would disgrace her children and their families if the details became public. She had to get home to destroy it, but she was too weak to leave this hospital bed.

The nurse noted her distress, misunderstanding it for pain caused by the cancer that was eating her alive. After another injection of morphine to ease her pain, the only word the nurse could make out was "Di—. My di—." The nurse touched her face and whispered, "I know, dear," believing she was anticipating her death.

Why couldn't she get out the words? Why had she written in that diary at all? As the room grew dimmer, what she had imagined an hour before to be a serene transition to the other side, was now a frustrating desperation and regret at having something important left undone.

CHAPTER 42

October 12, 2006
Flagstaff, Arizona

After setting the diary on the desk in the attic, Pilar decided to hide everything she found up here earlier. If someone had been here, she would not make it easy for them a second time. The trunks were heavy and she knew she could not move them alone. Besides, anyone that had searched here before would know their contents already.

On the other hand, she could confuse matters and move each item to different spots around the house. That childhood habit of hiding things kicked in again as it had at Lenore's home. She put the rifles in the hide-a-bed in one of the upstairs bedrooms, hung the uniforms in dry cleaner bags among the winter coats in the front hall closet, secured the loose ammunition in plastic baggies, and thrust them down into old sacks of flour in the kitchen pantry. She took the cover from a same-sized book to disguise the diary and slid it into a tight space on the bookshelf.

She congratulated herself, made another pot of coffee, and sat on the stool at the kitchen counter to think. Here she was with a truckload of facts that exposed a century-old mystery, but nothing concrete to point to Lenore's killer. Still, she believed her find this afternoon was the key and she did not doubt someone would be angry when he or she realized she knew.

The one clue was that this person had to have easy access to this house. Virginia was an old woman who had made her bedroom in the den on the ground floor. If she had a problem making it upstairs to her bedroom, what were the odds she could go into the attic for a quick read of an old diary or load up on guns and ammo?

Pilar guessed that someone had stumbled on the diary, and realized its significance. That person had needed time to set up an office up here with no fear of interruption. It had to be a family member, maybe Rod, but it could also be someone who had stumbled on the discovery during a maintenance job. Virginia would not be suspicious of workers that had to go to the attic or basement. From what she had read, Josefina did not tell Peter or Virginia about the diary or Virginia would most likely have destroyed it years before. It had to be someone, like Rod, who did many different chores on the property and had the best opportunity. This would not be a long list of possible suspects.

Pilar remembered her laptop, the CD, and the paperwork from Lenore's desk that Rod had not had destroyed. She pulled a bulky sweater over her sweatshirt and went outside to her car. After lifting her briefcase and computer from the back seat, she slammed closed the trunk lid. When she turned around, she looked down. She caught sight of footprints in the dusting of snow leading to her house.

A new snowfall had started in the past hour leaving the impressions of a large man's boot, faint but visible. Her eyes followed them around the side of the house where they disappeared in the flattened dead grass. Her heart pounded and her skin grew hot and moist under her clothes. She craned her neck to the side to get a look, but not seeing anyone. She relaxed, believing her imagination made her paranoid. Someone had taken a shortcut through her yard. Nothing more.

She returned to the kitchen and brewed another pot of coffee. She did not care if the caffeine ruined her sleep tonight. She set up her computer on the kitchen island and spread out Lenore's research papers. She was glad that she had not had time to tell Rod everything. Her hand involuntarily touched her throat remembering the force of his rage from the night before.

Lenore, without the benefit of the diary, had found historical clippings of the Rodchenkos, the Paralelos, and the Velasquezes. Included among the research, Pilar was impressed to read that Flagstaff had not been a "one trick pony" like many other small towns during that time, as Rod had told her. Multiple industries, such as the railroad, lumber, and livestock kept the Flagstaff economy flourishing throughout the years. A stable economy with high quality, well-paid citizens contrasted to some other small Arizona towns run by or corrupted by outlaws. These three families, respected pillars of the community, still made substantial contributions to the community, the church, and to the local college.

The tragedies of the Velasquez family's house fire were lamented as a great loss to the community in the news clippings. When the Rodchenko's were murdered, numerous articles demanding justice had compelled the local law enforcement to conclude the crime was not from within Flagstaff citizenry but by agents from Russia. Later articles denounced Lenin and the Bolsheviks and laid the issue to rest.

Lenore had tried to research the families before arriving in Flagstaff but had no luck. Her notes were NO SHIP RECORDS or NOT IN CENSUS. Pilar did not consider this strange since they were immigrants who might have immigrated to Mexico first or to a country in South America before coming to Flagstaff. The Paralelos, on the other hand, would only have had to travel across the border with their previous trips having taught them the best routes. Pilar was sure what Lenore was trying to prove by this research, but her methods had not proven anything but that they arrived in Flagstaff affluent and sophisticated. Bored and disappointed, she moved on the next set of papers.

In these papers, she found copies of local articles reporting robberies dating from 1879 to 1881. One story ended in Veit Spring, Arizona, where a band of five outlaws robbed a stagecoach in Canyon Diablo secreting a fortune in silver and gold in whiskey kegs hidden in mailbags. The posse killed all five men believing no one had lived who could tell the hiding place of the loot. Assumed hidden at their hideout in Veit Spring, searchers were unable to find a trace of it. Pilar grinned at she read, wondering if Lenore figured it out.

The second prominent story on Lenore's list was of two outlaws who stole eight large gold bars from a mine near Gillette, Arizona. Hiding out at Rogers Lake, they were reputed to hide their loot under the ice in the lake. In another story, four men made off with a total of two hundred sixty five thousand dollars in gold coins, sixty thousand dollars in currency and twenty-two gold bars in two different robberies. Pilar did not need a calculator to know that this combined loot was a fortune in any era. All four men met their deaths before they could reveal the location of their loot. Lenore's sidebar noted that no one ever found the loot, even though in the case of Rogers Lake, one of the original outlaws returned years later to search but was not successful.

While interesting, Pilar did not overlook the implication Lenore had made by combining the arrival of the three families to Flagstaff with the robberies. The diary was set from 1910 to 1920, twenty years later than the robberies. Pilar believed Lenore had pieced the story together on her own without learning the diary's back-story. Looking further, she found an additional note from Lenore, which said, TWENTY-TWO GOLD BARS— AJO. Lenore had been cryptic in her note taking and must have thought this important, but did not state why.

As Pilar drank her coffee, she let her mind wander back to those days to try to imagine the atmosphere in the home. The idea that these prominent individuals were common criminals who had fooled the entire community was nothing that she had not heard of in reality crime shows. Clever people lacking conscience have been doing that very thing from the beginning of time. It was the idea that the blood of those people ran through her veins that disconcerted her.

These days, did anyone care about one's ancestors, she wondered. While most people have relatives with no story at all, she thought that would be preferable to having a murderous bank robber for a great grandfather. She had to admit that the betrayal by her Pete stung. Had he lived all of his life without telling anyone? He knew the truth. She understood now why he moved east. Could it be he could not face Ralph Rodchenko once Ralph became his brother-in-law---knowing his father murdered Ralph's parents?

Tears pooled on her lids as she wondered how many more secrets she could stand to learn.

CHAPTER 43

October 13, 2006
Flagstaff, Arizona

After an evening of reflection and a night of bad dreams, Pilar woke in the morning with the resolve to go to Detective Macy with what she knew, including Rod's threats. Getting beyond the shock and embarrassment of her family's history, she knew that getting this knowledge out in the open was the best way for the police to figure out what happened to Lenore. So far, all they knew were the facts of the present family and their relationships to one another. With no reason to look beyond the obvious, they could formulate a motive based on minimal facts but enough to ruin someone's life with an accusation of murder.

By the time she arrived in downtown Phoenix, she was not as sure of herself as she had been earlier. So positive sitting in that attic, reading the diary with the ghosts of the past surrounding her, in essence if not in reality, she thought she had figured it out. A fortune of stolen loot might be hidden somewhere in the house waiting for someone to scoop it up and live happily ever after. Now, she did not like the sound of her own words that came out as juvenile and fantastic. She had to express the facts in a credible way.

Pilar was not sure how she planned to tell Detective Macy. Some of what she could say would be repetitive and speculative and she knew the police would regard her theories more as gossip than evidence, but she had to try.

After presenting herself to the sergeant inside the security cage at the entrance of the Downtown Police station, Detective Macy came to meet her and then led her to his desk on the third floor. She looked around at the gray cubicles established for each detective and realized again how nothing was ever as you imagined it. So much for her illusion of the open squad room, she had seen in movies and on television.

She waited for him to sit down, and took her time to decide where to begin. She looked over to find him staring at her. Her face flushed from irrational fear. What was she doing here? She had nerve acting like a lame television amateur detective. Fighting her urge to run out of the building and escape to her car, she started to talk.

"Detective Macy, I've come here because I'm convinced that Allegra is not responsible for killing anyone. I think this has more to do with something that happened in the family a long time ago."

"Tell me why you don't believe it," he said with an ironic smile.

"Why go to the trouble of luring Lenore downtown? If she were trying to make it look like suicide, Lenore dying at home would be more convincing. And how could she force Lenore to ingest those pills? Allegra's petite and not athletic. It makes much more sense for her to use a passive and non-confrontational method to kill someone. Don't you think?"

"You have good points there, but only if she were acting alone. Either of them could have crushed the pills or mixed the powder into her drink. My theory works better because I am not excluding the obvious. Allegra is immature, and probably gullible. She is a young woman who transferred her dependence from her mother to her new boyfriend. I think she would do whatever he told her. You're basing your theory on emotions and feelings, not on the facts. We cannot dismiss a prime suspect who had the opportunity, the motive, and access to the means, from consideration because you feel certain that she's not guilty."

"It isn't the feeling on its own. I've spent some time in the Flagstaff house and uncovered facts about my family from my great-grandparents' time. They were criminals who organized robberies in the 1880's through to 1910. From what I found of Lenore's research, I think she stumbled on it and that's why she was killed."

"You think someone killed Lenore because she found out about something that happened almost a hundred years ago? What would be the point?"

"A buried treasure hidden somewhere. If that's true and someone wanted it for themselves, don't you think that would be a motive to kill someone?"

"What proof do you have there's a treasure? Where is it? If it exists, why wouldn't the person have taken it long ago?"

"You're making me sound ridiculous, Detective. I may not have evidence yet, but I'm sure that someone more cunning than Allegra or Charlie is responsible for Lenore's death. Virginia may not have died a natural death either. The doctors believed she died of old age and there was nothing suspicious about her passing, so they didn't order an autopsy. I think this all has to do with the family's money and not the trust set up for Allegra."

"Listen, I sympathize with your position but I can't act on feelings. If you can bring me evidence of what you suspect or of whom you suspect, I'll consider it and investigate further. I'm obliged to follow the leads I have and to proceed as I see justifies the evidence. I realize she's your cousin, but we have rules to follow and every accusation has to have sound evidence in order for us to consider it. Otherwise, everyone who dislikes someone could come in here to accuse him or her of a crime. Or a guilty person accuses an innocent person to deflect blame. You'd be surprised at how much of that we get."

"What about this? I've been to the Flagstaff house and found a diary and other evidence that suggests Virginia's parents and her husband's parents were outlaws who might have stashed gold somewhere. The robberies went unsolved and no one officially found the gold. What if someone killed Lenore because the gold is still there? She was in that house every summer and could have figured it out or stumbled onto something. She was doing research on the family history and the old crimes. What if she told someone who also figured it out?"

"What evidence?"

"A diary that was written by Virginia's mother, Josefina. She talks about the stash boxes they built in the basement of the house. I haven't checked it out yet, but isn't it at least possible that the money and gold were left there all this time?"

"That would be a motive if the amount is substantial. Do you have someone in mind?"

"Well ..."

"What's wrong?"

"Being here and voicing my suspicions to you is scary. It's official. And it affects lives"

"If you have something tangible that relates to the present case, it's best to tell me."

Once she started, she found it difficult to stop long enough to take a breath. His eyes were set on her as she detailed the meeting with the sisters, Allegra and Sylvie; Lenore's research; Rod's reaction and everything she found in Flagstaff.

"I think Rod did it. I don't know how, but I cannot understand his reaction if he doesn't have anything to hide."

"That story might have some merit but you haven't brought me anything concrete that I can act on, but I'll look into it as far as I can, recheck his alibi. We don't want to ignore leads, but there is a practical side to police work. Without just cause, we can't get search warrants and pick someone up for questioning on feelings. I understand that you want to help Allegra. She's a tragic figure and maybe deserves sympathy, but that doesn't mean she could not commit murder. Keep that in mind. They could be playing you."

Pilar thought he was with her theory up to the point she

heard that patronizing tone in his voice. "That's it then, I guess," she said.

"No, I'll look into what you've told me about Rod, but I'm not making any promises that Allegra is out of hot water. You need to be careful about prying and let us investigate. You did the right thing coming here to tell me what you found out. Providing information to us creates leads we might not have arrived at ourselves. Guilty or not, most folks don't like feeling their privacy is invaded. With the police, they don't like it but they have no choice. Be careful. Someone might not hesitate to convince you to mind your own business."

"Thanks for your time." Pilar got up, as did Detective Macy, and she walked away. At the elevator, she shook her head and rolled her eyes. She would have to do his work for him, she thought in wonderment of her own arrogance. In the back of her mind, she had the slightest hint of doubt, though, because she knew the scenario he presented was plausible and possible. As the elevator descended, she lost the anger and anxiety.

She hoped she would not have cause later to regret taking his stand by finding out Detective Macy was right.

CHAPTER 44

October 13, 2006
Flagstaff, Arizona

Before she left Flagstaff, Pilar had called Allegra to schedule a visit to compare notes.

"Hello," Allegra said, sounding tired and diminutive.

"How are you holding up?"

"Oh, Pilar. Hi, I'm fine. Glad to hear from you."

"I'll be back in Phoenix this afternoon. I'd like to drop by to tell you what I've learned."

"Sure," Allegra said. "You know, I was thinking I would invite Tasha and Sylvie to join us.

Pilar's stomach lurched. She had reservations about meeting more relatives after her experience with Rod, but she went along. "If you think it will help."

◆ ◆ ◆

Phoenix, Arizona

Tasha sat on a stool holding a plate of pie under her chin

when Pilar arrived at Charlie's condo. Pilar considered it a small blessing that by the time Sylvie arrived, she would have little chance to be alone with her.

Given the events with Rod, Pilar planned to conceal some facts when she knew Tasha and Sylvie were coming. She did not know whom to trust. Tasha was Rod's sister, after all. How could she be sure they weren't on speaking terms? Who could say it was not Tasha that killed Lenore? She had the same motive as Rod.

"It's nice to meet you," Pilar said, when Allegra introduced them. Tasha pointed her index finger at her chewing mouth, and nodded. Before she had time to swallow, the doorbell rang.

Tasha and Allegra turned to Pilar, as if waiting for a cue. Allegra moved to open the door. Sylvie walked in without a greeting. Her eyes surveyed the interior of the condo, not noticing or acknowledging the other three women.

"Nice place," Sylvie said. "I had no idea your boyfriend did so well."

"Charlie was an executive until a couple of weeks ago. He does all right for himself. I'll give him your compliment," Allegra said.

Pilar thought the expression about tension so thick you could cut it with a knife applied here. This situation required a machete, wondering if this meeting might have been a mistake.

"Are you hungry? I made sandwiches," Allegra said, pointing at the food tray.

"No thanks. Let's get down to business."

Each woman took a stool around the island. Pilar noticed that Sylvie's mood had little effect on Tasha. Allegra's relaxed demeanor retreated into a submissive nervousness. Sylvie stared beyond them, to the sky beyond the balcony, Pilar guessed.

"While I was staying up in Flagstaff, I stopped by the historical society and found old newspaper clippings. I think Lenore figured out that Virginia's and Pete's parents and their friends robbed stagecoaches and railroads in the 1880s and later. That explains how they made their money. The six of them, Ricardo and Josefina with the Velasquez and Rodchenko couples.

"I also did a little research about unsolved crimes in the surrounding areas at that time. Six unidentified men robbed trains and a couple of banks. Most of what they stole was gold, but there were other items, such as jewelry, that never surfaced. The gang got away with their crimes for years, and then the robberies suddenly stopped. The law back in the day never figured out who it was, but there was talk by one of the witnesses that they thought one or two of the men were actually women. What if …?"

Tasha said, "Well, that sounds romantic but what proof is there to tie them to the crimes? How do we know there'd be anything left after all these years? Where would it have been all this time? Wouldn't they have spent it?"

"Of course, it doesn't make sense," Pilar said. "But could it be a coincidence that Lenore had researched all this now and found out the truth? I know I'm speculating, but I believe there's a real chance these six people were criminal masterminds who might have had others working for them. If they stashed stolen loot, someone other than a family member could be trying to find it. What I learned from the old newspapers was how close the three families were. Nothing new there. From the newspaper articles, I read of the deaths, the six of them, with their children, were all the others had, but what about their relatives from the old country. No one knew if Varvara died for certain, and she must have known what went on. What if she lived and had children who want to get back what they feel is owed to them?"

"Well, that's farfetched," Tasha said. "Grandpa Ralph's sister returned to Russia to fight the Bolsheviks and was never heard of again, more than likely killed. Don't you think she would have been in touch with her brother at some point?"

"If she could," Allegra said.

"Any ideas about other descendants of the Rodchenkos and Velasquezes that would still be alive to implicate the Paralelos?" Pilar said. "The Velasquez children died with their parents in a house fire, but there could have been relatives back in Spain interested in what happened."

"That would make sense if the gold and coins were kept in one place to be shared by the three couples, but never got divided because of the deaths," Tasha said. "There could be Spanish relatives who knew what they were up to, but why would anyone wait until now? It feels like every move forward turns into two moves back or sideways"

"Let's say relatives from Russia and Spain knew, but for whatever reason had to wait until now to come for it," Pilar said. "It's not cheap to cross the Atlantic and political circumstances could have prevented the trip as well."

"Okay," Tasha said, "Suppose we say this is real and not a cozy fire mystery, I can't see how we can turn up any treasures after all of this time on our own without clues to where it should be. You realize that the only two people who might know anything now are Mom or Uncle Nikolas. Gran would have had to talk about all of this to them, but she was too controlling to let anyone know something that could be used against her. For another thing, if there was an inkling of buried treasure somewhere, I think that either of them, or both, would be digging up the yard looking for it right now. No, I can't see that."

Pilar, who had not meant to exclude Sylvie, realized Sylvie had not said anything since she arrived. She looked over, unnerved by her startled expression. "Sylvie, are you alright? You look pale all of a sudden."

"I'm okay. It's disturbing to hear us talking in this casual way about them after all of this time and after everything that's happened."

"Let's not worry about that right now," Pilar said. "I think we tossed around a few ideas about what direction to take as far as finding out new information. I still have to say that this history that Lenore researched has to be important, no matter what the police might say."

"You've told this to the police?" Sylvie said.

"Yes. I spoke with Detective Macy about my theories. I don't know if he took me seriously. I thought it would be good for him to look at robbery as a motive in case some of the gold was still around. Tasha, do you remember anything hidden or secret hiding places when you visited as children?"

"Not me. Lenore played with us outside most of the time unless she was playing house in the basement. Rod was out with the neighbor boys all day long. I don't remember anything weird that hints of hidden treasure. What about you, Allegra? You spent some time during the summers when you were small."

"Nothing unusual and I would have noticed in that spooky house. I still remember how cold it got in my room at night, even in the summer. That's about it."

"Well, that's all I learned. I had hoped that one of you might have known something about it, or know of someone outside the family that the police should look at."

"I don't know if all your trouble has done much to help Allegra, but at least you're trying to help," Tasha said. She wiped her mouth with a napkin and stood up. "Allegra, can I help you clear up before I go?"

"No, but thanks for asking."

"Call me if you need me."

"I will," Allegra said, hugging Tasha as she opened the door to leave.

"I've got to go," Sylvie said. "It's too bad you didn't come up with anything helpful, but keep at it."

"Thanks. I think," Pilar said, suddenly awkward and uncomfortable.

"I appreciate you coming," Allegra said. Pilar thought she saw Allegra cower.

Pilar and Allegra exchanged frowned expressions, but did not verbalize their thoughts. "Let's sit down."

"Is there something bothering you that you haven't mentioned?" Allegra said. "If you learned something bad, I have a right to know." She reached out to take Pilar's hand. "I'm scared right now but I want to know the worst."

"I'm worried about something. It's what I ..."

At that moment, Charlie entered through the front door, interrupted Pilar in mid-sentence.

"Hey, how did it go?" Seeing Pilar, he stopped at the

doorway into the kitchen. "I thought everyone had gone."

"Pilar stayed to help me clean up, but she was getting ready to tell me something she was worried about that she had not mentioned before," Allegra said, looking at Charlie.

With both sets of eyes on her, Pilar said, "Well, I guess you have a right to know more than the rest considering you're under suspicion. When I went to the Flagstaff house, I found a diary up in the attic and a desk set up in the center of the room. I could tell someone has been up there using the room. It was too clean. Virginia couldn't go upstairs to the second floor, much less the attic. I'm sure she wasn't the one."

"So what's in the diary?" Allegra said, leaning forward.

"I found out that everything I talked about today happened. Josefina Paralelos wrote it all down. I'm starting to get scared because I think Rod is behind all of this. He was always up there doing who-knows-what around the place. He's the one that would have the best opportunity to search without making Virginia suspicious."

Charlie whistled and Allegra gasped. "I knew he was too good to be true," Allegra said. "What about Sylvie? Do you think she's in on it with him on it?"

"That's difficult to say. On the one hand, she had seemed sincere in her attempt to help you before. The obvious way she loves her husband and children, I can't see her lifting a finger to help you if it meant harming her husband. On the other hand, she didn't seem too happy about all the talk about the past today. It's easy to get the wrong impression sometimes, but Rod was clear in his threats. I've never been so afraid in my life."

Charlie cleared his throat and drew the attention of both women.

"Listen, I think I should tell both of you something I learned about Rod."

Their full attention on him, he told them about Den meeting Rod, the circumstances under which he met him and how he recognized him. "He makes his drug runs at night, which means he's able to leave his job without anyone knowing. That would have given him opportunity, even without a motive."

"Well," Pilar said. "Now that we are all agreed that Rod is not the paragon of virtue he appears to be, I think we can see him as the type who might be searching for a hidden family treasure and keep it away from the rest of his family. But what does this have to do with Lenore? I think I'm going to have to see Madera after all. She's the only one left that could know."

"Are you sure you should go back to her house?" Allegra leaned forward. "If she gets wind of hidden treasure, she'll want to get into the Flagstaff house to search. I don't see her being concerned about my well-being, so it would end up being about her getting what she thinks she deserves."

"If only," Charlie said.

"There's no way I'm going over there now anyway. Best to leave her out except as a last resort. I'm heading back to Flagstaff. That house might have more secrets to give up. If I could find any evidence of my theories, we can convince Detective Macy to look in a different direction."

"That's a good idea. If you get worried about anything, call us. You can stay here, right, Charlie? Here's both our cell numbers." She scribbled the numbers on a small note and handed it to Pilar. "Let us know what you're doing. I don't want anything to happen to you because you're trying to help me."

"I promise I will. I guess I should get going now."

"Be careful," Allegra said.

"Yeah, real careful," Charlie added.

As Pilar descended inside the ornate elevator, Charlie's words echoed in her mind. She relived Rod's threatening demeanor. As terrifying as that experience had been, she shuddered imagining how menacing he would appear if he wanted to kill her.

CHAPTER 45

October 13, 2006
Phoenix, Arizona

Detective Macy had little patience for lawyers. In his view, they were overpriced and unprincipled in their representation of anyone who could afford them. However, he had to admit he had gathered useful information on several cases when legal issues had been vague and incomprehensible to him.

He was not too sure how useful this lawyer could be in this business. For his purposes, the facts were obvious enough and unambiguous. With that said, he wanted to learn what made Virginia tick, and what drove her. With some cases, everything boiled down to greed, revenge, or both. Why this old woman would cut out the daughter who had taken care of her for the son who abandoned her? I guess the reason she told her daughter she would get everything was to manipulate her. Still, it seems harsh, even for a bad mother.

♦ ♦ ♦

Alfred Whitney sat across the long conference table again, longing to be extricated from this family's business affairs. Did it not always seem to be that the smaller the client, the larger the headache? Unbillable time sitting here talking with a police officer about facts that were laid out in the will, he struggled to appear cooperative. He figured the sooner he told the detective what he wanted to know, the sooner he could get back to his real clients.

"What can I do for you this morning, Detective Macy?"

"As you know, Lenore Santos was found dead under suspicious circumstances. Keeping in mind that her grandmother died a short time ago, we're looking into the affairs of the grandmother to determine if there's a connection."

"I thought Virginia died of natural causes. I hadn't heard of anything suspicious in that."

"As far as we know, she did. However, sometimes one event leads to another, so I'm looking into the impact her passing had on the rest of her family. It sounds like a good deal of bad blood went on. Do you have any knowledge of the root of the problems?"

"As far as Virginia told me, the reason she left her home and its contents to her brother's descendants had to do with fulfilling an old obligation. Her parents' philosophy was that family tangible assets passed through male heirs, since they expected their daughters to marry well and acquire through their husbands. When their parents died, Peter signed the house over to Virginia for her lifetime with no right to sell. The property would revert to him if she moved or died. It was a way for both of them to benefit and keep the property in the family. That was a mutual decision."

"That's extraordinary; not something you hear about in modest families. Now what about everything else that was left to her son in Beverly Hills?"

"Now I thought that was rude," Alfred said expressing his distaste. "When I tried to challenge her on it, she wouldn't hear it. Mind you, we're not talking a great fortune. The woman knew how to stretch a penny but that was because she did not have much to work with. Her daughter, Madera, is under the assumption that there are millions going to her brother, but after debts and other obligations, there is around $100,000 to split. I would say that Madera is lucky to get the monthly allowance. Her share will go further than if she received a lump sum."

"Did you also handle the trust for Allegra Santos set up by her father?"

"Yes, I did. It was straightforward. When Allegra was about a year old, he came in to talk to me about it. Some friends told him he should think about his daughter's future should he die before she was of age. I set up the trust giving the bank the authority as trustee until she's twenty-five. Before that, the arrangements were that Lenore would receive thirty-five hundred per month until Allegra was eighteen or until she graduated from college. That arrangement would change if Allegra moved into a dorm or moved out of state to go to school. At that time, the trustee would pay her education along with books and incidentals and allow for a reasonable amount for her living expenses. Lenore would have to submit expense reports to be reimbursed for Allegra's education expenses."

"So, Allegra was not exaggerating her mother's concerns about losing the trust money. What do you know about the current situation?"

"The fact that Lenore was determined to claim Allegra unstable and incapable of taking care of herself, would have put her mother in the position to continue receiving payments on her behalf indefinitely. I'm not going to speculate on the future events if Lenore were alive, but I anticipated an ugly legal battle. Allegra came to me for advice. I believed Allegra's position was weak based on what her mother told me, and I told her so. Afterward, she consulted another attorney about forcing her mother out of her financial affairs and out as her legal guardian. She told me when she called to confirm the attorney-client confidentiality that I should not talk about anything we discussed to her mother."

"Allegra told me she was ready to fight to prove she was not incompetent. Did her mother and grandmother know about this?"

"Not as far as I know. I was under no obligation to tell them since she consulted me as an individual about general legal matters. After speaking with her, I was surprised at her maturity and clarity. Her mother told awful stories that, in retrospect, were probably exaggerations. I'm sorry for the girl when it comes down to it. Even one million is motivation enough for most people."

"That much! Where did that come from?"

"Mr. Santos owned several businesses, all of which were sold or liquidated when he died, per his instructions. Due to the specific nature of his instructions, all of it went to his daughter with a minimal allowance for his wife. It was unfair, but I think it was more of a symbolic gesture of a father to a daughter. Keep in mind he was a young man and did not expect to die so soon. I would guess he expected to dispose of his business concerns gradually over time, as anyone would. By the time that happened, his daughter would be an adult and on her own. He may have left everything to his wife at that point or at least split it. Who knows?"

"I think I know the answer to this already, but was anyone else involved in the distribution of his assets?"

"It's funny that you ask. He had a life insurance policy with a beneficiary not related to him, an individual named Claire Spencer."

"Who is she?"

"No idea, but Mr. Santos left instructions that in the event of his death, I was to give her any assistance in confidence. I followed my client's instructions and provided the insurance company with the appropriate paperwork and death certificate. My secretary can give you her name and address if you like. Now if there is nothing else, I must get back to work." He stood, extended his hand for a parting handshake, and left the conference room.

He left Detective Macy to sit for several minutes taking notes. After speaking to his secretary, giving her instructions on the information to provide, he went back to his office.

This was not looking good for Allegra, he thought. Although her father might have had a mistress, Allegra was still the person with the most to gain by her mother's death. What he did not tell the detective was that Lenore was preparing for a fight to institutionalize Allegra. He had not even told that odious grandmother of hers when she was here. Better not to add flames to the fire. He confessed that he looked at Lenore's death as divine intervention and the best for Allegra.

CHAPTER 46

October 14, 2006
Phoenix, Arizona

Allegra set down the telephone, her hands shaking with panic. Detective Macy wanted her to come to his office to answer more questions. What did he know today that he did not know the last time he interviewed her? Charlie came in from the patio in time to see her standing stiff, her eyes wild and out of focus.

"What's happened?"

"Detective Macy. He wants to talk to me again, downtown at his office. He knows. He's figured out what I did."

"I don't believe that. How could he? "

"How should I know? What am I going to do? It's one thing to stand up to Gran when you're standing beside me, but I don't know if I can stand the pressure from a cop interrogating me on my own. Don't they take suspects into a tiny room and question them for hours without a break?"

"Come here," Charlie said. He met her halfway and held her close. "You don't know that's what he'll do. For all you know, he wants more background on the family. He could have a suspect in mind and needs to confirm facts. From what I've heard, they haven't had time to get the chemical analysis back, so he won't know that your prescription drugs killed her. Besides that, not all the drugs found in her car were your prescriptions. Let's not fall to pieces yet."

"You'll go with me, right?"

"I'll drive you, but I won't go in. Before you say anything, the reason is that if I'm there, I'll be making myself available for questions. We'll feed off each other's reactions. I can picture you looking over at me before you answer a question. That's the kind of thing cops notice. No, you need to do this on your own. I know you can do this. You have to convince yourself that you're not responsible for her death. Period. Once you believe it, you'll be able to answer his questions with confidence. If you start to feel concerned, tell him you want your lawyer present before you'll answer any more questions."

"You think I can do this without you?"

"Of course I do. You're going to find out soon enough that you don't need me as much as you think you do. Come on. Let's get this over with."

◆ ◆ ◆

Allegra leaned over to kiss Charlie when he pulled up in front of the station. She hesitated before she got out of the car. She looked up at the building, then back at Charlie.

"You're going to be fine. I promise."

"If you say so," she said, giving him a skeptical look.

"I'll be at the Rusty Hammer, that new English pub on Second Avenue. Call me when you're done and I'll pick you up. Okay?"

She grunted and stepped out onto the curb. As soon as she walked into the front door of the station, she convinced herself she would never be free again. Melodramatic, she thought, but her life had been that way. Nothing worked out the way she wanted. A lot of disappointment and the loss of the people she trusted. She answered the officer at the window that she had an appointment with Detective Macy. A loud buzzing allowed her access into his side of the room, where another officer escorted her to his office.

Detective Macy stood by a desk and reached out his hand to her as she approached. In her stressed state, she flinched with embarrassment at the sweatiness of her hands.

"Thanks for coming down here, Ms. Santos. I needed to speak with you in an official setting. Some serious issues have come out and when that happens, we like to address them before we determine if they're relevant to the case. I think you could help me with that."

When she did not respond, he continued. "I've spoken to Mr. Whitney about your father's trust. He informed me you've had problems with your mother. We have to consider everyone for motive, as well as opportunity and means. You had a strong motive to get away from your mother. From what I've learned, you've every right to feel that way."

"I didn't kill my mother."

"Well, let's talk about the days before your mother died. What were you doing?"

"I was at Charlie's. We talked a lot about how I was trying to take control of my life and what I should do next. The first thing I did was to move in with him. Mom didn't know it yet because I knew I'd be in for a battle."

"No doubt coming into a fortune has something to do with that?"

"That's not fair. Everything isn't always about money. Sometimes it's about freedom and dignity. Of course, I'll share what I have with Charlie, but who wouldn't? Anyway, he didn't know these details until I started talking about needing a lawyer who would be on my side. Before that, he encouraged me to go to school, be independent. He said that would prove my competence. So, I don't care what you think about us." She paused, took deep breaths to calm down. "Listen, I've told you everything I know. I have no idea where those drugs came from and I don't know who she would've met downtown in the middle of the night. Is there anything else?"

"Tell me about Rod. Your cousin Pilar was here and seems to believe he's responsible. Do you agree with her?"

"I told Charlie the other day that I'm uncomfortable around him. I can't say why, but whenever I was in Flagstaff at Gran's house, he treated me as if I was a stranger he wanted gone. I guess she told you about how he threatened her?"

"Tell me about that. What did she tell you?"

"She'd been staying there. When she came from my mom's house and started showing him what she'd learned about the family's history, he tore up the papers and threw her out. That's when she left for Flagstaff. She inherited that house, you see. Mr. Whitney had sent the key, so she went to stay there."

"Why do you think Rod did that?"

"I think she got close to something he doesn't want anyone to know about, obviously." Her confidence increased with the focus off her and Charlie.

"What about his wife? Is she the type to lie for him?"

"God, yes," she said.

"No hesitation about it?"

"No. If you want to know the truth, he thought he was going to inherit the house because Gran Virginia told him. But she told everyone the same thing. I know because I heard her. People forget about children. Pilar told us how Mr. Whitney explained about the legal arrangement. Once Gran died, the house went back to her brother. I bet Rod was pissed about that. Gran was always making comments like, "When this place is yours.""

"How do you feel about his wife?"

"Oh, her. I guess she's okay, but you can't tell her anything that she won't run back to tell Rod. She must love him to have put up with the abuse all these years from Gran and Virginia. Even my mom was mean to her. They could be pretty horrible."

"Tell me what you know about Pilar. She came along in time to witness a lot of drama."

"True, but that's a coincidence. I think she's a sad person who hides that from people. She's had a lot of death in her family. At least, she had a loving family in the first place. I think she came out here to find family again. She had no way of knowing she'd walked into a big mess."

"So you like you her?"

"Yes, I do. She's nice and I know she's trying to help since you think I killed my mother."

"Did I say that?"

"Not directly."

Macy grinned at her. "You can go for now, but don't go far. I might need to *consult* with you again."

Allegra stood up, surprised at his relaxed manner and her assertiveness. "I understand. I'm happy to help. "She shook his hand when he extended it, more surprised to be in an adult role for once instead of the kid hanging behind the grownups.

Outside in the fresh air and bright sunshine, she leaned against the side of the concrete building to process what had just happened. Her knees shook and her chest pounded, she guessed from the release of so much unaccustomed self-control. Once steady on her feet, she smiled, repressing a guttural laugh. She had experienced her first reality shift. Going from helpless little girl to strong woman, not realizing she had taken the mental leap to seeing herself as others did. She reached for her cell phone and called Charlie.

"Everything went okay, I guess," she said when he asked about the interview.

"He didn't ask about any tampered meds or anything about me?"

"At first, he asked about the days before Mom's death, about my trust, and the trouble I had with Mom. Then he asked about Rod, Sylvie, and Pilar. I stood up for myself and for you. I couldn't believe I was the person talking."

"I knew you'd be fine. I'll be right over to pick you up, and then we'll come back here for lunch. Play a game of darts."

"Sounds good. Anything to take my mind off the police station," Allegra said. "Thank God that's over."

◆ ◆ ◆

Detective Macy had a curious expression as he watched her walk toward the elevator. He had studied her during the interview. On her flushed face and tearful eyes, he saw a passionate woman who might have a fiery temper. For someone who until recently could not stand up for herself against her mother, she not only stood up for herself but showed a protectiveness over her boyfriend. The question now was whether the change happened because her mother is dead, or was the change the catalyst that instigated her to kill her mother. That is what he had to figure out about her.

CHAPTER 47

October 14, 2006
Phoenix, Arizona

Charlie sank back in a booth at the Rusty Hammer to figure out how he would expose Rod. Bringing him down by working with the cops to save his dealer friend, said aloud sounded bizarre. Like some of the Indi movies he watched, this could be tricky, as well as risky if Rod found him out.

As interesting as it was to think of Rod as having killed his sister, the big question would have to be why he would bother. As he told Den, he could not see any way Lenore, as insecure and anti-social as she was, not to mention straight, could have stumbled somewhere she could have learned of his secrets.

Lenore rarely went anywhere other than to her parents' home, the Flagstaff house, and work. She and Rod had bad feelings, reason unclear, so that eliminated the opportunity for her to find out something at his home or from Sylvie. Besides, Rod would be smart enough not to leave incriminating evidence of another wife anywhere Sylvie might find it. If he killed Lenore, his motive had to be family-related, and something valuable enough to risk endangering the status quo. The only thing a man like Rod would care about more than duplicity would be money, or something intrinsically valuable, like hidden treasure.

Den's motivation was self-preservation, but what if his knowledge of Rod's secret turned out to be the key. Until he heard Den's story, he had no more reason to suspect Rod than the cops did. Den had another good point when he said he had time to think up a way. Sitting in the dim light of the booth, feeling isolated and anonymous, he decided calling the tip line would be the best. People were always calling in tips to Crime Stop without giving their name to protect themselves against retaliation. Now, how to say what he wanted in a short span of time.

"Sam, I'll be right back," he said to the bartender. "I have to make a call before I pick up Allegra. We'll be back for lunch." Sam nodded with a smile and went back to wiping off his bar.

Once enclosed inside the old-fashioned telephone booth, Charlie practiced several times in a whispered voice before he thought he sounded different enough, and called the number. "I'm calling about the Lenore Santos murder. You should look at her relationship with her brother, Rod Folsom, if you're looking for a motive for murder. No, I'm not looking for a reward; I just want to make sure justice is served and that the wrong person isn't accused."

As if on cue, Allegra started to rap on his window. "Are we leaving?

He hung up the receiver. "No, I had to make a quick call. You didn't have to walk."

"I know. I wanted to burn off the stress. It isn't that far on a day like this. I'm starving now."

"My booth is probably still empty. Let's go eat."

She dropped her purse and sweater on the opposite side of the booth, and scooted in so Charlie could follow her. She squeezed his arm and rested her head on his shoulder. "I was scared, but I got through it. I thought for sure he could hear my heart beating through my sweater. I did better than I thought I would. Thank goodness that's over with for now."

"He'll want to talk to you again, you know."

"I know, but not again today. What have you been doing? Is something wrong that you couldn't use your cell phone? You seem upset."

"I've been thinking about everything, including the fact that I haven't looked for job and I need to get my ass in gear. I've developed some anxiety over that."

"I told you not to worry about money. I have plenty now."

"While that's generous of you, you know what I've said about that. We can't allow it to appear that you're vulnerable and have a freeloader planning to take your fortune away from you. That's what your grandmother and the cops would need. No, I need to work as I did before. There'll be plenty of time later for you to lavish me with an expensive lifestyle." Charlie smiled, and kissed her on her forehead.

"Maybe you're right about that, but I can at least buy groceries and put gas in the car if you run out of money. Speaking of Gran, I haven't heard anything from her. That makes me nervous."

"Have you heard from Sylvie or Rod?"

"Nope. I spoke with Pilar earlier and she said she was in Flagstaff still checking things out. I hope she comes back again today, but she might stay overnight again. I'd find it creepy to sleep in that big house by myself, but she might not feel that way."

"Not if she's busy hunting for hidden treasure."

CHAPTER 48

October 14, 2006
Phoenix, Arizona

Reading the transcript of the anonymous call from the tips hotline, Detective Macy thought this might be the break he needed. With few potential suspects, he had not looked further than Allegra. Her motive was strongest both financially and psychologically. She had the opportunity. And her alibi was her boyfriend. For means, the prevalence of the drugs on the street made it easy for anyone to get about anything they wanted with little trouble. He admitted to himself that he had allowed the money to blindside him, but Allegra was right. Everything was not always about money.

What made him a good detective had been his willingness to look for any motive, not only the financial ones. With this third person pointing a finger at Rod, he had a duty to look into it, however obscure the motive seemed. In his experience, innocent people do not get their names reported on hotlines and named by family members. He found in a couple situations that even when the individual turned out to be innocent of the specific crimes, they had been guilty of something else.

He had run a background check on Rod Folsom before, but

had not found anything unusual. He knew that he worked at Cinetel Electronics, was married, and lived with his wife and three children in a good neighborhood, had good credit, and no outstanding warrants. Not even a traffic ticket. He sounded too good to be true, which made him look suspicious. It might be useful to interview him again with more scrutiny.

Another one he wanted to speak to again was that newcomer, Pilar. He recalled that she had come to Arizona on a pilgrimage to meet her extended family. Could it be a coincidence that her arrival *appeared* to trigger the events that followed? Sometimes, a coincidence is just a coincidence. Sometimes the coincidence is a set of contrived circumstances meant to look like a coincidence. Other times, one unusual event is significant in its relationship to other events. Someone like Pilar could provide an outside perspective, more forthcoming than the tighter-bound family. During her visit here, she was willing to put herself in the mix to defend someone she thought was innocent. If she went further, she could dig up facts he did not know to look for.

Now that he made the decision to question Folsom, he had to find him. He called his office but received no answer, then remembered he worked the late shift. He called him at home but his wife said he was out taking care of unspecified errands.

Detective Macy heard his inner-detective confirming he had stumbled onto the right track. For this man to threaten Pilar and make her leave late at night meant something. Considering Rod knew the police suspected his niece of murder, he also wondered why he did not want to participate in proving her innocence. The anonymous tipster popped into his mind, and he decided to drive over to Cinetel Electronics tonight and have a talk with Mr. Folsom and his co-workers.

◆ ◆ ◆

Security was tight at the Cinetel Electronics complex, more so at night with limited staff. The Cinetel executives had requested additional perimeter protection from the Phoenix

Police Department that added to the efforts of a private security firm after a security breach one night.

After showing his badge and identification, the security guard issued a visitor's pass that he was to keep visible at all times while inside the gates. Before going to the lab where Rod worked, he took on a casual approach as he did while investigating friends and coworkers of a suspect. This approach worked most of the time, like tonight with the security guard.

"I guess you know we're investigating the death of Mr. Folsom's sister."

Shifting taller in his seat, the security guard looked into the Detective's face before responding, "Yeah. We all heard about it. That was a real tragedy."

"Have you known Mr. Folsom long?"

"We've worked here about the same length of time. I started two weeks before him. We're not friends, but we're friendly."

"How does this night shift work for both of you? I would get worn out trying to stay awake all night, missing the family because I slept during the day."

"It's not that bad. You find ways to make it work. I take short naps during my breaks and lunch hour."

"How does Mr. Folsom manage? He has an attractive wife and three small kids. It must really wear him out."

"To be honest, he has it easier because he's in the office alone. No one around to see if he sleeps or leaves. Of course, I wouldn't know either. I see him when he gets here and when he goes."

"Not even during breaks?"

"Like I said, I don't see him except when he arrives and when he leaves. We have different break areas. Besides, he's an engineer assistant and I'm security. We got nothing in common to want to go out of our ways to meet each other for."

"Are there other ways out than through here?"

Taken aback by the abrupt change of subject, the man hesitated, and said, "Uh, well, there're emergency exits but they're not large enough for vehicles, only for people. The problem there is you trigger an alarm when the gates open.

You'd need a key to override the alarm. I guess this is the only way out."

"Who's here when you're on break?"

Macy noticed that nerves or some other anxiety had taken hold of the man because beads of sweat started forming on his forehead. Macy thought that maybe he had stumbled onto something after all.

"Well, Hank from maintenance comes out to relieve me most of the time."

"Most of the time?"

"Listen, I don't want to lose my job. I've got a pension to think about."

"Tell me and it won't go any further than right here. I'm investigating a murder. I'm not trying to get you fired."

The man took a deep breath and let out a loud sigh, "I knew this would catch up to me one day. Here's the thing. Since it's in the middle of the night, I don't wait for anyone to relieve me. I just go. I don't go far, but the gate is unattended for an hour every night, and sometimes on my breaks. I'm supposed to take my lunch and breaks in there." He pointed to a door Macy had not noticed which led into a small anteroom that extended to the back of the guard window.

"Where do you go? The cafeteria inside?"

"Yeah. Sometimes I stretch out in the lounge for a nap. I swear I'm not gone longer than I'm allowed."

After his years on the force, Macy could still not get over how self-absorbed people were. Just as in this instance, an employee lies to protect his indiscretion on the job, even if it meant protecting a murder suspect. "When you told the other officer that Mr. Folsom never left the compound, you were lying because you didn't want to admit you were off your post and have no idea if he left or not?"

As if the proverbial light went off, the man's face deadened to ashen white. He stared out into the parking lot searching for the answers. "Oh, my God. I didn't think ..."

"That's an understatement. As soon as your shift is over, you're going downtown to revise your statement. I'll tell them you're coming, so don't get any ideas about not showing."

Macy saw the man's face go through a series of emotions, sweating worse, and tugging on his collar. "Officer, I'm sorry. I don't know what else to say."

Macy decided not to let him off the hook with lamentations about how anyone would have done the same. Damn it, this was a serious situation and this man had better learn his lesson.

"Just do it," he said before going back to his car. Damn again, he thought. If it had not been for that tip, he would not have looked at Folsom again and would have missed Rod's lack of an alibi. "He's supposed to be working tonight. Please tell him I'm here and need to speak with him."

"I'm sorry, but he didn't come in yet. His shift starts at eleven o'clock. It's not like him to be late."

"Damn," Macy said, heading back to his car. Time to find Mr. Folsom.

CHAPTER 49

October 15, 2006 6:45 pm
Phoenix, Arizona

Macy did not get the search warrant he wanted for Rod's home for lack of probable cause. Times like this, he wished he could make use of Global Positioning Systems or GPS trackers. The invasion of privacy controversy left too many debatable areas regarding its use, the potential of putting a conviction at risk if a judge dismissed evidence collected derived from GPS surveillance data. Learning where a suspect went often established his criminal activity but also pointed the police to the identities of more important players. But in a murder case, he did not want a defense attorney claiming rogue police procedures as a technicality.

Instead, he put out a broadcast alert for Rod Folsom and his vehicle as a person of interest. He had stationed a patrol car at his home and at Cinetel. The frightened security guard agreed to call when Rod arrived at work.

With that situation handled, Macy decided it was a good time to speak with Pilar again. He looked up her mobile number from his notepad, dialed and waited. No answer. He left her a message to call him, and then he returned to his notepad to look up

Allegra's number.

"Hello," Allegra said.

"Allegra, Detective Macy here. I'm looking for Pilar. Have you seen her?"

With relief in her voice that he did not miss, she said, "She was here but she left for Flagstaff again. Is something wrong?"

"No. When did she leave?"

"About two hours ago. She should be there by now or soon will be."

"If you hear from her, have her call me right away."

"Okay, I will."

He disconnected the call and wondered if he should drive up there when his phone rang.

"Macy, Reiner here. Folsom arrived at work. He only stayed fifteen minutes before leaving five minutes ago. I thought you should know he's driving north on the seventeen. He's not going home, because he passed that exit."

"Good work. I think he's going to Flagstaff, so I'm heading that way, too."

Macy still was not convinced about all of this long-forgotten treasure stuff, but he was certain something was going on. Thankful he always kept a thermos of hot coffee in the car, he drove as fast as he could without attracting attention of either Rod or the Highway Patrol. The cover of darkness on Arizona highways was a blessing. His senses were almost on fire as his eyes focused on the curves of the mountain roads and the cars in front of him.

CHAPTER 50

October 15, 2006
Flagstaff, Arizona

Pilar held up her cell phone to the sky. "Damn, no service." She had put on her running shoes and jacket, and decided to take a brisk walk through her new Flagstaff neighborhood, hoping to run into cell service along the way. She needed to clear her head to regain perspective. She walked through the winter air, waving back to neighbors walking dogs and a pair of small boys finding enough snow to use their snowboards in the neighboring yards. Without the intense sun of the afternoon and the intermittent winds, by nine at night, the icy air stung her face and hands on contact. This break away from searching the house opened her mind to other issues she had chosen to ignore until the current crisis passed.

Throughout her life, bearing up to personal losses only some could imagine, she never felt alone or at a disadvantage. She had survived the funeral for her parents and brothers, then Pete's passing last year, comforted by her faith that her family would always be with her. A family with integrity, unity, religious faith, and law-abiding honesty, had been her foothold in the world.

Now, the one person she valued over everyone else, the one who embodied those qualities, her dear grandfather, she helped to expose as a fake. If their family foundation was built on lies, where did that leave her?

By the time she returned to the house, she had forgotten that she wanted to make a call. Detective Macy needed tangible evidence that this house contained something valuable enough to kill for and she intended to find it. She looked around her, as if seeing the place for the first time. She had been over every bedroom and bathroom upstairs, all of the ground floor rooms, even under seat cushions in the living room for cryptic clues. One place she had not seen yet was the basement, on purpose.

Her childhood fear of the boogeyman kept her spooked enough all her life to avoid going into dark basements alone. She weighed her irrational fears against the logical process of elimination. After thinking about it, she decided to chance it. Face fears first. If there had ever been something to fear since coming to Arizona, it had been human beings rather than imaginary monsters.

The basement door between the kitchen and pantry had an off-putting appearance. Chipped paint concealed by a large corkboard glued to the inside panel held shopping lists and recipes. A sloppy job she would tend to later. She swung the door open on squeaky hinges and stuck her head into the darkness. She reached for the light switch and watched as the deep stairwell filled with an incandescent glow. She took cautious steps down to the painted concrete floor, surprised by its welcoming warmth.

She saw a key hanging on a hook in the recess of the exposed wall next to her and slipped it into her pocket to figure out its lock later. By the time she found another light switch, she had arrived on the bottom of the stairs, her eyes squeezed closed. Her finger lifted the switch while she braced herself for a dirty, unkempt basement moldy with age and neglect.

She staggered back in disbelief when she opened her eyes. To her right, she saw a finished basement furnished in Spanish Colonial, fitted out with a compact kitchen, a stone fireplace, and a door to the back yard. Cobwebs and dusty shelves showed evidence of a beautiful space unused for a long time. Although the sun had gone down, she saw the large windows and ten-foot ceilings a modern feature in homes today that made use of otherwise unusable space.

Behind her to the left of the stairwell, she saw a cozy room with a desk, chair, and recliner designed to be a small bedroom or an office. This space was smaller than the other side in height and depth but still quaint. While the main switch turned on a series of lights that lit the entire basement, she saw this room had separate lighting. At the desk, she turned on the lamp, and a picture light positioned over a grand western landscape. Almost at once, she noticed the built out wall behind the desk holding the painting. This might be a secreted closet or a Murphy bed.

She looked for a door handle or a drawer pull but saw neither. She ran her fingers along the outer edges for a spring lock or lever, anything that would release it. She performed the same examination on the other side with the same results. Frustration made her determined. Thinking that if she moved the chair away, she could get a better perspective to see how it opened, she tried to move the chair to the right. She expected a smooth movement, but almost fell across the chair when it stopped abruptly. She looked down to see one of the casters attached to a metal lever. With all her strength, she pushed on the chair until it gave way and rolled to the corner. As she did this, she heard metal snap metal and the large box moved a foot out from the wall.

She thought she might never have been this excited in her life. The adrenaline rush she experienced could have sent her into orbit. Her heart beat in her ears and her mouth went dry. She used her shaking hands and inched forward to look inside, not sure what she expected to see. She smiled, thinking as long as she did not find a dead body she was good.

Edging in sideways into the foot wide area, she saw that most of the wall was stone, rough, cold, and damp. In three steps, as she neared the center, in the dimness she could see a flattened area. Once in front of it, she saw metal drawer fronts displaying metal rings welded on as handles. She pulled but it did not move. Six of them all locked or fixed in place. Deflated, she thought these drawers might not have been opened or used for years and could be rusted shut.

It took another five minutes of feeling around in near darkness when her fingers touched a lock to the left of the stack of drawers. On a whim, she used the key she found at the top of the stairs, not expecting it to work. To her amazement, the skeleton key turned inside the ancient padlock. The sound was subtle, a click and a loosening of a bolt.

Her pulse raced when she pulled on the top drawer that gave way now. All six drawers opened, but all were empty except for one at the bottom. It held a thick packet of old documents. Her high hopes of finding gold and old money vanished. Doubt crept in that maybe she had nothing after all, except a vivid imagination. At least, she had a great old house even if it did not help her yield a treasure.

The house had gone quiet. She leaned against the wall in the tiny space to think, resting her head on its rough surface. She had just closed her eyes, when she heard noises. Someone was walking upstairs. Had she locked the front door, she could not remember. Then she cursed aloud for not checking the back door. The adrenaline rushed through her veins, pounding her heart, paralyzing her legs. The panic created confusion about what to do next.

She stood, frozen, listening for new sounds. She thought of the lights illuminating the hall and most of the basement. She wondered if a burglar would bother with a basement. Maybe not, unless they noticed the lights. Had she closed the door at the top of the basement staircase? She rushed over, flipped off the light switch, and waited again in the dark. When she looked up, she saw the closed door and relaxed. Everything was quiet now. Maybe she had only imagined the sounds were footsteps.

She stood motionless for another five minutes. She remembered the papers in the drawer and put them back. She was surprised at how quiet she could be as she shoved the drawer back in place, turned the key, and withdrew from the space. When she had gathered her nerve, she used her cell phone as a light to find her way up the stairs to the kitchen. Her contradictory emotions—one minute fearful, the next angry—she did not know which instinct to follow. She tiptoed up the stairs. When she reached out for the handle, she saw the door was open. Only a crack, but not latched as she had thought.

She pushed the door in a fluid movement, her head leading her body into the room to peek from side to side. Before she had time to understand what happened, muscular arms wrapped around her neck, lifting her off the floor while covering her head with plastic. She clawed at the bag, kicking her assailant with the force of her strong legs. For a few seconds, she sensed a pause when the pressure around her throat lessened and the hands moved from her throat. She started to raise her hands to the plastic still tight against her face, braced to run.

The unexpected blow to her stomach, both vicious and powerful, knocked the wind from her lungs and doubled her over. She reeled backward and took in another blow more brutal than the first. The impact slammed her into a hard surface. Unable to suck air, her head started to spin, her legs buckled beneath her, and she slid down the side of wall. She choked for air, but only plastic filled her screaming mouth. Moaning on the floor, she thought he was done with her until he pressed a large boot deep into her stomach making her strain harder for breath. After a second that seemed like an hour, he moved his foot, and gave her one last kick in the side.

She heard his heavy footsteps running across the kitchen, out the backdoor, and down the porch stairs. She tore at the plastic, shredding it with her fingernails. When she could feel the air on her face, she expanded her chest to breathe before losing consciousness.

CHAPTER 51

October 15, 2006
Flagstaff, Arizona

When Detective Macy arrived at the Flagstaff residence, he looked at the grand old house for a minute before walking up the front steps to the porch. He could see lights on inside but they were incongruous to normal lighting in a home with occupants, even at ten o'clock at night. Ringing the doorbell and knocking on the wooden door with no response made him uneasy. He tried the knob, but it would not turn. When he peeked around the side of the house, he saw Pilar's rental car parked under the porte-cochère. He pulled out his flashlight and made his way to the back of the house.

The melted snow had left the ground moist and soggy. When he walked toward the rear of the house, he saw the long strides of a man's footprints. The depth of the shoe impressions and the distance between them indicated the man was running. Macy approached the back door with care, pulling his gun from its holster as he walked. He reached the last step and aiming the light inside, peered in through the kitchen window. That is when he saw Pilar on the floor.

He tried the doorknob. This time, an unlocked door swung inward. He stepped inside, Glock raised and ready as he checked the room with his back to the wall. He squatted down beside Pilar to check her pulse. Relieved to find her pulse strong, he stood up, pulled out his cell phone, and called 911. After identifying himself and his own description, he explained the situation and Pilar's condition as he saw it. Once he knew help was on the way, he checked to be sure that the rest of the house was clear and secure, before he returned to Pilar.

Within minutes, he heard the sirens approaching. He had grabbed a blanket from the closet and covered her. Seeing the plastic pull tie around her neck and the black garbage bag it secured outraged him. His instinct told him to remove it, but he knew that action might compromise evidence. She was lucky to be breathing; lucky for the ripped plastic, lucky she managed to save her own life.

◆ ◆ ◆

While the paramedics attended to Pilar, Macy checked in with Reiner for the status of the BOLO on Rod's Tahoe. They might not have anything on him yet for his sister's murder, but Macy believed they could place him here by the footprints and traffic cameras. Officers waited for Rod at his office and a discreet distance from his home. One way or another, they would have him in custody soon. It was a matter of waiting.

Following the ambulance to the hospital, Macy let his mind go back to everyone he had interviewed, but this time with a fresh eye. He had failed to make an important connection by not being thorough in verifying Rod's work alibi. By the time he reached the hospital emergency room, and waited around to speak to the doctor on call, he knew this was a simple case of greed for property. Real estate property, not the gold Pilar believed. The case was still circumstantial, but now that he considered Rod a viable suspect for Lenore's death, Macy bet he could find CCTV footage of his vehicle in the area around the bus station.

"Pilar suffered a mild concussion," the emergency room physician said. "The blows to her stomach while she was being suffocated forced out air from her lungs quicker and caused her to lose consciousness. Someone knew what he or she was doing. If she had not had the strength to tear open the bag, she would be in the morgue instead of the emergency room. She's awake with a bad headache and lots of contusions, and a few broken ribs. I want to keep her overnight for observation, but I don't expect further complications. The forensic people have already processed her."

"I'm sticking around until she's released. It's not a good idea to leave her unguarded, and I need to interview her while the incident is fresh in her mind."

"I'll take care of the patient's health. You take care of her protection," the doctor said. "If you'll excuse me, I'm needed. If you have any concerns, one of the nurses can find me."

Macy watched the doctor disappear down the hallway before he went into Pilar's room. A nurse was getting her comfortable for the night and both looked up at him when he entered. Pilar smiled at him, overtly expressing the effects of the pain medications. He was relieved she was going to be fine, but could not help but blame himself for not taking her seriously.

◆　◆　◆

Tucson, Arizona

Rod sat in the passenger seat of Sheila's vintage El Camino looking out into the darkness. He stared at the dim lights from the I-10 access road east of Exit 236, and the bright Chevron sign on the road ahead without seeing them. After all his careful planning, his world was falling down around him. Once the cops took a harder look at him, they were smart enough to put the pieces together. He should not have lost his cool with Pilar and kicked her out. Just the survival instinct took over, he thought. Then to find her in the basement at the Flagstaff house, he had been sure she found the gold. But when he thought she was dead, he went back to find nothing but papers.

"Baby, what's the matter? You're brooding. I don't like you like this. It scares me," Sheila said.

Rod looked over at the woman he had known the last five years. She called him Nick and he liked that. She was rough, uncontrollable, with a hard edge about her that had roused him from the tedium of his life. In contrast, Sylvie was compliant, even-tempered, good qualities in a wife, but not exciting. Sylvie's toxic neediness had driven him into Sheila's bed, and into their separate life in Tucson.

"We've got to get out of state. It's all going to come out soon and I don't want you and Barbie getting caught in the trouble."

She reached over to kiss him and let her long black hair brush against his skin. "We have the fake passports and our money already transferred to Belize. Why bother to go back?"

"You're right. Forget the Tahoe. Let's go back home and pack, and then get the hell out of here. I have a bad feeling."

"Just keep your temper under control. That's when shit happens," Sheila said, turning the key in the ignition. Before she put the car in gear, the reflection in the rear view mirror of flashing lights from a patrol car blinded her.

Rod looked at Sheila. She placed her hand on his arm, and said, "Don't react. Stay cool. It's probably nothing."

She rolled down her window as two officers approached with flashlights, one on each side of the car. The beams of light crossed over the interior of their vehicle.

"Good evening, Ma'am. You've been parked here for a half hour. Is there a problem?"

"No, Officer. I was dropping off my husband and we lost track of time talking," Sheila said, pointing to the Tahoe parked in front of them.

The second officer leaned in to look at Rod, and said, "I'd like to see both of your driver's licenses, the car registration, and insurance."

Shelia pulled her license from her wallet and reached across to the glove box for the car's documents. She twisted her head around to look into Rod's face. He had not moved. He sat frozen, not aware that she was looking at him.

"Get your license out. They'll get suspicious if you don't," Sheila said, nudging him.

He considered his situation. He would not be surprised to find out he had a warrant issued against him. His life with Sheila was bound to lead to more questions and more digging into their financial affairs in Tucson. As soon as he had the chance, he would make Sylvie pay for this mess.

He reached into his pocket, pulled out his wallet, and handed the license to the officer at his window. They watched as one of the officers went to the patrol car to run their names and plate number. Rod knew he had been right when the officer walked back at a faster pace, rigid, and primed for confrontation.

"Sir, please step out of the car slowly and keep your hands where I can see them," the officer said.

The officer at Sheila's window looked down at her, ready to say something, not prepared for her reaction. "Get your fucking hands off my husband, asshole." Rod heard Sheila's raised voice and tried to turn toward her, but the second officer misunderstood his movement, slammed him face down on the hood of the car, and handcuffed his wrists at his back.

"You son-of-a-bitch! What are you doing to him?" Sheila opened the car door and stood up in an attempt to rescue Rod. The officer moved out of the way of the moving door, but leaned toward her to stop her. Rod watched as she swung a fisted hand into the officer's jaw, and could do nothing but lower his head. The sickening sight of the woman he cherished thrown to the ground, kicking, and clawing all the way down, sent a rage through him he had never experienced.

"Sheila, stop!" Rod said. "You're making things worse. Think of Barbie. She won't have anyone if something happens to you." He knew the sound of their daughter's name would have the effect he intended. She came to an abrupt stop, causing the officer trying to contain her to stumble at the loss of momentum.

With the two Mirandized, and seated in the back of the patrol car in handcuffs, the second officer held Sheila's license.

"The name of your license lists you as Sheila Folsom.," he said to her through the open door.

"Yeah, so what? He's my husband. I took his last name," Sheila said, still defiant, but subdued.

"Mr. Folsom, our records show you living in Phoenix, and sharing a home with Sylvie Folsom. Care to explain that?"

Rod remained quiet.

"Look in my purse. I have our marriage license. You can see for yourself," Sheila said.

"You always carry that around with you?"

"I happened to need it yesterday and forgot to put it back in the safe."

The first officer pulled the document from her purse, and held it up in front of the light. "It looks good, but the security markings are missing."

"It's a copy, not the original, dumbass," Sheila said.

"We should have a lot to talk about at the station," he said.

CHAPTER 52

October 16, 2006
Flagstaff, Arizona

By eight thirty in the morning, Pilar had settled in a recliner in the basement den, explaining to Detective Macy and a Flagstaff Officer Ron Spatz how she came to be downstairs to look around when she thought she heard walking upstairs.

"I must not have checked the back door and that's how he got in."

"Or he already had a key," Detective Macy said.

"That's possible. Could've been a worker that came here and stole a key," Spatz said. "Anyone would know Virginia lived here alone. An easy mark," Macy had told her earlier that Spatz did not believe Rod, a man he had known since childhood, could be capable of any kind of brutality. "You say you believe Rod assaulted you? It'll be his word against yours that he threatened you before and that he was here."

"I guess you'll be satisfied when he kills me. I'll see if I can get him to leave evidence behind before he does the deed."

"Being melodramatic and sarcastic is not going to get you

anywhere, Miss Sagasta."

Detective Macy cleared his throat, "He's a person of interest in his sister's death down in Phoenix. You have CCTV footage placing him in the neighborhood, and a neighbor called in a suspicious parked vehicle providing his license plate number. We know he was here during the time of the attack. Why come up here when he should be at work anyway? If he's not involved in this, he's involved in something."

Detective Spatz hesitated. "Let's take a look at this cabinet, or whatever it is. Ma'am, how do we get in this closet?"

After Pilar explained how to move the furniture, she handed Macy the skeleton key. The two men went through the same procedure, and opened the drawers one by one.

"Interesting," Detective Spatz said. "Look here, Macy." Spatz backed up, and then pulled out a pair of latex gloves from his pocket before he opened the drawers one by one. Unlike Pilar, they had the advantage of a powerful flashlight that illuminated the interior surface. "See the scrape marks, metal on metal does that. It's the same in each one. How long ago, I couldn't say. I might have to retract what I said about something hidden down here. The drawers are big. There'd be enough room to fit a lot of loot in here."

Pilar gave Macy a dour look that was part sarcastic, part satisfaction.

"I know the robberies she's talking about," Spatz said. "I grew up here and heard all the stories when I was a boy. Every few years, someone writes an article about one of the robberies or there's a special on television. You get treasure hunters tearing through every site related to the robberies. No one finds anything. If this young lady figures it out, it'll be the biggest story in Arizona history. Especially if it turns out that three of the most prominent Flagstaff families of the day were outlaws. I'm going to call the forensic team to fingerprint this area. While they're at it, I'll ask them if they can determine what was in here before."

"Whatever," Pilar said.

"Are you staying here alone?" Spatz said.

"I don't have any place to go unless I check in at a motel. I'd prefer to be here."

"In that case, I'll have patrol keep an eye out on your place tonight," Spatz said. "The forensic team will be here in the morning. I'm sure you know not to touch anything else down here."

"If she doesn't mind," Macy said. "I'll stay on here tonight."

She answered his questioning nod with a smile, and said, "I appreciate that. Being alone and injured is not easy."

Spatz left after he and Macy helped Pilar upstairs. Pilar settled into Virginia's bedroom, wondering if she could sleep in a room where someone recently died.

♦ ♦ ♦

Macy positioned a comfortable chair to give him a view of the front of the house and easy access to the back. Once he settled down, he checked in with Phoenix. He listened at first, expecting to hear that his suspect had been picked up. Instead, he shot questions to the person on the other end in quick succession.

"What do you mean, you lost him? How could that happen? Are you saying he never showed up at home or at work? What do mean he's in Marana?"

Pilar opened the door, walking with cautious reserve, bent now that the abdominal pain had set in. He saw her face drawn with concern listening to the conversation. When he disconnected, he decided to play down his concern.

"Do you know anyone who lives in Marana or Tucson?"

"No. Why do you ask?"

"Sit down, please."

"Oh my God! Is the news that bad?"

"No, I just get nervous seeing you lean over like that."

Laughing, she said, "Geez. You're not supposed to be funny. It hurts when I laugh." She had taken hold of a chair back and walked around to sit on its soft cushion. "Okay. What happened?"

"We anticipated that Rod would return to work or go home, so we had a patrol car in both locations. Instead, Tucson PD spotted his Tahoe off the I-10 in Marana parked at the side of the road. He's not with the vehicle, so they'll keep an eye out for when he returns. We'll see who drops him off. It's unlikely he's on foot."

"I'm confused," Pilar said. "Why would he take a road trip this time of the night?"

"We're trying to figure that out. By all accounts, he should be at work. I bet his timecard shows he's still on the job."

Pilar shifted in her seat, closing her eyes at each painful movement. "You're probably wondering why I came out here to begin with," she said, in an abrupt change of topic.

"The thought crossed my mind. You have a good life back in Cincinnati from what I've learned. Accomplished athlete, great job, loving family, lots of friends, most of the good stuff most folks want."

"That's all true, except in the last few years I lost my parents and my two brothers in a car accident. Then the restaurant I managed closed and I retired from professional sports. So many changes at once, that I ..." Pilar stopped to choke down her spiraling emotions.

"I'm sorry, especially about your family. That's a huge loss."

"I had my grandfather until he died last year. He was Virginia's brother. The only ones left back home are my Great Aunts Marian and Gladys. I was so naïve to think I could create a new family out of strangers because they're blood relations. Not only did that not happen, but on top of that blow, I've learned my hero might have been part of the gang. Even if he didn't participate, he had to know. Coming here has destroyed my hero."

"He would've been a child back then. What can you expect a child to do even if he did know?"

"I guess not taking the inheritance. Telling his family about it, at least."

"That's not realistic. People that grow up accustomed to a certain standard of living are not eager to give it away. You would have him walk away penniless, and allow his sister to have it all? Heck, people that didn't grow up with money would think twice. Some might say that a practical son would not have denied his parents' inheritance, especially during the Depression. As for telling his family, he might have been too ashamed to admit that."

"You're right. Once this is over and I have more time to think it over and talk with my Aunt Marian, I might see it in a different light."

Macy kept quiet, allowing her time to process. He sympathized with her. A long way from home, in trouble, with no one around she could call for immediate help. A lonely little girl who needs rescuing. Yes, he knew he was old-fashioned.

"Do you think they'll catch him tonight?"

"As soon as he returns to the vehicle, he'll be picked up for aggravated assault and transported to Phoenix. I don't know when since we don't know where he went and how long he'll be gone, but we'll get him. Until that happens, I've spoken to the Flagstaff Police Sergeant, and he has agreed to keep an officer posted for protection duty until he's caught."

"Thank you. Thank you for saving me and for staying here tonight. I'm sorry, but I need to get back in bed. The pain pill is stronger than I expected." Leveraging herself off the chair, she stood up and waived a hand at his offer of assistance. "There's coffee, tea, stuff for sandwiches in the kitchen. Help yourself. Goodnight."

He watched as she made her way to the door, noticing the effects of the pain medication in her careful steps. He did not take to the notion that women were as equipped as men to handle physical brutality. Imagining that bastard striking out at her in that way infuriated him. The enjoyment would be all his when he had him in the interrogation room.

♦ ♦ ♦

Rod called his lawyer in Tucson his first opportunity, who posted bail for both of them after booking. The bigamy issue had not been resolved, although that would not take long. After they retrieved their vehicles from the impound lot, Sheila met him outside the gate.

"I have something to take care of in Flagstaff. Get our stuff together and book three tickets to Venezuela on any flight out of here today. I'll call you when I'm on my way back. Be ready. I should be back in five or six hours."

"Okay, I will," Sheila said. "Are you sure you need to do this? We don't need the money."

"I want it because it's mine. Virginia told me the whole story two weeks before she died. She was going to show me where it was the next time I came up. I would have had the time to take it if Sylvie hadn't killed her, regardless of who inherited the house."

"I understand all that, but now the risk is too high. I don't like the idea of something happening to you up there."

"Just do as I say. Get everything ready. We'll be on that plane before you know it." He pulled her to him, and kissed her forehead, the tip of her nose, and her lips. He jumped into his Tahoe, and leaned out of the window. "Whatever happens, you and Barbie get on that plane."

CHAPTER 53

October 16, 2006
Flagstaff, Arizona

Detective Macy got an early start the next morning, driving on I-17 southbound to Phoenix by six-thirty. Flagstaff PD agreed to post a patrol car outside. That eased his mind about her safety. He had cleaned up and left before she got up. He had not intended to leave before she woke up, but when he got the call at six-fifteen that Rod Folsom was in custody, he thought Pilar would understand his rudeness to wrap up this case.

Receiving the call this morning about Rod had set his pulse racing. Rod had returned to his vehicle around five o'clock, and had been taken into custody on the aggravated assault charge. Macy expected to find Rod in an interview room in Phoenix by the time he arrived at the station.

"You're not going to believe this," the officer said. "The woman who drove him back to his Tahoe claimed to be his wife. She had the marriage certificate in her purse, if you can believe that. The officers thought the certificate looked forged, so they're checking the records. They think she knows about the other wife. When she saw the officers cuffing Rod, she went nuts, kicking, punching, and biting. They arrested her for aggravated assault on a police officer. What can of worms did you pop open?"

"This keeps getting better. So have they processed him?"

"Yes, on the Flagstaff aggravated assault charge. One of them called their attorney. He arrived before they finished. The lawyer demanded their release on bail, claiming there was no probable cause to detain him for Phoenix PD. You might not get the opportunity to question him."

"Damn. Anymore bad news?"

"He's lawyered up, refuses to comment on any of the charges without his attorney. For the really bad news, wife number two said he couldn't have killed Lenore because during that entire night, he was with her in the emergency room. Their four-year old had developed a blistering rash and they had taken her in around eleven that night. That's what cinched the lawyer's claim."

"That's not what I wanted to hear." Macy frowned. A partial victory was better than watching him walk free. Disappointed as he was, he had to tell Pilar that Allegra, and maybe Charlie, were back on as prime suspects. Unless Pilar came up with someone else, he had no choice.

"Just one more thing. Tucson PD received a call from Scottsdale PD. Apparently, they've had a GPS tracker on his vehicle since last week. They had a tip that he was dealing drugs in Tucson, but there was no evidence. They needed to know where he went and when he had the opportunity."

"That could be what we need. I'd like to know what that guy's been up to myself. I'll talk to them when I get back. Leave the name and number on my desk."

"Already done, sir. A complicated case, I'd say."

Macy chuckled, "That's an understatement. Every lead we get a lead, instead of finding answer, we find more questions."

♦ ♦ ♦

Glendale, Arizona

Sylvie sat in her kitchen with the morning paper, and glanced at the wall clock. Eight-thirty. Rod got off work at seven and could get home in less than a half hour. If he were going to be late, he'd always let her know. Something happened. She called his cell phone, but it went straight to voicemail. She had no idea who to call. Their friends were limited to a handful of couples, all of whom worked the day shift at the plant. She decided to do nothing. That is what Rod would expect.

At nine o'clock, still sitting in the same position at the table, she jumped when her house phone rang. "Finally," she whispered and rushed over to grab the receiver.

"Hello."

"Sylvie, this is Pilar. How are you holding up?"

"What do you mean?"

"Detective Macy called to tell me about Rod's arrest. You know, in Marana, this morning."

"That's ridiculous. Rod's been at work all night. What would he be doing down there, anyway?"

Sylvie heard the hesitant silence at the end of the call. A silence she recognized when someone revealed facts assumed already known, but who then realizes it's too late to take it back.

"Pilar, tell me what you're talking about. Right now," she said, holding back hysteria and anger from coming through her voice.

"Sylvie, I don't want to hurt you."

"Spit it out!"

"Okay," Pilar said. Sylvie noted how Pilar's voice dropped to a whisper, the tone both alarming and unnatural.

"I went back to Flagstaff yesterday and while I was there, Rod attacked me."

"That's bullshit."

"If you don't want me to tell you, just say so," Pilar said.

"Go ahead with your fairytale."

"It's not a fairytale. I didn't see his face, but the police are sure he's the one. They can place his Tahoe there and he has a key to the house to get in."

"A-ha! I knew it. No one actually saw him attack you, including you. What is it you have against my husband anyway? Going around telling lies that he's attacked you. I could have killed you when you made up that story that he threatened you and kicked you out of the house. What have we done to you to make you treat us like this?"

"Oh, I don't know. I guess I'm the one who's crazy," Pilar gave in to the temptation to lash out at her. "At least I hear his other woman agrees with you."

"You lying sack of shit. How dare you. I'll not stand for anyone slandering my husband. You'd better keep away from me if you know what's good for you." Every nerve in her body trembled with rage. Sylvie slammed the phone into its cradle, and stumbled backward, reaching out for a surface to support her.

None of that was true. How could it be? Why would she say those things? She looked around her kitchen, clean, organized, and normal, a calm realization that this was her life with Rod. Nothing obtuse about it. They had built a straightforward, middle-class life with no secrets and no blame. She would overcome this karmic misfire. She knew many people were jealous when they see you are happy and loved. They try to tear you down and make you weak. That would not happen to her.

This would not be the first time she had to pull it out to protect her family and she guessed this would not be the last. This is an easy one to fix. All she had to do was call that detective working on Lenore's case and tell him about Pilar's call. She will be the one he starts looking at in a different light.

"I'll fix you, Pilar!"

CHAPTER 54

October 16, 2006
Phoenix, Arizona

Detective Macy found himself impressed as he looked around the front room of Charlie's condo and then back to the man. Previous checking had confirmed the executive position he had held for many years. With that salary, he could afford to surround himself with quality. The industrial loft feeling could have been severe but warm woods in accents pieces and the muted tones of the throw pillows softened the harshness of cold steel. Not bad, and not new either. Enough wear to know he had acquired this long before he knew Allegra.

Allegra came from the kitchen carrying a tray of hot chocolate and cookies. Macy thought she was not as recognizable as she should be. In this environment, her diminutive stature and dark features gave her a regal presence, and a contrasting softness against the steel backdrop of the structural elements. She had an underlying strength behind her confidence that must have been there all along, but not nurtured. Remembering what she had said in previous interviews about her relationship with Charlie, Macy found himself coming around to the same conclusion that Charlie was good for her.

"Thanks for seeing me on short notice. We've had some developments that you need to know about. I also have more questions."

"Sure. We'll do what we can to help. Have a seat, Detective," Charlie said, motioning to the sofas.

Allegra joined Charlie on the opposite sofa after setting the tray between them on the glass coffee table. Handing a cup to Macy, and then to Charlie, she picked up her own and started to sip. "What's going on?"

"Your uncle Rod has been arrested for aggravated assault against Pilar," Macy said.

"You're kidding! I knew he was too good to be true. Wait a minute, *not murder*?" Allegra frowned.

Charlie said nothing but looked on with an innocent expression. Something about his reaction gave Macy an inkling that he was looking at the anonymous caller, but kept it to himself. Better to leave that for another time.

"Wait a minute!" Allegra said. "I didn't know she had been attacked. She should've called. Is she alright?" Her hands shook as she reached over to set down her cup.

"She's going to be fine," Macy said.

"That's a relief," Charlie said, reaching over to take Allegra's hand.

"I can't discuss those details, but the reason I'm here is because he has an alibi for the night of Lenore's death. He was at the emergency room in Tucson with *another* woman and daughter from eleven until the morning. I have to admit I thought I was on the right track, but now we're back to the beginning."

"No, you can't mean that you're back to suspecting us?" Charlie said.

"The truth is that the more I know both of you, the more I don't believe. My problem is that Lenore led a solitary life except for her immediate family. We didn't find any leads to suggest an internet stalker or any new individual introduced into her life that would explain it. It keeps coming back to her family. Tell me again about the relationships, starting when your great grandmother was living."

"When Gran was alive," Allegra said. "Everyone was expected to visit her in Flagstaff every Sunday. She was controlling and mean and liked to pick at everyone's open sores, like telling Gran Madera how she warned her having children with Grandpa Bert would produce defective children. That was always a good one because she got two shots with one arrow."

"Nice people," Charlie said.

"She would go on that Aunt Tasha was gay because her father Grandpa Bert is spineless. She taunted my Mom that she was too ugly to attract another man and she should have been grateful that she had been able to catch one at all. Of course, then there was me. She kept telling me how no money in the world would cure mental illness, and that I should be grateful not to be in an institution. It was horrible to go there. I was glad when she died."

"What about Rod?"

"Rod was the one she wasn't mean to. Sylvie got it instead. I couldn't believe he would let his wife be talked to like that, but Mom said it was because Gran had promised him a special gift when she died."

"Really," Macy said. "I heard he thought he was supposed to get the house. I thought your grandmother was under that same impression."

"No, she wasn't. Not about the house. I heard her talking to Grandpa one day about it. I think I knew that Gran was lying to everybody about what she was going to leave them, but no one would have believed me."

"How mean was the old woman to Sylvie?" Macy said, visualizing the delicate image of Sylvie fending off her attackers.

"Vicious. They all ganged up on her to humiliate her. You know, pick on her about her looks, her hair, and her clothes, make fun of her sick mother, and accuse her of stealing things they had given her as a gift. I don't know how any of us kept taking it, except that you get trapped by someone that overbearing and become afraid of making them mad."

"Tell me about your Aunt Tasha."

"A couple of years ago, I'm not sure when, she didn't show up one Sunday. Gran was furious. She had Grandma call everywhere to leave messages. Tasha never called back. Gran told Grandma that she was not to have anything to do with her until Tasha came to her to apologize. Gran said she would not give Grandma a dime if she allowed her children to be disrespectful to her. Tasha never called, and I didn't see her again until she was here."

"How do all of you get along with each other?"

"We don't. Everyone lived in fear Gran would find out. You know about the big blow up with Sylvie the day Pilar arrived? Sylvie stood up against Gran and the others because they were horrible to Pilar. Mom said Sylvie screamed, 'You'll see your grandchildren over my dead body,' or something like that. Gran died that night. Come to think of it, mom said someone almost ran her down the side of the canyon on the way home."

"I'm surprised Virginia wasn't the one murdered," Charlie said, his face tight with anger.

"That's something to consider," Macy said. "More things go on inside families than outsiders can fathom."

Allegra and Charlie nodded, but said nothing.

"Did your mother ever mention learning about a secret hiding place in Virginia's basement?"

Allegra looked surprised, frowned. "Not that I remember. She might have known about something like that. All the grandchildren spent part of the summer there every year until they were teenagers. Why?"

Ignoring her question, he said, "This gives me a few things to think about that I need to investigate further. All the same, keep yourselves available if I need to speak with you again." Extending his hand to Charlie as he stood, he thanked them both and left.

Macy walked toward the elevator, meditating on the effect law enforcement has on individuals propelled into a criminal investigation through family or circumstances. Why is it when I talk to those two, I get the feeling they are hiding something?

CHAPTER 55

October 16, 2006
Phoenix, Arizona

Outside Charlie's condo, the heat of the afternoon sun had penetrated the interior atmosphere of Macy's car, forcing him to remove his jacket and open the window. Winter in Phoenix had surprised him at first. He laughed, remembering his car experiences in the eastern climates. That plastic scraper he used to chip away the accumulated snow and ice on the windshield and the endless waiting for the car heater to warm enough for the defroster to clear the fog on the inside. Even when the car was in the garage, he recalled with a grimace the exertion of shoveling a thirty-foot driveway after a night of snow or ice freeze. Blinking back to the present, he looked up and said, "Thank you for sending me here."

He pulled out from his parking space and left the underground garage. Within moments, his mind was back to the case. He trusted his instincts. He believed Rod was responsible for Lenore's death, and maybe even for his grandmother's death. With a solid alibi, though, he had nothing. If the alibi had been provided by the second wife only, he could break it, but not with dozens of emergency room staff to corroborate.

Back at his office, he reviewed his notes, made new notes, tried to see a pattern or an anomaly. As far as he could determine, Rod was Johnny-on-the-Spot when it came to who could have found the gold and who would have had the leisure to remove it at his own pace without arousing suspicion.

Money was the motive, but Lenore's knowledge could have been the motive if she also knew about it. She was the oldest child, the one placed with the duty of watching the younger siblings. Maybe she knew about a secret hiding place and Rod was concerned she would mention it to someone else before he removed the contents.

What if he tried to kill Pilar for the same reason? He did not expect Pilar to inherit that house. Imagine his panic that she would find exactly what she found, the secret hiding place. What did not make sense about that reasoning is that the drawers were empty. If he had removed the contents prior, why worry that Pilar would find the hideaway, but it would make sense if he had not found it yet.

The desk phone in front of him interrupted his thoughts. Detective Spatz, after the amenities, said the forensic team found traces of gold inside the compartments but they could not determine if the gold scrape marks had been left by the stolen bars or not. After thanking him, Macy called his partner over to discuss the case.

Detective Martin Stokes, a veteran detective, had been on vacation all week. His first in five years, he had returned today looking happier than Macy had seen him since his wife died. He watched as his friend settled his ample frame into the visitor chair.

"Well, what's been going on while I was away?"

"Have I got a case for you to chew on."

"Oh, yeah? Let's hear it."

When Macy had brought Stokes up to date, Stokes said, "What about the wife, Sylvie? You haven't mentioned too much about her."

With an open mouth and half smile, Macy followed his

thoughts through the details until he realized that the facts fitted Sylvie as much as they fitted Rod. Why had he not given her a second thought? He knew it was because of that double standard, chauvinistic attitude he could not overcome even after years of working in law enforcement: The notion that murder was not lady-like.

The taunting chuckling coming from Stokes brought him back. His partner knew him well and most likely knew what he was thinking and found it amusing. "We can laugh about it, but one day you might be laughing out of your backside if you're not careful."

A voice from around the corner of his cubicle called out to Macy that his search warrant for Rod Folsom's home had come through. Rod was no longer a viable suspect for his sister's murder, but could be an accessory before or after the fact. Within fifteen minutes, Macy had his team ready.

CHAPTER 56

October 16, 2006
Glendale, Arizona

After placing the phone back in its cradle, Sylvie went weak. The ticking of the clock caught her attention to let her know it was after three o'clock. She had not heard from Rod all day. Looking around her, she saw the commonplace interior of her kitchen but found it confusing and frightening. What was going on that she could not trust herself to recognize any of it? She moved to the coffeemaker and poured the dark liquid into her mug. She leaned over the counter looking out onto the tropical landscaping, and glittering kidney bean shaped pool with the afternoon sun casting shadows that played hide-and-go-seek behind the foliage. The soothing sight calmed her down.

Pilar's call would not have disturbed her had she been able to find Rod. If he had been arrested, he would have called her to put up his bail. Whatever Pilar was up to, she was not going to let her place a wedge between her and Rod. The idea that Rod would have threatened Pilar to leave was ridiculous since he knew how important it was to her to have Pilar close. She did not know anything, and once she went back to Ohio, they would have plenty of time to search the house. Once she had a chance to talk to Rod, everything would be fine. He would know what to do.

Looking down at her hands, she saw they were no longer shaking and smiled at her recuperative powers.

When the doorbell rang, she had relaxed, unconcerned when she saw Detective Macy and several men behind him. Handing her an official-looking folded paper, he said something about searching the house, but she was not listening. She placed her hand on his forearm, and said, "Can I speak with you?"

"Sure."

"I want to know how to go about pressing charges against someone."

"Anyone in particular?"

"Yes. That Pilar person. She had the nerve to call here this morning to tell me the police arrested my husband for attacking her *and* that he has another woman claiming to be his wife. She put on the act as if she was concerned, but she's trying to make trouble. I want to put a stop to her saying those things about my husband."

Detective Macy looked at her but did not answer right away. He took her arm, led her to the sofa, and sat next to her. Oblivious to the men searching her bedrooms, she kept her focus on him and waited for an answer.

"Mrs. Folsom, I have some bad news for you. Pilar was not lying to you. Rod *was* arrested early this morning in Tucson. His lawyer got both of them out on bail."

Sylvie rolled her eyes. "Come on, Detective. Let's be serious. My husband would not do those things."

"I'm afraid you're wrong, Mrs. Folsom. I'd also like to ask you a few questions, if you don't mind coming downtown."

She looked into the interior of her home, realizing for the first time that officers were searching her home, looking through her family's private things. "What are these people doing in my house? What right do you have to burst in here and disrupt my household? What about my neighbors? What will they think?

What about my children? Where's my husband? I demand to know what's going on here." Sylvie rested her hand on her throat, mouth open, gasping loudly. Her eyes were wild, glassy and out of focus.

"As I explained at the door, we have a search warrant that gives us the right to search your home for evidence that might be pertinent to the death of Lenore Santos."

"This is all bullshit! Get out of my house!"

"That's not going to happen, Mrs. Folsom. I suggest you calm down and cooperate."

"I'm not answering any questions until you tell me what you've done to my husband. You're with the others who are jealous of me and want to disgrace me."

"Officer Darrow is going to assist you downtown," he said motioning toward the tall, female that had remained standing to his right since he sat down.

Sylvie looked up at the woman towering over her in the dark blue uniform and flinched.

"Let's go, Ma'am," Darrow said. "You don't want to make things bad for yourself. You have your children to consider. You wouldn't want the neighbors to see you in handcuffs, either."

"Yes, you're right. Let's get this over with so I can get back. The sooner all of this is cleared up the better."

Sylvie turned her attention to the searchers, and flinched when she heard a male voice call out, "Jackpot!"

CHAPTER 57

October 16, 2006
Phoenix Police Department, Interrogation Room 1

An odor of stale perspiration, stale cigarette smoke, and a noxious vomit smell pervaded the interrogation room and assaulted her senses. Sylvie sat erect with her feet flat on the floor and her hands clasped together on the tabletop. Wondering how long this was going to take since she had to pick up the children, she glanced at the door every few minutes. No large mirrored wall, but she guessed a camera was focused on her with Macy watching to see how she was coping. All she had to do was sit still and wait. All of this would be over soon.

After what seemed like more than an hour, she sighed in relief when saw the door creaked open. Another step closer to going home, she thought and smiled at Detective Macy. He's an asshole, she thought, but if she did not play the game, they would not let her go.

Macy took one of the matching industrial chairs across from her and sat down in a casual manner. She found it amusing to watch his deliberate manner in doing everything from sitting to opening the notebook. This was another test of her patience and she would not make the same mistake she had made at home.

"I see you're feeling better, Mrs. Folsom. Before we go any further, I need to read you your rights. You have the right to remain silent. Anything you say can and will be used against you in a court of law. You have the right to an attorney. If you cannot afford an attorney, one will be provided for you. Do you understand the rights I have just read to you? With these rights in mind, do you wish to speak to me?"

"Fire away," she said, and smiled.

"How did you feel about Virginia, your husband's grandmother?"

"I hated her guts to the very depths of my soul. She was a viper."

"That's very candid."

"You want me to be honest, don't you?"

"Absolutely. I'm guessing you were happy she died."

"I could have killed her a hundred times," Sylvie whispered, leaning over the table.

"But you only killed her once?"

"You're putting words into my mouth, Detective."

"Okay, are you saying you did not kill her?"

"No, but I don't like anyone to tell me what I'm saying."

"I see. Do you want to tell me what happened in your own words?"

"Naturally, I planned her murder as a mental exercise for a long time during those drives home after those wretched Sunday visits. I had rehearsed so many times that putting it into action was easy.

"When Rod left for work that night, I had already given the children over-the-counter sleeping pills to keep them asleep until I returned. I know, it sounds like a miserable thing for a mother to do but I did it to protect them. You see, I set the alarms and during an emergency the sounds would wake them up and they would be safe. I did a test run one night and found that the fire and burglar alarms woke them up even if they had the sleeping pills in their systems. The drugs were mild, but enough to keep them sleeping while I went to Flagstaff. I'm a *good* mother."

Sylvie waited for Macy to nod his head in agreement before she went on.

"I left around midnight and drove within the speed limits. When I got there, I parked down the hill from Virginia's house behind an empty house. I walked up the hill, cut through the back of the property and across the yard to house. I had Rod's key, you see. I was just about to let myself in through the basement door when that nosy old bat from next door came charging up with a blackjack. When she saw me, she let down her guard, but I had to kill her or she would have told the police I was there after she found out Virginia died the same night. It took all my strength to get her back to her own house."

Macy made a choking sound, but waved her to go on.

"Anyway, dear old Virginia still had good hearing so I was as quiet as I could be when I opened her bedroom door. I found it infuriating seeing her sleep as if she had the soul of a saint. That made it easy. I walked over, grabbing the extra pillow next to her and pressed it over her ugly face. I can't say if she struggled because I was shaking from anger. I kept pressing down and didn't notice her arms and legs move. When I'd finished, I had concerns that I might have caused bruising, but it turned out to be fine."

Sylvie's shoulders relaxed as she finished speaking,

Macy shivered, his eyes not leaving hers. "Was it for revenge for the way she treated you?"

"That was a bonus. I did it to help my husband."

"How did that help him?"

"So he could get the house, of course. I knew he wanted to get in there and find the stolen loot. A good wife does what she can to keep her husband happy. I did what I could," Sylvie said, her tone remained pleasant, still careful not to show signs of emotion.

"Is there anything you can tell us about Lenore?"

"Detective," she said, smiling "You know very well I do. You see, she had called me and wanted to be friends. She said she was impressed with how I told off the family and was going to do the same. She was sorry for the way she had treated me before and could I ever forgive her. Well, I went along with the joke. I thought it took some kind of nerve to think all you have to do is say you're sorry and that wipes out fifteen years of abuse and humiliation. Don't you agree?"

"Absolutely," Macy said.

"Before I decided to kill her, Rod told me that the gold he wanted was not in the Flagstaff house where it was supposed to be. Virginia had told him about the stories. When he looked in the hidden compartments in the basement after she died, nothing was there. Well, he wasn't sure what to think. Then he thought how Lenore must have found it when they were kids, but he said he couldn't believe she had he balls to take it. I could believe it, no matter what kind of act she put on."

"So, you decided to get her to tell you?"

"I asked her to meet me downtown. I told her I wanted to plan a surprise for Rod, which wasn't exactly lying," Sylvie let out a chuckle. "I asked her to meet me at the bus station where we could go in and have a sandwich. That way, I didn't have to worry about Allegra or my children being a witness. She fell for it. She was happy that we were friends, she said. The people in Rod's family are something else. Anyway, I got into her car and handed her a small hot chocolate. I had stirred in the drugs I crushed up earlier. I watched while she drank, and stayed until she started to get sick. I dropped the empty medicine bottles.

"When I was sure she was past help, I got out and walked away. I parked my car on a side street on the other side of the station in a dark neighborhood. Can you believe how stupid some people are?" Sylvie rolled her eyes, grinning.

"After Rod called to tell me the news, I went over to her house on the pretext of trying to help, so I could look around for the gold. No gold, not even a clue to where she put it. I still don't know. Maybe she never had it. While I was there, I slipped all the prescription bottles in Lenore's medicine cabinet to confuse things when I heard the officers thought her death was suspicious. Hell, I'm not a cop. I hadn't thought they'd make a big deal out of it. It's not like anyone will miss her."

Macy still sat motionless. Sylvie tried to read him, but found his impassive expression annoying.

"I'm tired now. I want go home now. My children will be wondering where I am."

"I arranged for your mother to pick up your children. You don't have to worry."

"Thank you," Sylvie said, giving him her sweetest smile.

"Did your husband know any of this?"

"Oh, yes. We tell each other everything. We were pleased when Virginia's death looked like heart failure. You see, Rod said that if anyone got suspicious, we could point the finger at Pilar. The day she visits, Virginia dies and she inherits the house. Rod found out about Virginia's will a couple days before I killed her. After I told him what I did, and he told me he wasn't getting the house, I knew we had to have her with us in case we needed to frame her for the murders. One way or another...," Sylvie took a sip of water, keeping her eyes on Macy.

"Rod wasn't happy when Pilar started helping Allegra. When she went to Flagstaff instead of going back to Ohio, he got worried she'd find where he'd been working in the attic or find the gold. At first, he was just going to scare her, but when he saw through the basement door that she was getting close to the hiding place, he panicked. I guess you know the rest. He should have stayed to make sure she was dead. That was careless."

Sylvie inhaled and blew out a heavy breath. For the first time, she looked worried. "Now, please tell me something, Detective. What is all this nonsense about another woman?"

"Her name is Sheila and they have a four-year-old daughter named Varvara, but they call her Barbie."

"That was his great aunt's name! Varvara is Russian for Barbara. That bastard! If I'd known, I'd have killed him, too."

♦ ♦ ♦

"Shit!" Macy said, once he was back with the other detectives. "That is one spooky Stepford wife. I feel like I need to take a bath in holy water."

"If we didn't have this on tape, I don't think anyone would

believe what we just heard," Stokes said. "I almost can't believe a sweet-looking woman like her could be that evil."

"It's the company she keeps," Macy said. "What's the status on her husband?"

"We need to have him picked up again, now that we know he was an accomplice. Scottsdale PD agreed to share the GPS data if we needed it."

"Do we have his current location?"

"Yes. Right here," he said pointing to his monitor.

The vehicle was heading on the seventeen north. Macy knew that if he was on his way to Flagstaff, he was heading to Pilar. Rod did not know about Sylvie's confession, and would think he still had a clear path. He notified Flagstaff PD that he was on his way and the situation while he veered his car out of the parking lot. Then, he spent the next half hour trying to reach Pilar but his call kept going straight to voicemail.

CHAPTER 58

S leeping through the grogginess from the pain medication, Pilar was startled when the house phone rang. Detective Macy started speaking in his slow, concise voice, "Lock up the house and hide in a safe place until I get there. I'll explain everything when I get there, but the short version is that Rod is out on bail and he's on his way to Flagstaff, at least his Tahoe is. This sudden snowstorm has done a number on the roads up there. They had to pull the officer watching your house due to several emergencies. Don't worry. I'll be there as soon as I can."

Before she had time to respond, she heard the click disconnecting the call. Her pain vanished from a sudden jolt of adrenaline. She was back in survival mode. At least the pain medication kept her discomfort at a minimum. She looked out of the window and did not see the patrol car. She went to every room and locked every window and door.

Not knowing what time Rod or Macy left Phoenix, she thought it best to jumpstart into panic mode now. She barricaded herself in the middle bedroom on the second floor that had the strategic window over the porte-cochère. She watched the snow-dusted streets for movement. The momentum of the snowfall took her by surprise as the street surfaces disappeared before her eyes. Every nerve in her body was on fire as she sat in front of the window straining her eyes to see any sign of movement through almost zero visibility.

As she sat there, afraid and anxious, she had a change of perspective come over her. She was not going to sit still waiting for Rod to murder her or count on Macy to arrive at the crucial moment to save her. Rod was a desperate and angry man who had nothing more to lose. If he had the opportunity to get to her, she would not live to tell. Better for her if she took advantage of the two physical attributes she excelled in that Rod could not match, her stamina and her running speed. Pilar guessed she could outrun him even in her weakened condition as long as she avoided a direct confrontation. She looked down over the rooftop below the window and started planning.

She heard the door downstairs open and shut. She froze, and listened for sounds.

"Bitch, I know you're here," Rod yelled from the first floor. His weight on the ground floor echoed hasty groans as she heard him running from one room to another. "I want the money. Show me where you hid it and I might not wring your thieving neck."

Pilar bolted upright. Her breath coming in short, fast gasps. Her heart raced. For a long minute, her fear paralyzed her. A part of her said this was not happening. Then she heard the creaking boards on the stairs. She heard him grunt and curse, his deep voice bellowing inside the open stairwell. He was getting closer and she knew she had to do something.

She needed a way to delay him to get a head start. Something told her to look in the closet for something she could use as a weapon. She could not believe her eyes when she saw one of the old rifles propped up in the corner. Her knowledge of firearms was limited, so she grabbed it and stood behind the door.

The doorknob turned counterclockwise, and she heard Rod try to push the door. Sure, she thought, he knew she was in the only locked room. Then she heard the key in the lock and saw the door move. A ripple of fear seized the back of neck while she watched him start to make his way inside. She thought of every offensive tactic she knew. Be positive. Be confident of your abilities. Focus. Don't miss. She took the batter's stance and swung the rifle by its barrel into Rod's face. He stumbled back into the hall and fell on his back. She slammed the door shut and locked it again. She could not let her guard down wondering if he was more than stunned.

She pushed up the window and leaned out to survey the area. The icy air rushed in around her, allowing the heat to escape with the steam of her breath. She had already dressed in warm clothing to counter the drafty house. Her thermal underwear, two sweaters, two pairs of socks and ski pants left her needing only a jacket, cap, and gloves that she found in the closet. She stepped outside onto the roof. She closed the window behind her, and then ducked down to get a bird's eye view of the area to plan what she would do.

Blinking to focus, she was stunned to see Rod's Tahoe parked two houses down on the street. Pilar wondered how she had not seen it before. She heard gentle movements outside the door, and then heard his low grumbling. She had to go now. Then, she found the perfect spot.

With a careful calculation, and praying she would not break any bones, she bent her knees, took a deep breath, and propelled herself off the roof. She landed on a snowdrift next to the pile of boxes. She noticed a box cutter and tucked it in her jacket. She took a moment to take a deep breath, looked to be sure he had not seen her, and took off running down the slippery snow-covered road.

Her heart was racing more from fear than physical exertion. She stopped, gasping, and looked behind her. She still could not see him. She kept running until she passed his Tahoe. She stopped, deciding to double back. Not knowing how much time she had before Rod realized she was out of the house and on foot, she knew that if she could disable his wheels, he would be forced to follow her on foot where she had a better chance to outrun him. She pulled out the box cutter and stabbed at the tires. No time to be sure how much damage she caused, but she hoped he could not get away before Macy arrived.

She circled around back onto the snow-covered street, and squatted behind his Tahoe. She peered past the windshield but still did not see him. Running again, she did not stop this time until she was three blocks farther away. The snow still came down like a blanket. She hid behind someone's evergreen bushes and looked out. She heard a slicing sound getting closer. To her horror, she saw Rod snowboarding down the middle of the road, swaying side-to-side, taking the time to look in yards and behind cars. She had lost her advantage. He was now faster and he knew the area better than she did.

"Think, think," she said.

She watched him getting nearer, then she had the idea that he was faster going downhill but not going uphill. He would also have to be on foot to chase her through the neighborhood backyards. At his current speed, he would go a long way before he stopped to reassess his situation. By the time he returned to the house, Macy should be there. When she saw Rod swish past, she started running to her left, uphill through a neighbor's yard. She had run through two yards, when she heard the awful sounds.

She heard brakes, followed by an impact with the car, and then a horrible thud when his body landed on the icy ground. The sound of the snowboard hitting glass seemed like minutes. She heard the driver get out of his car, hurling expletives.

"Damn teenagers," the man said. "His parents better have insurance or their ass is mine for Christmas!"

"Calm down," said a woman from inside the car. "Don't you think you should check to see if he's alright?"

"Call 9-1-1. I think he's unconscious." The man went over to check on the person spread out on the pavement. "Look, this is that Folsom boy. What the hell is a grown man doing pulling a stunt like this? Some people never grow up."

Pilar froze in her steps, not sure what to do. She made her way over to the couple, keeping alert for movement when she saw Rod face up on the icy pavement.

"Did you see what happened," the man asked.

"No, but I heard it," Pilar said. "Is he alright?"

"Between you and me, I think he'd dead. I tried to find a pulse a minute ago, but didn't find one. Shit, what is this going to do to my insurance premiums," the man said with a groan.

Pilar looked down at Rod's face. Her grandfather's features, now relaxed without the distortions of cruelty. She bent down to feel for a pulse on his wrist, then on his neck. No movement. Only cool damp skin. She noticed a greyish hue to his coloring, and knew the man was right. Rod was dead. She felt lightheaded and nauseated.

"I need to get back home. I have an injury and need to get my pain meds. I live in Virginia's place on the corner," Pilar said, pointing up the hill. "Please tell the police I can make a statement about what happened. My name is Pilar Sagasta. I don't feel well."

She heard the sirens behind her as the ambulance made its way up the hill, feeling a guilty relief at someone else's expense. She was sure he had to be dead, but she still used caution walking up the hill, looking behind her several times before reaching the house and closing the front door.

While she waited for the police to interview her, she made a large mug of hot chocolate, poured out an entire box of cookies into a bowl, and cozied up on the sofa wrapped in a blanket with Josefina's diary beside her, and let herself cry.

CHAPTER 59

October 16, 2006
Flagstaff, Arizona

D etective Macy pulled into an empty space next to the ambulance in time to see the two paramedics lift the gurney into the back. He walked over to ask for an update on Rod Folsom's condition.

"There's nothing we can do for him," the first paramedic said.

"An impact to the head at that speed …," the second paramedic said, allowing his sentence to hang.

Macy knew not to expect a good outcome. If paramedics had the authority to pronounce death, they would do so in this instance. He took a last look at the boots sticking out from under the sheet, and then drove the few blocks to Pilar's house.

He met an officer leaving when he arrived at her door, and let himself inside. He was relieved to find that she had not suffered new injuries, but the physical exertion had taken its toll. Her eyes expressed her discomfort lying back into the sofa cushions, her knees at her chest, her arms wrapped around her midsection. Macy could not help but blame himself for this, and for Rod's death. The 'what-ifs' kept popping into his head.

She answered the unspoken concern in his expression, "I'm alright. I'm more shaken up that anyone would want to hurt me."

"Thank God you're alright. It's been a helluva twenty four hours."

"I don't understand most of this. What did he expect to get out of killing me?"

"He was desperate. His last chance to get what he thought you had found. Arrogance makes you stupid. He could've gotten away if he'd been clearheaded."

Macy watched as Pilar reached for a glass of water and swallowed several pills. "Are you alright to be left on your own?"

"I think so. I doubled the pain meds, and took the tranquilizer the doctor suggested. I should fall asleep fast, but I wouldn't protest if you stayed."

◆ ◆ ◆

The bright morning sun had started to melt the icy surfaces. Macy stood on Pilar's front porch calculating road conditions to Phoenix. When he heard movement inside, he went back indoors to Pilar pouring a cup of coffee.

"Thanks for staying. I slept like a rock," she said, easing down on a side chair. "It's like a dream now that it's over."

"Rod didn't stand a chance," Macy said. He settled into the chair next to her where he had slept the night before. "The impact with the car did some damage, but when he landed on his head, well, there wasn't anything anyone could do."

"I wish I could be sorry, but all I feel is relief. I've never been so terrified."

"No one can say he didn't deserve it. He was into way more than trying to find his family's treasure," he said. "A true Machiavellian man. To get what he wanted, he didn't hesitate to use whatever means necessary to achieve his end. It takes a certain intelligence to master that level of deception."

"I'm just glad it's over. I think I'll forget the notion of

looking up anymore long, lost relatives. I am as incredibly naïve as my friend, Tammy, says. This whole time, I had no suspicions of Sylvie, not even at the end. What's going to happen to her?"

"I'm not sure. That's up to the lawyers and the court to decide. Right now, she's in a facility for observation. She might stand trial, but as long as she stays locked up anywhere, I'm good."

"And the other woman, Sheila?"

"Interesting story. She and her daughter left on a plane en route for Venezuela before Rod was pronounced dead. She knew she was a person of interest in the Scottsdale investigation, and probably thought she should get out while she could."

"The good news is that Allegra and Charlie are off the hook."

"Yes," Macy said. He wondered if they were as innocent as Pilar said, or just not guilty in this situation.

"At least I knew they were innocent," Pilar said.

"I read Josefina's diary," Macy said. "I know a couple of historians who'll flip over this information."

"I think it's the right thing to do to put it on permanent loan to a museum. Seeing it will mean more to people in Arizona. And who doesn't love stories that expose old crimes?"

"Well, this little book solves the mystery of several robberies," Macy said, running his forefinger over the delicate missive. "Imagine an organized gang in Arizona back then. No one had any idea a few men coordinated the seemingly unrelated robberies over twenty years. The outlaws who rode for the gang never gave them up or weren't able to identify them. Could have been hired by the lieutenants of the gang. Not much different from today, to be honest." Macy laughed. "Being a lawman myself, I bet the sheriff and his men back then would roll over in their graves to hear about this."

Pilar laughed, too. "But what I don't get is if the posse started after them right away, how could the gang have had time to make the switch?"

"The way it seems to have worked, they were given prearranged drop stops where they'd leave their loot. They'd continue as decoys with empty containers. Paralelos,

Rodchenko, and Velasquez came by at some point, picked it up, and went on their way. They could even have been part of the posse chasing them. Josefina didn't put every detail in her diary."

"Interesting twist," Pilar said. "So, the ones who got caught or killed were at the bottom of the pyramid, following orders with no significant knowledge."

"That part is all speculation, of course, but Josefina wrote how the six of them brought the loot to their house in Mexico, split the cash between them, and stored the rest until it was safe to move. Then Rodchenko and Velasquez went back to Europe with their money. After a while, they had political reasons to leave their respective countries. They had more than enough to live on so they didn't need to continue to steal, but they had to hold onto the gold and coins that were still hot."

"That must be what Lenore had been researching."

"Right," Macy said. "When Paralelos knew he had to leave Mexico, they transported everything to the new Paralelos house in Flagstaff. I'm sure they designed the basement part of the house for their meetings and hidden stashes. From what she wrote in the diary, Paralelos had held onto an old grudge for years before he decided he didn't want to share anymore. He murdered his partners in cold blood. She knew what he had done. He must have lived a miserable old age seeing the look in her eyes every day."

Pilar smiled, "I think he knew she would kill him. Living with her was his prison. Never able to leave, never able to get rid of the stink of his betrayals. Justice is not always served in prison or at an execution."

"Very true," Macy said. "In the end, Ricardo must have found it difficult to move the gold and coins inside Arizona due to the notoriety of the crimes. As he got older, times changed. More technology, tougher sheriffs, tighter borders, who knows why he never cashed out. Unless you find it, there's a good chance Virginia or Lenore found it and moved it somewhere that we'll never know."

"Quite a legacy," Pilar said.

"What they were has nothing to do with you. I tend toward

the nurture position. I don't believe that our fates are sealed by our genetic codes."

"That's something to hope for," Pilar said.

"What the descendants did had more to do with who influenced them as children. As Josefina wrote, Virginia was evil. She was cruel and sadistic to the people closest to her. You'd have to be a person of strong moral fiber to overcome a childhood like that."

"I hope Allegra turns out alright."

"She might. She is her father's daughter, too," Macy said. "You can keep in touch with her; be an influence."

Pilar laughed, "I don't want the responsibility of being a role model. I said as much about Rod's children to the social worker. I heard they went to stay with Sylvie's mother and the care attendant."

"They're getting a rough start in life," Macy said. "Time for me to get back."

"I can't tell you how grateful I am for everything you've done. I'm keeping the house, by the way. I can't turn over this history to strangers. When I come back, I hope to see you. Don't plan on being a stranger."

"Let's hope no one gets murdered next time we meet."

♦ ♦ ♦

Pilar watched him walk down the sidewalk to the curb. He turned and nodded, and then he took in a breath. She watched the cloudy mist escape his mouth when he took a last look at the house before getting in his car. Pilar smiled. At last, she would not have to look over her shoulder anymore.

She ran her fingers over the diary again, and placed it in the tissue-papered lining of the wood box she found for its transport. Something felt incomplete about the story. Nothing left of the gold and coins but residue in the boxes. Maybe Lenore figured out what she had, but what did she do with all that gold? Where is it now?

CHAPTER 60

October 30, 2006
Phoenix, Arizona

Madera sat on her back porch, watching hummingbirds hover around the feeder hanging from the patio roof rafter. She was still having trouble coming to terms with her losses, the greatest one being her only son. The way she saw the situation, Sylvie must have been the one who corrupted him. He was such a good boy. That was how she played the drama over in her mind every day, hoping for an alternate conclusion.

She supposed with everything that had happened, she was lucky to have the monthly check her mother set up for her. The very idea that Nikolas got so much still riled her, but he was not the only undeserving one. That Pilar bitch had no right to the house. She was a stranger. Then for her to donate the diary, uniforms, and guns to the museum without so much as asking her if she wanted them made her blood boil. She could have auctioned off the lot for a pretty penny.

More than losing the money, since it all came out in the papers, she was ashamed to show her face in public, especially at church. She knew they were talking about her, the granddaughter of common criminals, and the mother of a two-timing murderer. She saw the looks they gave her now. What's worse is she had to face the humiliation alone.

Of all she had anticipated at this age, the last thing she imagined was that Al would abandon her. He was her husband. He was supposed to stand by her, for better or for worse. He told her that if she had wanted him to stay around, she should have treated him better all those years, not worse. "Asshole," she said. The intrusion of her voice scattered the birds. She watched them resettle on a power line in the distance, and said, "That's right. Go and leave me."

Bert, of all people leaving her. And since when can he afford to move to Hawaii? She would not be surprised that Pilar found the gold and gave him some of it. They were so chummy now. She squinted her eyes, sensing her blood pressure spiking. "If I ever find out you have my gold, I will kill you in cold blood, Albert Folsom."

The telephone rang, and Madera reached over to pick up the cordless. When she saw the call was from Tasha, she decided not to answer. Another sympathy call. No thank you. She rested back into the chair cushions, and started to cry. "What did I ever do to deserve this?"

EPILOGUE

November 30, 2006
Amberly Village, Ohio

Pilar reached for a fresh biscuit from the baking pan that Marian placed on the trivet at the center of the table. The old-fashioned kitchen, utilitarian and cozy, made life appear simple and joy come easy, no matter what. Pilar experienced her happier moments sitting around this large wooden table. She cherished the familiarity of tall kitchen windows, the flowers on the sills, the oak hutch with the pullout cutting board, and the pantry shelves lined with Marian's homemade preserves.

She pulled apart a biscuit and smeared a large tab of butter over the flaky insides. The aromas in this kitchen took her back to her childhood, a place of good memories where she felt safe and loved.

"I can't believe what you had to go through. It's a mercy you're alive to tell the tale," Marian said, setting down the sausage gravy before Pilar.

"You and me, both. I made it easy for them to draw me into their troubles. I hope I've learned my lesson."

"You're too goodhearted to stop caring about people. Just temper that empathy with common sense."

Pilar grinned wide. "I've got that out of my system, that desperate need to find family. I've all the love and support that I need right here in this kitchen." Pilar went quiet while she finished her breakfast. She shivered thinking about Marian's age, and how before she knew it, Marian would be gone. She gulped down an urge to cry.

"You hear anything from Allegra?" Marian's voice startled her.

"Yes, I got a postcard from her yesterday. She and Charlie got married in Vegas. They invited Claire to the wedding but no one from the family. She sounds happy, normal even."

"That's a blessing. I'll pray for her to stay that way."

"I've had enough strolling down memory lane with distant relatives," Pilar said lopping up the end of the gravy with the last piece of biscuit.

"You're sure about that?" Marian said.

"Positive."

"Then maybe I shouldn't give you this letter from Nikolas Rodchenko?"

Pilar looked at the letter, postmarked Beverly Hills, California, and turned it over a few times. She looked over to Marian, "I'll deal with this later," she said. Her inner voice told her that she was about to be drawn into another family drama.

ACKNOWLEDGMENTS

I am indebted to Deanna Martinez Patnode for sharing her valuable family history that turned out to be the inspiration I needed to complete the story.

Without the following individuals, I never would have finished this book: Marilyn Janson, of Janson Literary Services, who twice provided her valuable manuscript evaluation and professional critique; Deborah J Ledford for her full manuscript edit that led me closer to completing this book than I had gotten before; Bob Arthur, of Global Investigations & Security Consulting in Scottsdale, Arizona, and Timothy Moore, Detective with the Phoenix Police Department for their technical advice.

My deepest appreciation to my beta readers, Alice Laird, Deanna Martinez Patnode, and Kurt Granberg, for sharing their particular insights and for pointing out the last few manuscript hiccups.

Finally, thanks to all the friends over the years who patiently listened to me talk about writing this book, and who then encouraged me to "just do it."

ABOUT THE AUTHOR

Born and raised an only child in Cincinnati, Ohio, Cathy Ann Rogers spent her early years listening to vivid stories by parents, relatives, and other elders.

After establishing her accounting and tax business, Cathy refined her writing craft through a series of published short stories. Her first novel displays her penchant for creating literary characters who imitate reality through their skewed sense of justice as well as their bittersweet victories.

She lives in the Arizona desert, where she shares her home with two Bichon Frises, Whitney and Sophie. She is currently writing the next installment in the Pilar Sagasta series.

THE HISTORY BEHIND THE STORY

E ach character in this story is a figment of my imagination, but the historical references were taken from actual nineteenth century and twentieth century events. I have also used artistic license with the timelines of certain crimes for the sake of the plot.

The robberies mentioned in Arizona took place, but to my knowledge, remain unsolved. Even when the perpetrators were arrested or killed, the gold and coins referred to in this book are still missing today. I offer a solution that is derived purely from my own devious imagination.

As I brought these characters to life, I attempted to show both sides of their countries' revolutions through their eyes. During my research, I discovered the underappreciated Mexican women, known as the Soldaderas. These women, mostly unknown in American culture, deserve a special mention for their active participation at the frontlines of battle.

Cathy Ann Rogers

www.ingramcontent.com/pod-product-compliance
Lightning Source LLC
Chambersburg PA
CBHW050019180626
46810CB00002B/495